I0669969

SPRING'S DESCENT

A SINFUL SEASON'S NOVEL
BOOK ONE

C.L. BRIAR

Copyright © 2024 by C.L. Briar

All rights reserved.

No part of this book may be reproduced in any form or by any electronic or mechanical means, including information storage and retrieval systems, without written permission from the author, except for the use of brief quotations in a book review.

Cover design: Artscandare Book Cover Design

Map design: C.L. Briar Books

IBSNs

Hardcover: 978-1-956829-20-4

Paperback: 978-1-956829-21-1

Ebook: 978-1-956829-17-4

Special Editions: 978-1-956829-22-8

DARKLANDS

Leche

POMEGRANATE
GROVE

ASPHODEL PLA

Phlegethon

TARTARUS

COCYTUS

MOUNTAINS OF
MOURNING

ELYSIAN

Styx

THE
UNDERWORLD

DARK PALACE

ARCHERON

COCYTUS

For the dark fantasy girls who dream of being stolen away by their very own shadow daddy.
This one's for you.

TRIGGER WARNINGS

Trigger warnings for Spring's Descent contain intense and potentially upsetting themes including:

- Emotional distress.
- Relationship complexities, forced proximity
- Abduction
- Violence, blood, and gore.
- Mental health struggles including suicidal thoughts.
- References to sexual assault
- Explicit scenes including breath play, anal play, bondage, praise kink, and exhibitionism.
- References and mentions of an eating disorder, fat shaming.

CONTENT WARNINGS

Content warnings for *Spring's Descent* include intense and potentially upsetting themes such as:
- Emotional distress
- Relationship complexities, forced proximity
- Abduction
- Violence, blood, and gore
- Mental health struggles including suicidal thoughts
- References to sexual assault
- Sexually explicit scenes including breath play, anal play, bondage, praise kink, and exhibitionism
- References and mentions of an eating disorder, fat shaming

PERSEPHONE

I JUST NEEDED AN ORGASM. MY KNEES DUG INTO THE FIELD OF wildflowers as I rocked over the stablehand's toned body. The long layers of my cotton dress pooled across the chiseled muscles of his stomach as the heat from our combined breaths puffed into the cool spring air around us.

"Gods above, Korae," he said as his blue eyes roved over my body, snagging on the loose ties over my breasts. They were on the verge of slipping out, exposing me to the curious eyes of any person wandering this part of the forest. I didn't mind the thought of others watching, so long as I could finish.

His grip on my ass tightened as I picked up the pace, arching my back. My hands trailed up to my chest, brushing my nipples through the thin, cotton fabric as I let a moan tumble from my lips—fake it till you make it, right?

"Gods," he panted, head falling back. At least *he* seemed to be enjoying himself.

Closing my eyes, I focused on finding the rhythm I needed, grinding along Oliver's length—Orein? Odin? Never mind. I just needed to come. Not only would an orgasm grant me a much needed stress relief, but I also craved a glimpse of the magic lurking in my veins.

Magic was addictive, especially when you were as weak as I was. Each burst was euphoria. Every hit, a taste of the type of power I'd never get to experience. Release magic was all I could muster—power derived from an emotional release. Sex was the most common, but mending a heartbreak, forgiving those who have wronged you, all contained power. It wasn't a type of magic that could be controlled, though, and I'd only ever been able to feel power through an orgasm.

Other earth witches didn't need sex to access their magic before their awakening, but even the strongest among us had admitted to flares of magic shortly after climax. Something to do with how sex was linked to life magic, not that any of them would fess up to Demeter about it.

We were supposed to be chaste, docile things whose only care in the world was ensuring our magic lines continued. Sex was for reproduction purposes only, not something to find pleasure in. At least not for women.

Much to my mother's dismay, I thought the entire idea of being a man's breeding toy was totally fucked. She'd wanted me to be her perfect daughter, one pure and above reproach. So, naturally, I had done everything possible to rage against the destiny she'd crafted for me.

Which was how I found myself in the middle of a field, fucking a stableboy whose name I couldn't remember.

Adjusting my angle, I braced my palms on his chest, working my clit. There. A real moan fell from my lips as I concentrated on chasing that growing heat low in my belly.

Grass stained my knees and wildlife flitted around us, but I welcomed the extra connection to the earth. I needed it.

"You're a ray of beauty in a dismal world," the stableboy panted, his body writhing up and down as I moved. "A marvel to behold, Korae."

I squeezed my eyes shut tighter, attempting to block him out. I hated my name, the very sound of it feeling like daggers dragged across stone. Larkspur said this guy was a good fuck—and I was so desperately in need of a good fuck—but this was seriously taking a turn for the worse.

"Your eyes are like fresh grass. Your hair like the golden-red of a blazing fire—"

"Stop talking," I ground out, pressing my hand over his mouth as I angled my hips forward.

If he could keep his mouth shut for a little longer, I might have a chance—

"You have got to be shitting me," I muttered, slipping off him as I felt his entire body tense. I angled his pulsing dick down just as he came, spraying his own chest with the mess.

A long, contented sigh escaped him as his eyes fluttered open with something close to hope. "Did you finish?"

Is he serious? If he thought *that* was what it sounded like when a girl came, I would have to have a very serious conversation with Lark. Pressing my lips together against a very candid and extremely unhelpful retort, I pushed to a stand and focused instead on retying the bodice of my dress.

"Not even close, Orwin."

"It's Owen," he said, using his discarded shirt to mop up the mess. Stepping into his pants, he lifted a bushy brow in my direction as if I were lying. "I've never not made a girl come before."

A snort ripped through me, the sound only darkening the look of suspicion in his eyes—eyes that shifted over my shoulder to the tree line in the distance.

"Get behind me," he ordered, retrieving a small dagger from the pocket of his pants.

Rolling my eyes, I continued brushing out my dress. His actions were commendable but pointless. Only the strongest witches were granted life after our twenty-first birthdays, and I was anything but.

I was the daughter to the great Demeter Thornbrook, the witch who had single-handedly led our people to safety after The Dark Faction's infamous attack on The Crystal City. She was powerful enough to keep us hidden, single-handedly maintaining the glamor these past ten years.

There were whispers the gods would invite her to join them in The Aboveworld. Some claimed she had already conversed with Zeus and Hera, that she had been given Hestia's blessing for selecting our new home in The Black Forest. Every witch here worshiped her, but they didn't know her the way I did.

"Put the blade down," I said to Owen as the pungent smell of lilac reached me. Power rippled through the field, causing my spine to stiffen and my pulse to race, but Owen stood his ground, having no idea who was walking toward us.

There is nothing to fear, I reminded myself. I only had one month left until Hecate decided if I was worthy of her blessing —her power—or if what little magic lingering in my veins would serve the coven better in death.

I already knew what my fate would be.

That's what gods and goddesses did after all—killed mortals. Aphrodite and Ares visited The Realm of the Living often enough to play their games, sometimes joined by Athena or the twins, Artemis and Apollo. There had even been whispers of Poseidon thrashing about, but they always returned to The Aboveworld the moment a tendril of Hades's death magic surfaced.

Don't get me wrong, if I were an immortal, I'd run from the one thing that could kill me, too.

But I wasn't a god. I wasn't even really a witch—not without magic.

Inhaling through my nose, I let out a long breath, schooling my features into a taunting smirk that was sure to get a rise out of her. I would see the same sneer of disgust staring back at me from her cold, pale-blue eyes either way. The same disappointment I always saw when she looked at me.

"Head Matriarch," I said, letting my lips stretch into a lopsided smirk. "How kind of you to drop in. To what do we own this great honor?"

Mother lingered on the edge of the forest, refusing to draw nearer, but I could see the revulsion in her eyes from here. Our strength as a coven was dwindling with each witch claimed at her awakening. Their initial deaths did return a flicker of earth magic to the coven for a brief period, but eventually, the rush faded. And we were left weaker for it.

Once upon a time, *I* was meant to be the savior. Mother used to tell me tales of how we would become the most powerful earth witches in centuries. She said that one day, we would banish Hades and all traces of The Dark Faction to The Underworld. We were going to restore the balance of power in our favor. It turned out, I was the biggest let down of them all.

"High Matriarch," stumbled Owen, dropping the dagger to fix his clothes. "I was just admiring your daughter. Her grace and poise are unrivaled—"

"Yes," my mother cut in, stopping him mid-lie with a single word. The condescending tilt of her chin and her appraising gaze had me feeling like I was a child again. "My *daughter* has such elegance acting like a common pig rutting in a field."

My cheeks blazed as Owen sputtered a response, somehow agreeing with her while also professing his honorable intentions for me.

Male witches possessed magic as well, though they anchored in nature as opposed to our casting abilities. They were a tether to the earth, a grounding presence—but I'd made sure to select Owen because he was purely mortal. Not a single drop of magic in him. Something my bitch-of-a-mother would loathe.

"And marriage does tend to increase a woman's odds of

6 | SPRING'S DESCENT

surviving the awakening, or so I'm told," Owen continued, the pitch of his tone taking on a familiar arrogance.

"Get to your point," Mother warned, still glaring at me as if she were worried I'd drop to my knees for him right in front of her. I held her gaze unflinchingly, wondering how such a stuck up, hateful thing could ever bring a child into this world.

"I'd like to ask for Korae's hand in marriage."

My head snapped to Owen, eyes wide with disbelief. Life was harsh. Every day wasn't guaranteed. Other witches like me realized we'd probably be dead long before we felt true magic.

But marriage? I'd rather take my chances in The Underworld.

"You can't be serious," I breathed.

Anger flickered in his eyes for all of a heartbeat before it was replaced with a self-assuredness that had probably gotten him through every obstacle in life.

"We'll wed the night before your awakening," Owens said, turning down the edges of his soiled collar as if the cum sprayed across it were some sort of trophy. "It will increase your odds of survival—"

"While also giving you access to my power," I cut in.

"What power, daughter?" Mother's voice was low, but it shot through the clearing and into my chest with the accuracy of a skilled archer.

Owen's lips twitched, a triumphant smirk twisting his lips.

"A kind offer to preserve what scraps of dignity my daughter's reputation clings to," Mother said, her voice dripping with false kindness. She took a step forward, looking me over as if I were a prized cow raised for slaughter only to fall short at the auction. "But I'm afraid she can't wed you."

Disbelief clashed with hope as my gaze bounced between them. Was she sticking up for me? Despite everything she'd put me through, maybe there was a piece of my mother that still cared. Somewhere, deep down, maybe there was a lingering seed of compassion pushing its way to the surface now that my time on this earth was coming to an end.

Mother's lips twisted into an evil, pitiful grin. "Korae is already betrothed."

2

PERSEPHONE

"Betrothed?" I echoed, brows furrowing. My mother stepped back with a twisted smile on her face, one that showed she was enjoying every moment of this. The lilac scent of her magic shifted with the breeze, transitioning into one of cedar. I fought the urge to run, my stomach twisting, as a figure behind her emerged from the trees.

Cyrus's long blond hair had been left down, stretching well past his broad shoulders and defined chest. Despite the crisp, early spring air, he was clad only in a thin tunic and pants, revealing the sword strapped to his waist. The sight of the weapon was almost enough to break the mounting tension in the clearing.

Though a strong grounder, Cyrus's skills with a blade were pitiful. He was the type of man that relied on others for protection, his wealth and high rank in the Green Coven sheltering him from life's bitter realities. I could've had him disarmed and at the pointy end of the blade in no time if it were a fair fight. But life wasn't fair.

"I've asked Cyrus to help Korae through her transition,"

Demeter said, her upper lip curling as she said my name. "And he has accepted."

"You've got to be kidding." A harsh laugh left my lips. "Cyrus isn't even in our coven. He'll barely increase the odds of my survival—"

"Enough," Cyrus snapped, his silver eyes blazing.

He strutted forward, scaring the stableboy into a retreat, until he was positioned just before me. Electricity pricked the air as Cyrus drew power toward him, but I refused to cower.

This asshole wanted me meek and trembling. He enjoyed the sight of me bruised and bleeding before him after one of Mother's outbursts, waiting for him to heal whatever bones she'd fractured. I'd been many things in my short life—weak, useless, a complete fuck up—but never broken.

"I decide my future," I challenged, lifting my chin in an attempt to hide how my hands shook both from anger and a hint of conditioned fear. Cyrus may be terrible with a sword, but he and mother wielded a lot of magic. Not to mention he was double my size.

"I've given Demeter my word," Cyrus said. "You will be mine, Korae, in one month on the eve of your twenty-first birthday."

"Ko-rae," I said, enunciating each syllable as I gestured with my hands to be even more obnoxious. I hated my name, but he sure as shit was going to get it right. "Like a ray of fucking sunshine."

"My apologies, Lord Cyrus," Owen muttered, completely ignoring me as he held out a muddy hand for him to shake. "I had no idea she was yours."

"I'm not anyones," I growled through clenched teeth as my cheeks flamed, no doubt growing nearly as red as my hair.

Marriage was the one exception to covens remaining on their own. Cyrus and his followers joined us in hiding just after we split from The Crystal City. Unlike the strong casters of the Earth Coven, green witches were known for leading quiet lives focused on healing, but they'd shown up one day kissing Mother's ass and hadn't left.

"Don't let it happen again," Cyrus warned, looking down his nose at the stableboy. "From this point on, Korae is my future wife and will be treated as such."

"Of course." Owen bowed—*bowed* to this asshole—before dashing from the field and leaving me alone with my two least favorite people in the world.

If it wasn't for the threat of the Dark Faction finding me—finding us all—I would've fled ages ago. I was trapped here, or at least I had been. I'd begun realizing that this was all going to end one way or another, and when it did, I wanted to go out on my own terms.

Death was waiting for me.

It could be worse. I could be forced into marriage with the piece-of-shit-witch Cyrus, and have my powers bound to his for all time.

"I'm not marrying you," I seethed, trampling over blossoms as I pushed past the two of them into the pine forest. The pads of my fingers grazed the fire opal dangling from the golden chain around my neck, seeking comfort in the stone.

I'd made it all of three steps before vines lashed at my ankles and chest, winding up my knees and across my shoulders. Others coiled along my wrists, jerking my arms behind my back until it was everything I could do just to remain standing.

"Do. Not. Walk away from me, child."

Shame-tinted anger coursed through my veins as her magic spun me to face her. I worked to fix the flippant smirk in place —the one she liked so much. It wasn't much, but it was the only form of protection I had. She might chip away at my body, force me to scream and cry, but I'd never let her see how wounded my soul was.

Looking at the loathing in her gaze, I wondered if she secretly prayed for Hecate to kill me.

"Do you have any idea how much of a mess you've made? I'm the head of the Earth Coven, the strongest witch ever known in The Realm of the Living, and yet my name has been dragged through the rat-infested gutters because my whore-of-a-daughter can't keep her legs shut."

The vines tightened, dragging a ragged breath from my lips as my skin split. My chest heaved and tears pricked my eyes, but I bit my lip against the cry, even as fat droplets of blood welled and splashed along the petals of wildflowers below.

My blood soaked her vines, the red linking together to carve trails down my fingers. All the while, the large emerald around Demeter's neck flared, flashing with her power.

Gritting my teeth against the slicing pain along my ankles and wrists, I met Mother's gaze, imparting everything I was too cowardly to say out loud.

Cyrus drank in my pain, his pupils dilating as my body shook. He tracked each slash across my skin, every flinch of agony I failed to conceal, before gazing at my mother with raw, unbridled desire.

Tears pricked my eyes, but I refused to let a single one fall. Instead, I focused on my rage. On the flicker of satisfaction I got from forcing my mother to expose who she really was. Nobody else saw this side of the High Matriarch—the vile, ugly soul lurking beneath her polished exterior—only me. And Cyrus.

She stepped closer, her pale eyes blazing with disgust. I ignored the way her revulsion pricked, the way my stomach clenched at her blatant abhorrence of me. I had stopped striving for her acceptance long ago.

"You will marry Cyrus on the eve of your awakening. He is a powerful grounder who might just be able to help you survive with the marriage bond complete and your magic merged."

Merged, as in we'd have to consummate the marriage as well as bind our souls to one another. There would be no separation.

Unable to stop myself, I glanced toward Cyrus and immediately regretted it. The hungry look plastered across his face was enough to make me nauseous. Bile burned the back of my throat as I thought about what the two of them would force me to endure. I would never be anything other than a hole for Cyrus to fill and a power source to exploit—both in name for my mother and body for my would-be husband.

"Don't be such a prude, Korae," Mother chided.

"Prude or whore, Mother? Which one is it?"

Her hand lashed out before I had time to brace for the impact. The slap was vicious, jerking my head to the side and splitting my lip. Heat bloomed beneath the stinging impact, and the tears I'd worked so hard to hold back tumbled free.

I focused on the warmth of my blood coating my fingers, on the faint traces of fresh air and wildflowers surrounding me. And then I poured every last drop of my concentration on counting to ten.

There was nothing else to do. Mother never stopped with one strike. I was useless. Powerless to do anything but find a way to survive, I focused on making it through the next ten seconds as she unleashed all her pent up fury.

One. Two.

"Pathetic waste of a witch." I doubled over as far as her vines would allow, gasping for breath as her fist collided with my stomach.

Three. Four. Five.

"An embarrassment." Quick flicks of her wrists had the vines drawing back. The crack of the whip rang through the air as they lashed at my chest, slicing through my clothing and skin mercilessly.

"More," Cyrus growled as a tortured cry rang in my throat.

Six. They couldn't touch me—not the real me. I only needed to fixate on the infinite rage I kept smoldering inside. The relentless fire that burned right next to my endless self-loathing.

Knuckles collided with my cheek. Vines devouring my legs.

Slice and sting. Blood and pain.

What number was I on?

"Earth witches are meant to be poised," Mother spat. "Balanced and beautiful always. But *you*. Just look at you. There's nothing beautiful. Nothing worthy. Just a fat, attention-seeking *waste*."

Humiliation burned in my gut, worse than my cracked ribs or the dozens of cuts marring my body. Worse than *any* physical pain. Because despite how desperately I didn't want to… that self-conscious little girl inside of me believed her.

Demeter smiled triumphantly, as if sensing my shame. She stepped back next to Cyrus, surveying my shattered body as she rested her long fingers on his shoulder.

"All that is required, daughter, is for you to fuck the night of the wedding. We won't need to share him indefinitely."

My stomach heaved as she leaned in, her lips pressing against Cyrus's neck as her cold gaze stayed fixed to mine.

Just once, I wondered what it would be like to have a mother who fucking *cared*. One who did her best to calm my fears, who loved me enough to lie and say that everything was going to be all right.

"I'd rather die," I breathed, spitting out blood. I hated the way I was too weak to prevent my voice from shaking. Loathed that my only options were to bind my body and soul to my mother's fuck boy or meet my fate in The Underworld.

"Careful what you ask for," Mother cooed.

A gasp tore from my lips as the vines along my wrists and ankles tighten, slicing through my flayed skin, digging into muscle as they lifted me from the ground. I wanted to rage, to fight and scream, but only a tormented whimper came.

"I won't be made a fool, daughter. Not even by you."

The vines withdrew a moment later, dropping me to the blood-stained ground with a harsh thud. Having gotten her point across, she turned and walked away without bothering to look back.

"Clean her up," she called to Cyrus over her shoulder. The maliciousness of her voice had cooled into a contained politeness as if she had spent the last few minutes admiring the flowers. "I don't want any proof of what happened."

My bitch-of-a-mother covered her tracks well. She always had, but with Cyrus here to clean up her messes, she'd become fearless.

I wondered if all people were like that. Able to flash a smile and a few soothing words for the public but commit vile acts in the shadows. Did compassion even really exist, or was it simply something we pretended to feel? Another tool to keep the weak and impressionable people of the world oppressed?

"Come now, Korae," Cyrus tsked as he bent down beside me, careful to step outside the pool of blood flowing freely from my lacerated wrists and ankles. My left eye was swollen shut, and there was a bubbling wheeze in my lungs. Maybe this time my injuries would be too great, and I'd finally get some peace. "Hate me all you like, but we both know you'll do as you're told."

I recoiled from his touch, the jarring motion causing my vision to spot. Mother had used her magic on me before, but this was pushing it. If I were awakened, I'd be stronger and able to heal, but right now, I was as good as human. If I kept bleeding for just a few moments longer, this would all be over...

Cyrus's cruel laugh pulled me back to the present as his hands clamped around the raw, ripped tissue of my wrists.

"Don't worry, Korae." His breath heated my cheek as he leaned in, the smell of lilac clinging to his skin—my mother's scent. "Once you're awakened, things will be different. You'll see."

Cold energy flooded into me from Cyrus's grip, slowly working its way up my arms. It felt like sludge, like clumps of rotting grass clogged my veins, forcing its way through my body. Splintered bones snapped back into place as vessels knit themselves back together.

"That was close," Cyrus said, rolling out his shoulders as fell back, catching myself on my hands.

My palms dug into the blood-stained grass as I panted for air. All of my injuries had been healed as if I hadn't been on the verge of death moments before. My body might be free of scars, but I was left with an oily residue of his magic violating the crisp cleanness of my own. And though I knew Cyrus had saved my life, had given instead of taken, I couldn't help but feel as if I've been used.

"But now we know how much fun you can handle." Cyrus dragged me to stand, pinching my chin between his fingers as he pressed a disgustingly soft kiss to my forehead. "Once you bind yourself to me, we can play every day."

3

HADES

BLOOD DRIPPED FROM THE MORTAL'S MOUTH, THE STEADY DRIBBLE running down his neck and staining his ruined tunic as he struggled to breathe. My shadows held him by the throat, keeping his boots just barely scraping the smooth white rock of my torture chamber. Red was everywhere, spraying the walls, pooling along the floor. It looked like a grotesque painting from a mad artist.

And gods, was I creating a masterpiece.

Allowing my head to drop back, I inhaled deeply, relishing the metallic tang of copper and fear. My lips stretched into a satisfied grin as I spotted ruby drops splashed across the ceiling.

Delightful.

"Please," the man cried, tears squeezing out beneath the swollen pulp of skin that was once his face. "What do you want? I'll give you anything."

My fists clenched, the veins along my forearms standing out as I fought the urge to punch him again. The sound of his voice alone was nearly enough to send me into a blind rage all over again.

I hadn't bothered to ask questions when I'd found him.

Hadn't been able to think around the scent of *her* clinging to his body—a faint hint of wildflowers among the rot of stale beer and horses. Even now, with the walls decorated in his blood, it took every fiber of my wretched being not to let my shadows rip him to pieces.

This was how it had been for the last hundred years. Nothing but rage and pain and the occasional partner I used for pleasure. I remembered feeling other emotions before. Joy. Lust. Maybe even something close to love, once. But not anymore. The Underworld was crumbling. An entire realm full of souls relied on me to keep them safe... and I was failing.

With deliberate slowness, I crept toward him, allowing my ram horns to shimmer into being as I fed on his terror. I was The Devil Beneath, the monster those in the Realm of the Living ran from. Fuck, even my brothers and sisters chose to avoid The Underworld, fearful of my wrath. And right now, with my great, leathery wings cast wide and the normal cerulean blue of my eyes eclipsed in black, I looked every bit the creature of darkness that I was.

"Where is she?"

His chest heaved as his breath came in rapid pants, each expansion causing a wince. "Who?"

My shadows tightened around his throat, yanking him off the floor completely. He struggled, his fingers clawing at the band of darkness around his neck as his eyes bulged.

Nostrils flaring, I gripped his chin between my fingers, forcing him to meet my cursed gaze.

"Look at me," I commanded, my upper lip curling as the scent of his terror spiked.

"Please," he cried as his eyes met mine, his body trembling around a silent scream.

Slipping into his mind, I called forward the horror of his nightmares, forcing him to relive each one. It was one of my many talents as Lord of the Underworld, one that I enjoyed quite a bit. I grew strong on his suffering, watching as the pulse in his neck thrummed, as his skin paled and his body quaked.

Delightful.

Only after a hopeless whimper tore itself from his throat did I let up.

"The woman you sank your cock into," I snarled, shadows growing denser around us as the temperature dropped.

"I—I didn't do anything she didn't want," he stammered as my fists flexed. As much as I wished he weren't, I knew when it came to Persephone he was telling the truth. But he couldn't hide his past from me—couldn't erase the black haze of his soul from what he'd done to the first girl who'd trusted him to keep her safe. For that, for every second he'd lived unencumbered by guilt while that girl lived haunted by his touch, I'd make him pay.

"She's *mine*," I seethed, my fist colliding with his face, splintering the bones beneath. "Where?"

Blood ran freely from his nose, mixing with the drool and bits of chipped teeth that splattered the white tiles on the floor.

"Willowcrest," he mumbled between tears. "Korae is there. In the heart of The Black Forest."

Korae. That's what Demeter was calling her. My upper lip curled, already knowing why she picked it. Korae meant maiden. Another earth witch Demeter had raised this past decade to be quiet and tame. Though the piece-of-shit before me proved she wasn't one to follow the rules, I knew my betrothed—my soon-to-be-wife—would be another witch poisoned with a hatred for my kind.

No matter. She would be mine one way or another. And if she was fucking around with this guy, someone who wouldn't know where a clit was if it had an arrow pointing to it—Well, I'd enjoy showing her what it meant to be fucked by a god.

Ignoring the stench of the mortal's fear and the metallic tang of blood, I honed in on her sweetness. Inhaling deeply, I committed her scent to memory—vanilla with a hint of wild-flower. My mouth salivated. Gods, she smelled delicious.

The time for hiding was over. Soon, I'd have my little witch in my arms. I hoped she begged. My cock twitched at the idea of her on her knees before me, pleading for a mercy that wouldn't come.

"Thanatos, it's time." I stepped away from the shaking human as my shadows descended. I let his screams echo in the chamber for a moment longer, relishing that he knew the God of Death was on his way to greet him, before abruptly cutting them off with a sharp snap of his neck.

The air shifted as the gentle beating of wings reached me. Thanatos's white feathers and striking silhouette appeared a moment later, complete with the scythe he used to reap wicked souls. The God of Death stood a few inches taller than my six-foot-three, all lean muscle and speed where I was thicker across the chest and thighs. His silver-blond hair was longer than mine, his skin a pale, bone-white hue. His bright blue eyes and full pink lips paired with the white wings had him the picture of what mortals called 'angels'. Little did they know, Thanatos was the one sent to collect souls when their life strings were cut and drag them into The Underworld for me to keep.

A brow quirked as his sharp gaze looked over the mess I'd created.

"What did that poor bastard do?"

"He slept with my wife."

Thanatos's lips twitched. "I thought the wedding wasn't until next month. And then there's the whole problem of finding the bride in time."

"We have her location," I said, turning from the room, rolling out my shoulders as I head for the door. "It's time to collect my betrothed."

"She's going to fight you," Thanatos warned, falling in line behind me. "Demeter has filled her head with nothing but hatred for those in The Underworld. You most of all."

"Then I'll hide my identity until she gives herself to me, body and soul."

Only then would The Underworld stabilize. Death was powerful, but without life to offer balance, it was an unstoppable void, ravaging not only my realm but that of the living as well. My little witch needed to join my side, to take her rightful place as my bride, ensuring all would be restored.

"Aidoneus should do nicely," I added. Thanatos lifted a brow at me. I shrugged. "Hecate insists I was once called that in another life."

"It's better, but she'll run either way," Thanatos said.

My wings bristled as my palms shoved the door open. The cool, crisp air felt like the first breath I'd had in hours. Letting my wings expand, I tilted my head up to the darkness above. "It's a good thing I love the hunt."

I'd been stalking her for years, my little witch always just out of reach. But tonight, I'd gotten her scent, and fuck if I didn't want to drown in it. She could run as fast and as far as she liked. It made no difference. I would find her. And when I did, I'd drag my little witch to The Underworld to be my bride. My queen. To be my goddess forever.

4

PERSEPHONE

"She wants you to marry Cyrus?" Larkspur asked, dragging the brush through my still damp hair. I'd scrubbed my skin until it was pink but couldn't erase the feel of Cyrus's magic. She knew what had happened the moment I returned to my room—the only other person in the world who saw the harsh realities of this coven like I did. Lark had brought up two steaming cups of tea seeping on the low-set table in front of the worn sitting couch while I was in the shower and was now working my favorite wildflower-scented oil thoroughly through my curls, gently tugging the knots free.

I allowed myself to sink into her touch, wondering if this was what it would've felt like to have a big sister.

"Yep." My voice was devoid of emotion as I looked my body over in the mirror. A thin silk robe hung low across my shoulders, exposing my collarbones and a large portion of my chest. They weren't sticking out nearly as much as Mother would have liked thanks to Lark sneaking me small loaves of bread from the kitchen whenever she could. Lark said it was a good thing I wasn't as thin as the others, despite how the rest of the coven whispered.

I had felt stronger and was able to keep up with Lark during our secret training sessions now, but it was hard not to feel like I'd failed somehow.

The tap of the brush on the counter drew my gaze up, finding Lark's hazel eyes swirling with concern. Her long hair was tied back, showing off her strong cheekbones and flawless dark skin. Gods above, I wished I could look like her.

"Cyrus as in the blond who is so far up Demeter's ass that he wouldn't be able to tell the difference between night and day?"

"That's the one. As if that wasn't bad enough, I'm pretty sure they're fucking."

"Eww." Lark wrinkled her nose as the two of us moved from the ensuite to the couch. The plush cushions were bleached by the sun, the rich yellow fading into a pale cream, and the whole thing was permanently sloped in the middle, but it was a safe place Lark and I had to shed the masks we were forced to wear.

According to Mother, my room was small compared to what was normal for the next leader of the Earth Coven. She talked often about the luxuries we were missing being out here in the woods rather than our rightful place in The Crystal City. I only wished it could leave my mother and this shitty coven behind.

"Let me get this straight," Lark continued as I sank into my side of the couch. "Your mother is sleeping with Cyrus but expects you to marry him anyway?"

My stomach churned, but I nodded. "I can't do it, Lark. Even if they weren't, I can't bind my soul to a man like him."

"Hold on." She turned toward the door, retrieving a bottle of wine from her bag hanging on a peg by the door before returning to my side. She had on her servant gown, the forest green a few shades darker than my eyes. Lark was forced to wear it every day—a beacon among the coven that she betrayed us, but it only seemed to compliment her umber curls. "I think we might need something stronger than tea tonight."

A smile tilted the edges of my lips as I saw the vintage label.

"Even if I had a bottle of this daily for the rest of my life, I couldn't go through with marrying him."

"I get it, Rae, but you know Demeter has a way of getting what she wants." The cushions dipped under Lark's curvy figure as she sat next to me. Lark's body was just like her powers: Seduction. Persuasion. Compulsion—none of which were powers from the Earth Coven. She hardly ever used her magic, but occasionally, when the moon was high, Lark would play.

We were told her types of gifts came from The Underworld, that anyone capable of such magic should be banished from the Realm of the Living immediately, but I wondered if all magic didn't come from Hecate herself.

"Demeter will deny having a relationship with him. Nobody else will understand why you won't marry Cyrus, especially since you've only had flickers of power."

"I don't care if anyone else gets it, Lark. Despite being the High Matriarch, Mother can't force me to bond."

Popping off the cork, Lark held the bottle out for me, the warm spices reaching across the space between us. "This conversation requires a drink."

I took it, the glass cool against my lips as I drank. I didn't want there to *be* a conversation. This was my decision. My choice. Even if it meant taking my chances with meeting Thanatos sooner rather than later.

But Lark was my friend, the only person to have shown me kindness in this life—beside Ruby. Ruby and I had been close as children in The Crystal City, our families having grown up together. At the time, Ruby's mother was in line to be High Matriarch before The Dark Faction destroyed everything.

Ruby was six years older than me, her magic showing signs even when we were children. She'd been the first person to hide with me when Mother was angry. She would create a distraction long enough for me to run or she would hold me when the tears wouldn't stop. She'd even stepped in front of me once, Mother's hand splitting her lip instead of mine.

I would never forget the fear in Ruby's eyes as she wiped away the blood. It was the first time I realized most parents didn't hit their children.

She promised she would save me, that we would tell her mother, and everything would be okay. But then The Dark Faction attacked. The two of us escaped the massacre, forced to bow to Demeter's whims in this new hell. I thought that was the worst of it until... until her awakening. She was one of the first claimed by Hecate. One of the first sacrificed to offset the death magic ravaging our world.

"Marriage could help," Lark said as I lifted the bottle to my lips again.

I coughed, choking down another gulp as I wiped the mess away from my lips with the back of my hand. "You can't be serious—"

"Not with Cyrus," Lark amended, snatching the bottle from my hands and taking her own sip. "Obviously. He's probably one of those guys who thinks he's great at sex, but the entire time he's been rubbing your left fold while thinking it's your clit."

I snorted a laugh as she continued.

"But the marriage part. That would give you a boost in power and increase your chances of surviving. Even Willow is set to marry a witch from the Green Coven next week, the night before her awakening."

"Why? Her powers have shown since she was thirteen."

"She wants to have the best chance at surviving, and Demeter made it pretty clear marrying green witches is the only way to do that." Lark sighed as I grimaced. "I don't like it either, Rae. My point is, that it's normal for witches to wed before their awakening. Expected even. Marriage is better than death."

Not entirely sure I agreed with that statement, I watched the dark liquid lap at the sides as I swirled the glass bottle. It *could* give me an edge if the person who I linked my life with was powerful.

Handing the bottle over, I reached for the tea. A bitter scent reached me, causing me to wrinkle my nose. *Not the chamomile I'd been expecting.* This was my monthly tonic to prevent pregnancy, and while it always made me sleepy, I felt drained after. Not rested. Lark reported no such issues with her tonic. I would have to choke it down eventually, but I'd wait until I was turning in for the night.

"There was another attack." Lark glanced to the wooden door, listening for signs of others. We were on the third floor—the top level of the tallest building in the little town our coven had crafted in The Black Forest. A glance toward the narrow windows showed nothing but branches and the night sky, meaning everyone should be asleep by now, but our lack of caution had earned Lark a few beatings in the past. "I overheard the kitchen staff. An entire village consumed by the darkness in the east near Green Coven territory."

"Gods," I breathed, my stomach twisting. "The Dark Faction?"

"Who else? Based on the number of deaths, witches think The Hound of Hell was there, slaughtering mortal souls to add to Hades's realm." She shook her head. "I only bring it up to point out that it isn't just the covens who are affected by the Dark Faction. The entire Realm of the Living is suffering. We need every witch possible to fight this. Maybe marriage wouldn't be so bad if it meant you got to live."

"No," I said after a long moment. "The only person I trust with my life is you. Everyone else here would fuck me over the first chance they got."

"You'd rather die?" Her voice was gentle, but I could hear the worry beneath it.

Unable to meet her gaze, I lifted the bottle to my lips once more, savoring the spices rolling over my tongue. I could almost see the earth where the grapes were grown. Nearly feel them ripening in the sun. Earth witches were meant to connect with nature and spend their lives bettering plants and forests around them. I wondered what my life would have looked like if the realms weren't set on war.

"I would rather die as myself than live as another."

Lark's shoulders slumped as she forced a long, low breath out. Her hazel eyes dropped to the floor for a moment before a forced smile was etched back in place.

"We should go out."

I snorted at the rapid change in topic. "To where? Her Royal Bitch-Witch is pissed at me for the stableboy *and* my refusal to marry Cyrus. There's bound to be extra eyes on our building tonight."

Her full lips tilted in a wicked smirk. "It's a good thing most everyone will be sleeping when we leave."

"Sneaking out?"

She nodded, seeing the hint of life spark in my eyes. "The kitchen staff have been talking about a traveling singer in the pub. His voice was so captivating that they think he's descended from faeries—Or that he's made a deal with Hades himself. The town hasn't decided which tale to believe, yet."

"The pub we went to last month?"

"Of course," Lark said. "Where else would we go around here?"

True. Willowcrest was the only town near enough for late night adventures. Adventures that had proven quite beneficial. I clenched my thighs together, remembering the last week when a tall green witch took me out back in a cluster of oak trees. The bark of the tree he'd pressed me against had bitten into my back as the sweet scent of moon flowers mixed with the musk of his body. The light from the tavern windows stretched across the night while the stars shone overhead.

Now *that* had been a good fuck.

"Most of the town will probably be there," Lark added, lifting a brow at the blush across my cheeks. "You might see that guy from last time."

I shook my head. "He was great in bed, but he started praising the Green Coven's teachings when we came back inside."

"Like their affinity for healing, or…?"

"More like, 'women shouldn't be burden with the pressures of running towns.'"

"Gross."

"Yep. He asked me if I was on a monthly tonic after we'd already fucked and then proceeded to tell me how he was against them and if a pregnancy was meant to be, we should let nature take its course."

"Fuck that," Lark said, shaking her head. "Just because the covens are shrinking doesn't mean we should be forced into parenthood."

Cyrus had been very vocal on the need to return the coven to what it once was. With more and more witches claimed at their awakenings and fewer people choosing to have children, he wanted to unite witches across The Realm of the Living with the aim of replenishing magic. It sounded good on the surface, but if he had his way, we'd be little more than breeders for the men. Our bodies theirs to use.

And now, I was betrothed to that asshole.

My stomach twisted as I forced out a breath. I reached for the bottle, intending to take another long swig, only to find it empty. My world was entirely fucked, but more wine and a night out with my best friend would go a long way to make things better.

5

HADES

CRISP SPRING AIR SWIRLED THROUGH THE OPEN MOUTH OF THE cave as the veil between our worlds lifted. The scent of pine mingled with night-blooming flowers as coarse stones crunched beneath my boots. Soft light of the moon illuminated the rocky alcove I was poised on, shining down on the forest below, as I surveyed the world before me.

Willowcrest was a little over a mile from here, but the full moon and clear skies allowed me to spot the thatched-roofed homes clustered around a boisterous inn. Humans swarmed the place, some pairing off and venturing into the forest while others remained in the spots of light spanning out from the tavern windows.

Mortals had a way of making noise. Like a hive of bees constantly humming. Even now, when the day had long since passed and stars filled the sky, they continued to buzz.

Like an infestation.

Before this century, it had been a hundred years since I'd left The Underworld. Since I'd had a reason to risk forgoing the comforts of my own kingdom to venture into The Realm of the Living. Thanatos and Hecate had been my scouts here for the better part of a decade while I searched every inch of The Underworld for a trace of Persephone.

But I'd lost track of time.

I'd joined Thanatos this past year as Hecate's ability to travel between realms grew harder, her magic weakening in time with the power of the covens. My little witch had evaded me for too long, and now both our worlds were suffering for it.

The night air shifted, bringing with it the scent of rosewood and the subtle sounds of large, feathered wings overhead. Thanatos dropped from the sky a moment later, the soles of his boots gentle on the hard earth. His silver blond hair was half bound, the long stands reaching well past his shoulders.

"Anything?" I asked, keeping my voice low as I scanned the trees. We'd told only Hecate of our plans to venture between realms, but that didn't mean my bastard-of-a-brother wouldn't have spies scattered across The Realm of the Living, just in case.

Zeus knew of the rapidly approaching deadline, as did the other gods in The Aboveworld, and did nothing.

Never mind that the death magic was running wild in my realm, as well. My brothers and sisters hadn't started this apocalypse, but they didn't particularly care if it came to fruition.

They were convinced I would fail. When I did, when every soul in The Realm of the Living was forced to The Underworld, Zeus would create a new generation of humans. Like a spoiled child exchanging his old toys for new ones.

Thanatos was one of the few gods who sided with me. Being the God of Death forced you to grasp the enormity of a soul transitioning between realms. He was my brother in every way that mattered, the one being who'd been by my side through it all—war, women, and curses. Hecate understood enough, but Thanatos felt each loss as I did.

"Not yet," he said, his white wings vanishing from view as he stepped beside me. "But the humans in town tell tales of powerful witches from the forest. Witches who enjoy music and drink... and the occasional partner."

My teeth clenched. It would seem my little witch enjoyed rebelling against Demeter more often than I realized. It should have been a relief that I wasn't marrying a pious bigot, a sign that perhaps I could get her to set aside her prejudices and join The Dark Faction willingly, but the thought of her scent clinging to another caused an unfamiliar burn in the pit of my stomach—was that jealousy?

I'd had fleeting nights of pleasure myself, but it was an exchange. A basic need being met—like eating or drinking. Everything, all emotion other than anger and pain had been stripped from me long ago. There was a time when it had been more, a fading memory of blood racing and bodies moving, but those days were gone.

This wasn't about love. It never would be. Love was a fool's notion, a ridiculous belief mortals concocted to lighten the harsh reality of their short, miserable lives.

This was about possession. Claiming my little witch would ensure power was returned to me.

That was all it was. All it could ever be. But the thought of her fucking another felt like a dull knife sawing through bone.

"I've had Orpheus playing ballads to lure witches for the last three days," Thanatos continued in a conversational tone, the same one he always got when trying to steer me away from a killing spree. I may not be as callous as my siblings, but there were always souls in need of punishment. "Word is circulating. If the Earth Coven is truly in The Black Forest, Persephone will appear within the week."

I nodded. "Demeter is calling her 'Korae'. I doubt she knows her true name."

"I've informed him," Thanatos said. "The witches who frequent the tavern never stay. Orpheus says some linger through the night if they choose to take a lover, but all return before the sun rises."

My nostrils flared but I pushed the flicker of anger from my mind and stepped forward, teetering on the cliff's edge. The tavern continued to fill, but I sensed no flash of power among its patrons. No promise of redemption. "We have a month, brother. One month until all is lost."

"We'll find her. Orpheus was sure a few witches visited yesterday. We only need to wait for the first to arrive and then follow them back to the coven."

"As we have done time and time again," I gritted out, the darkness inside of me spilling over. The sparse foliage peeking through the rocky cliff withered as the temperature around us dropped. "Another forest. Another coven, but I can't scent her. What if the stableboy was wrong? Who's to say we're any closer to finding her?"

"Don't do that. This is the last coven founded by earth witches originating from The Crystal City. I'll take the far edge of the forest while you stay near. She must be here," Thanatos said, taking a step back as shadows condensed around me. Frost fissured out along smooth stones as the plants alive and thriving only moments before blackened into husks devoid of life. But he didn't run. Didn't flinch under the might of the death magic.

He understood the strain I was under because he'd been the one cleaning up my messes.

Rolling out my shoulders, I took a deep breath and drew the darkness toward me, coiling it tightly within my being where it couldn't hurt anyone. The anger I'd felt moments ago chilled as the dark magic of The Underworld rushed through my veins, weaving its cold power through my very soul.

"You can't keep taking the power into yourself, Hades." Thanatos's voice was soft, not chiding but concerned. "You may be the God of The Underworld, but you are not immune to the effects of death magic."

I didn't bother responding. It had felt like an ice pick slicing through my ribs the first few times I'd taken back the death magic, but my heart had stopped beating long ago, frozen by the infinite darkness. I barely felt it now. Barely felt anything.

We'd had this conversation hundreds of times and the results were always the same: Thanatos cautioned me while I reminded him we had no other option.

Tilting my chin to the moon, I lifted my hands to the stars, expelling a fraction of the creeping cold, more to appease him than anything. The slim traces of moisture in the air froze into dozens of shimmering crystals before pinging in the branches of the trees below.

Those little displays no longer helped. I still felt cold, like the magic of The Underworld was slowly changing me into stone. With this much death magic flowing in my veins, I wondered if I would be cursed to remain. If Persephone escaped and the realms fell, would there be anything left of me to save?

"Shall I fetch Orpheus?"

"No," I said, allowing the tendrils of my magic to stretch along the edge of the forest. It was a risk to expose my power over such a large area of land. If Demeter sensed me, she'd pack up the witches and flee. But if my little witch was near, she'd be drawn toward me, like a moth to flame. "Let Orpheus play while he can. If he is as good as he claims, Persephone should be along shortly."

"And what happens when she does appear?" he asked, sounding like he already knew the answer. He shifted from foot to foot, shooting me a cautious glance. "She'll need to be eased into things, Hades. It's not her fault she's been lied to her whole life."

I knew he was right, but the gripping numbness of death magic had yet to fade... and couldn't find a way to connect to whatever empathy remained in my twisted soul. There was only one thought on my mind. A single need driving me forward.

"When my little witch finally reveals herself, I plan on showing her who she belongs to."

6

PERSEPHONE

"I HAVE THE PERFECT DRESS." LARK SPRANG UP FROM THE COUCH, the wine making her movements wobbly. The tea cups clamored against the wooden surface as her shins hit the edge of the table. "Gods above. Sorry Rae. I'll get another tea before we go."

"Don't worry about it," I said as I headed to the small cabinet to grab towels. "I'm betrothed now, remember? It's not like I'll be sleeping with anyone. Cyrus and Mother have no doubt spread the word that I'm off limits."

Lark knelt beside me, taking one of the towels to help mop up the mess.

"I'm off limits," I repeated, my hand stilling around the wet cloth.

"Rae?" Lark asked, lifting a brow. "What is it?"

"The stableboy, Ollie—"

"Owen."

"Yeah, Owen. He was my last fuck. And it was *terrible*." I threw my head back with a groan as the reality of my future sank in.

A drunken laugh escaped her. "I told you, you had to be on

top. He may not know what he's doing, but he's not bad to look at."

Agree to disagree.

"You probably scared the poor guy."

"Hardly." I huffed, gathering the damp towels and placing them in the laundry bin. "He offered to marry me before Cyrus showed up."

"He did?" Lark asked, her eyes swirling with that far-off look she got when she was hatching a plan.

"Don't get too excited. My mother shut him down and Cyrus confirmed I'm not to be touched."

"Shit. Why does it have to be Cyrus?"

"I don't know," I breathed, catching a glimpse of myself in the mirror. My fingers closed around the fire opal at the end of the gold chain, wishing I'd have the chance to claim a real conducting stone from the caverns of The Crystal City when the first tendrils of my power manifested, like every earth witch had done centuries before.

Just another thing to grieve.

"This is all I am, Lark. A tool to be used by Cyrus. A lump of clay to be shaped by my mother. A sacrifice to the goddess for the good of our coven."

"*This* is not all that you are, Rae." Lark grasped my hands, forcing me to meet her gaze. "This prison, that bitch of a High Matriarch, your fucking betrothed—*all of it* will be a bad memory one day. We're getting out of here."

"Of course," I said, not quite selling my false bravado. We'd made that promise to each other so many times in the last four years. I wondered when it started tasting like a lie.

"There may be a lot of things out of our control, but tonight isn't one of them," Lark said, dragging me toward the closet. "Let's make it a night to remember."

～

"LOOKING GOOD, RAE," LARK SMILED, BEFORE RETURNING TO fine-tuning the soft, umber curls falling perfectly falling past her shoulders. Her hazel eyes looked over her makeup, searching for any imperfection and finding nothing. I wasn't even sure why she bothered with powder. Her dark skin was flawless.

Not for the first time, I scrutinized the heavy spattering of freckles across my own face, their presence made only more pronounced from countless hours I'd spent in the sun. I knew it wasn't healthy, but I couldn't help but compare how Lark's dark skin was smooth, her nose sleek and strong, while mine was slightly upturned. My pale pink lips were lacking compared to the natural rose-colored hue of hers, and despite my nagging insecurities telling me to be thinner, I envied the roundness to her bust and hips. I was warm tones and sharp edges, while Lark was soft angles and bold lines—beautiful in a deadly sort of way.

And powerful. She'd survived her awakening just before Mother forced her to join us four years ago. Despite her servant status, Lark was important. She just had something about her that made others want to trust her. To listen to her. Sometimes I wondered if that was the real reason Mother punished her.

"Stop looking at me like that, Rae. You're making me blush."

"Ha-ha," I said, turning back to the mirror as I adjusted the laces of my corset. Lark was gorgeous, and the two of us had been through a lot, but we were friendship witches all the way.

I cinched the white panels of the corset just beneath my breasts, leaving the shimmering fabric of the gown beneath exposed. There were two long slits reaching up my thighs, the thin fabric and corset helping to exaggerate the narrow swell of my hips.

"You really outdid yourself this time," I said, looking myself over. Lark was seriously gifted when it came to making dresses.

She claimed there was no magic involved, but I'd never heard of another person being able to craft fabric like this.

Lark cocked her head to the side, taking in the outfit now that it was complete. "You look incredible."

"Are you sure it's not too much?"

"Absolutely not. Life is too short to be boring."

I fidgeted with the laces again, self-conscious without a bra. "Maybe I should wear the blue dress."

"The blue dress is for exploring the forest and seducing stableboys. *This* dress is perfect for attracting the types of men who know exactly what they want. The slits up to your pelvis will scare off the shy ones, leaving only those bold enough to act, which is your goal for tonight, right?"

Normally, it would be an easy 'yes'. Sneaking out to the tavern, finding a passing traveler who had no idea who or what I was exhilarating. Freeing in a way very little else in my life was.

For far too long, I'd been the quiet girl Mother wanted me to be. Then Lark showed up. Mother thought she'd serve as a warning: Mess-up-and-serve-the-coven-for-life sort of a thing. But Lark only ever made me stronger.

Even as a new witch, her abilities came naturally. We would creep into the forest trailing the other witches and had discovered Willowcrest. Every time we snuck out or trained, Lark practiced with her powers. She encouraged me to do the same, despite me only having wisps of magic accessible. Each small act of defiance felt like a win.

"Yes. My goal tonight is to remind myself that there's an entire world beyond The Black Forest. And maybe if I'm strong enough to survive, I won't always feel this way." Cyrus and Mother might have planted guards on our building, but I wasn't ready to give up my last few days of independence.

"*This* way?" Lark asked, her piercing hazel eyes not letting me look away.

If it were anyone else, I wouldn't have answered. I would have deflected and moved on... but this was Lark.

"I feel like... like I'm five sizes bigger than I'm supposed to be. Like I'm stretched to obscene proportions while everyone around me is the picture of beauty. I'm a giant in a room of faeries. A weed among a garden of pristine roses. And not just my body. It feels like me—*all of me*—is just too much."

"You're never too much." Lark squeezed my hands, refusing to let me retreat further. "This coven, hell, this entire section of the forest may make it seem that way, but there's nothing wrong with you. You're a wild bird who was born in a cage. A predator forced into submission. We only need to get you out of these bars and into the sky where you belong."

I swallowed around the tears working their way up. Lark's abilities allowed her to be more perceptive than most. She saw everything, the good and the bad. Sometimes it left me feeling vulnerable and too exposed, but in moments like this, it felt like being seen. Like maybe I wasn't invisible after all.

"Now," she said, straightening up before things got weird. "What are we going to do with your hair?"

"Up is probably best."

"Down it is," Lark said, reaching for a sleek black dress. The long-sleeved, floor-length gown covered Lark's body like a second skin, leaving little to the imagination.

"Black?" I asked. It was a foreboding color among our coven. Lark never cared much for superstitions, but black was the color of death—particularly, the color that was associated with The Dark Faction.

"The night to your light," she said, shooting me a wicked grin. "Not to mention, my eyes look incredible with heavy liner."

I rolled my eyes but couldn't argue.

"We could run tonight," I breathed, realizing this may be our last chance. We couldn't sneak out very often without getting caught and my birthday was next month.

Her eyes found mine in the mirror, waiting for me to make a joke. I didn't.

"I want to see you free of this place before..."

"The awakening will go off without a hitch," Lark said, spinning to pin me with her gaze. "You are the daughter of Demeter. As horrible as she is, she's the most powerful witch the Earth Coven has seen—the entire living *world* has seen—since Hecate. Some even level her skills to that of a goddess. She may be a bitch in every other regard, but the fates wouldn't take her only daughter. They wouldn't be that cruel."

Wouldn't they?

But I only shrugged as I sat on the edge of the couch to slip on my boots. They ruined the aesthetic Lark had worked so hard to create with the ethereal dress, but we had to make it through the forest before we reached the tavern. And I wasn't about to go slinking through the trees in the middle of the night in pointed heels.

"My fate is sealed either way. I'll die or I'll be forced to marry Cyrus. And right now, I'd prefer death."

"I can't say I blame you on that one." Lark's brows drew together, a frown forming on her red lips as she reached for the silver chain on the edge of the dresser. She lifted the necklace over her head, the crescent moon settling over her dress. An amethyst stone dangled from the tip, her conducting stone.

Pushing all thoughts of my awakening, of Cyrus, and my mother from my mind, I allowed Lark to cast a linking spell over my fire opal.

Earth witches' powers were tied to crystals, each precious stone connecting to a different aspect of magic. Not only were they emblems of pride, but the stones allowed a witch greater access to her magic. Those predisposed to protection spells drifted toward turquoise, intellectually driven witches focused on strengthening the spells in our grimoires chose lapis lazuli. Rose quartz and carnelian were popular with witches thought to have been blessed by both Aphrodite and Hecate, and amethyst was thought to help soothe the mind, particularly regarding harmful dreams.

Then there was an emerald, thought to increase the witch's affinity toward nature—a true earth witch. I'd read through every text in The Crystal City when I was younger. Fire opal had never been a conducting stone, but when Lark filled it with her magic and the shimmering stone warmed against my skin, I let myself believe it could be.

"Fuck buddies are limited to the immediate area," Lark began, going through her regular warnings. "If you need anything, hold your stone and say—"

"'The moon is high in the sky,'" I finished as I stumbled forward, the wine choosing that moment to catch up with me.

"Gods, you're already tipsy," Lark teased, looping her arm through mine as we snagged our cloaks and started toward the door. "We better get going or we'll miss the musician. I heard he was pining after a lost love. Maybe I'll be the one to mend his broken heart."

We started down the spiral stairs, careful to avoid the squeaky wooden floor boards beneath our steps and any stray witches roaming the halls. This was the hardest part of the evening. The one carrying the most risk. I'd almost died earlier today. I didn't want to think about what Demeter would do if I so publicly humiliated her. On second thought...

"Maybe we should let them catch us tonight," I whispered as we reached the ground floor and passed the first set of rooms. Lark lifted a brow, clearly waiting for me to elaborate. "If rumors of my whorish ways were confirmed throughout the coven, maybe Cyrus wouldn't want to marry me."

Lark's lips press thin, her eyes turning guarded as we passed more quiet rooms. "I don't think it's your virtue he's after, Rae. All it would achieve is another lashing."

Voices drifted through the night as we turned down the final corridor, light spilling into the dimly lit hallway a few paces up. It was coming from one of the studies, ones that were only ever used by green witches.

My pulse kicked up, every sense sharpening as the familiar tang of adrenaline flooded my veins. I should be worried someone would find us, but I felt more awake than ever. The potential of a fight—one that could quite possibly be my last—or the need to flee... it felt like a small flicker of life in my monotonous routine.

With nothing more than a glance, Lark and I hitched our dresses and cloaks up so that we were able to tiptoe forward.

"...that's right," Cyrus's familiar voice rang, the sound pricking the fine hairs along my arms. "Demeter said I can bend her daughter over and take whatever I want, however I want. It can be as bloody and brutal as I please, and I can share Korae with whomever I like as long as I marry the slut afterward."

7

PERSEPHONE

I HALTED AS CYRUS'S WORDS REGISTERED, FEELING AS THOUGH I'D been struck. Taking shaky breaths, I willed my body to stop trembling as I came to terms with just how evil my mother was. My own mother *sold* me to him, like I was nothing more than a trinket to barter. An annoyance to be rid of.

Shock gave way to disgust in the next second as I realized just how far Demeter would go to ensure her reputation and power remained intact.

Lark tugged on my arm, her eyes lifting to the ceiling in a silent question of if we should turn back.

"Why wait?" A feminine voice asked, before I could nod. There was a soft clatter, like a glass being set down before she spoke again. "Fuck her now and be done with it."

"I would enjoy seeing Korea on her knees, servicing me with bruises on her face, her lips split and bleeding from how hard I've used them."

My nostrils flared as the last remaining wisps of shock gave way to unbridled rage. That limp-dick-of-a-witch actually thought that I'd marry him? That I'd sacrifice every ounce of self-worth and yield to him because my mother said so?

Letting my anger guide me, I slipped my arm free of Lark's grasp and stalked forward until I was just outside the door. A quaint study composed of bookshelves and high-backed chairs centered around a small, rounded table came into view, but my attention snagged on the familiar sneer stretched across Cyrus's pompous face.

A roaring fire was blazing in the hearth behind him, the sharp planes of his face harsh in its light. The second chair was facing away, concealing everything of the other person, except a thin bracelet with a tear-drop diamond dangling from it. The gem rattled as she reached for her glass.

"It'll be a lot easier to make her death look like an accident if you're not married to the whore."

What the fuck?

Lark sucked in a breath, the two of us sharing a wide-eyed glance. She stretched forward, peering over my shoulder inside the room, but shook her head a moment later. She didn't know who the other person was either.

"I can't kill her until after the wedding," Cyrus chided. "She needs to be linked to me as well as the Earth Coven before her thread is cut, or else all that power will siphon back to them."

I lifted a brow toward Lark, but she was staring past me, her lips pressed into a hard line as she scanned the rest of the room.

"You're sure Demeter is okay with us killing her only daughter? I know she likes handling things herself."

A thin sheen of sweat broke across my brow as Lark wove her fingers through mine, urging me to retreat. My breath was coming in short bursts, my body already preparing for a fight, but Lark was right. Running in the middle of the night with little more than a threadbare gown and a cloak didn't make for a smart getaway.

"Not us. Me. Korae's life will be mine to claim—"

A loud creak sounded from the wooden floorboards as I stepped. I stilled, holding my breath as the conversation in the sitting room silenced. Lark and I were frozen to the spot, stranded in the shadows at the back of the hall.

Light blasted into the corridor as the door crashed open.

My lungs seized, a scream trapped in my throat. Every muscle in my body tensed as Cyrus's silhouette stepped into the hall with a second person poised behind him. I was rooted to the spot, my knees locked as a chilling smile stretched across his face.

Lark managed one word before they reached us.

"Run."

8

PERSEPHONE

MY HEART THUNDERED IN MY CHEST, THE FRANTIC BEAT NEARLY painful as Lark and I tore through the last stretch of hallway. She was quicker than me, blasting through the door and leading the way into the forest without hesitation.

Branches whipped against my arms and face, drawing blood from my exposed skin as my cloak billowed behind me, but the stinging pain was numbed by the potent fear permeating every inch of my body.

"Shit," Lark panted as the sound of heavy footsteps behind us grew louder. Her arms pumped as we veered to the north, finding our secret path toward Willowcrest, but the two of them were still gaining.

"We need to reach the village limits," I huffed, pushing my body to keep pace with hers. "Cyrus won't attack with witnesses—"

The underbrush of the forest folded around us. Vines reached for my legs, lashing at my ankles. A shriek tore from my throat as I ripped through them, fully knowing there was no going back. Bushes stretched inward, their thorns jutting forward to block our path. Even the trees seemed to bend, their great trunks curving to slow us down.

"Shit," Lark repeated, her hazel eyes taking on a red hue as her powers rose.

"Sleep," she commanded. The power of her voice echoed throughout the trees, able to coax the forest to lessen its grip on us—barely. "I won't be able to hold this for long. The woman with Cyrus must be a powerful earth witch. One of the best."

I bit back a scream as I ripped my ankle from the thin vine curling up my calf. The sharp thorns sank into my flesh, tearing through skin and muscle as I yanked my body from their grasp. Another wrapped around my shoulder with the next step, and another along my thigh a few breaths later. I couldn't stifle the whimper that fell from my lips even as I forced myself to keep going.

I was going to die here, torn apart at Cyrus's feet.

"We're not going to make it," I said, daring a glance behind. The forest was a tangled web of twisting vines and gnarled roots, but it parted for the two figures closing in on us.

"Keep running," Lark commanded.

And I did. I willed my legs to move faster, forcing myself to not think about the trail of blood and bits of flesh I was leaving behind. But they were only a few feet behind us now, and the edge of the forest was nowhere in sight.

Lark caught my gaze, having come to the same conclusion I had. A dozen emotions flitted through her eyes much too quick for me to decipher, but the sheen of tears and the slight tremble to her lip had worry clawing at my throat.

"At least we won't be alone," I breathed.

"Keep running, Rae." My brows furrowed even as she slowed, not comprehending what she was saying. "No matter what you hear, you keep running."

The forest grew calmer beneath my feet as the trees turned

their attention toward Lark. I reached for her, my hand gripping hers, willing her to keep pace with me. "We get out together, Lark. Together or not at all."

Wood splintered as the trees bowed to the witch's power, but I couldn't leave her. I wouldn't.

"Demeter has my sister," Lark said with tears in her eyes.

"What?"

The resounding resignation in her gaze nearly broke me. Her fingers traced the amethyst stone around her neck, my own fire opal necklace warming as hers did. "I was never getting out of here, Rae. But you are."

Before I could protest, Lark shoved me into the branches, the forest rippling under her command as it pulled me through the trees. The last thing I saw was Lark collapsing beneath Cyrus's towering form before I was thrust forward with the forest closed in behind me.

SOBS TORE THROUGH ME, TEARS SPILLING DOWN MY CHEEKS AS I pushed my body to its limits. Lark's blast of magic carried me through a large portion of the forest before it fizzled out, but I needed to reach Willowcrest before Cyrus and his witch caught up.

The muscles in my legs burned as the cold night air pricked the dozens of cuts covering my body. My cloak had long since been ripped away and the thin material of my dress was reduced to tatters held up by the laces of the corset over top, but warmth pulsed from the fire opal around my neck, spurring me on.

Lark was alive. She would be punished for this. In all actuality, she might be *killed* for this.

For me.

I should turn around. I should be fighting for her. With her.

And if my lack of powers were the reason I was killed, then I would die beside the only person who'd ever cared about me.

But I was a coward. Turning around would seal my fate. I'd be Cyrus's toy until he was finished with me. He might wait until my awakening to lay claim to whatever powers manifested, but once that was done, he would kill me.

And in that moment, I realized I very much wanted to live.

Somewhere along the way I'd accepted my life would end on my twenty-first birthday. That the entirety of my existence would be rendered down to a few stolen nights of fun amid years of misery.

But Lark had just given herself up for me, expending the whole of her earth magic so that I might escape my fate. I wouldn't let that be for nothing.

My boots pounded the ground, snapping twigs and crushing leaves as I raced through the night. Tears streamed down my face, falling freely as the cold night air burned my lungs with each stolen breath, but the forest was thinning. I could see the moon through the tops of the trees, illuminating the world around me.

A few yards more and I would reach the tavern.

A dark chill swept through the air, drawing a gasp from my lips and snapping my attention toward the east. It felt like ice was slithering beneath my skin, like little pieces of it were breaking off into my blood and pumping through my body. And then the cold was replaced by yearning.

My heart shuddered, my pupils dilating as I searched the trees for the source. In that moment, all the panic, the shame, the fear swirling through me was gone.

The trees shifted into fields as my feet carried me forward, deviating from the path toward a tall cliff in the distance.

I blinked, realizing that I had no idea where I was going. The village was less than a mile away... but the forbidden darkness on the edge of the mountainside was calling, drawing me closer with each passing second. I tilted my neck as the towering thick pines opened, finding a shadowed figure poised on the edge of the cliff.

My heart thundered against my chest, hammering as if it were trying to break free, as I gazed upon the chiseled body and broad shoulders clothed in black. The stone wall was bleached white in the moonlight, but shadows wove around him, shrouding most of his face from view.

Something in my soul yearned to reach him, to banish the darkness holding him captive and bring him back to life.

A forceful gust of wind swept down the cliffside, causing the branches of the trees to whip back and forth. I covered my eyes against the worst of it, looking toward the shadowy figure up above, only to find the darkness had gone.

Clouds blew over the moon, dimming its light. My arms came around my chest as a deep chill filled the air. My breath puffed out in ragged pants rising up before my eyes as frost grew across the forest floor.

I searched for an escape from the encroaching cold, my battered limbs tingling with the need to move. To run.

Turning toward the town in the distance, I stumbled through trees and shadows, feeling as if they were purposely trying to hold me in place, until I came to a small clearing. The only signs of life were the blooming white narcissus flowers sprouting among dark tendrils. They waited until I was in the center before winding up my legs, surrounding me in their deadly embrace. But it didn't feel painful. If anything, their presence dulled the sting from some of the cuts along my ankles.

"I hope you've enjoyed your freedom, little witch," a deep voice rumbled. I jerked my head to the right, to the left, searching for the source, but it was like the night itself was speaking. "Because now that I've found you, I'm never letting you go."

My vision spotted as the darkness grew, forming a taloned claw. The shadow limb reared back before striking the earth, splitting it beneath my feet. A piercing scream wrenched from my chest as I fell into the chasm, surrounded by nothing but air and the infinite night.

9

HADES

I'D FINALLY FOUND MY LITTLE WITCH. I TUCKED HER INTO ME, one of my hands wrapped around her shoulders while the other was positioned under her knees as crumbling shards of onyx crunched beneath my boots. Vast mountains composed of volcanic stone and thick forests stretched high into the sky, closing off the north. Heavy mist clung to the lowlands set before them, the ancient swamplands littered with gnarled trees, their bone-white bark stark against the black backdrop.

I turned south, already knowing what I'd find. The dark, onyx pebbles glinted in the early morning sun, the ground growing lighter the closer it got to the flowing river a few paces ahead. The river ignited under the sun's rays, casting the entirety of its surface in a brilliant yellow glow as the citrine gems glimmered. Its enchanted waters sprang from the Cave of Dreams, winding south along the western region of my kingdom.

The Lethe.

I'd captured my little witch only to drag us to The Darklands of the North. Under normal circumstances, it wouldn't have mattered, but with my powers waning, I couldn't be caught on the edge of Hypnos's territory, especially not with my little witch clutched to my chest. She was the key to restoring the full might of my power, and that was the last thing the north wanted.

My grip tightened around Persephone as I called on my wings, ready to fly us both out of here, but they didn't come. I tried again, still moving toward the river, focusing on bolstering my shadows, but only small tendrils answered my call. The rest of my power evaded me. It was there, hovering just beneath the surface, but I couldn't reach it.

Shit. The death magic coursing through my body wasn't meant to be contained. There was meant to be a balance between life and death, each proving problematic if left unchecked. But there was no light for my darkness to feed on.

It wouldn't kill me. Thanatos had ascertained as much after speaking with the fates, but each time I consumed death magic, each time the dark tendrils were drawn into my body, I was left with a yawning emptiness that extended a little deeper.

I refused to let it consume the souls of my realm. So, I turned the magic inward, protecting them the only way I knew how by offering up slivers of my soul for it to dine on. I'd do it all again to keep those in my realm safe, but I hadn't expected to be affected this significantly. Death magic had never dampened my powers this fully before.

Body tensing, I picked up the pace, glancing down at my queen. Streaks of blood covered her body from where thorns and branches had torn at her chest. Wisps of my shadows surrounded each one, urging them to heal. She'd fought bravely, my Persephone. Half-a-dozen witches had trailed her, all fully awakened, but my little witch never faltered. She kept pushing, even when faced with insurmountable odds.

I killed them all with a sweep of my hand, turning that entire section of the forest into blackened ash. I should have destroyed the two that were fleeing, but they held a witch between them that had saved Persephone. I hadn't seen her cast, but her magic clung to my little witch, carrying Persephone away from the others.

Something stirred in my chest as I watched Persephone's long lashes flutter in her sleep. Her fiery red curls fanned out around her freckled cheeks, and I couldn't help but notice how her pouty pink lips formed a flawless heart shape. Fuck, if she wasn't irresistible. The perfect fucking queen to my king.

Demeter had insisted on calling her 'Korae,' but Persephone was so much more than a meek maiden. Names held meaning for our kind. By keeping her true name hidden, Demeter tried to strip her of her identity. Of her destiny.

But her efforts hadn't made a difference.

I inhaled deeply, committing every inflection of my little witch's scent to memory. She smelled like vanilla mixed with the faintest trace of wildflowers. A flush still lingered on her cheeks from her run, her brow slick with a faint sheen of sweat. She was life, held in the embrace of death, returned to The Underworld where she belonged.

She stirred in my arms, her fingers curling into the thin fabric of my tunic as a soft moan fell from her lips. Fuck, if that sound didn't pierce right through me. Her bright green eyes blinked open, a soft pout tugging on her lips as she tried to get her bearings.

"You're safe, little witch."

Those piercing eyes of hers snapped to mine, widening as she realized she was tucked against the body of a monster. Fear doused the air as she screamed. I inhaled deeply, drawing all of her terror into myself—it was intoxicating. Like the sweetest ambrosia.

"You smell delicious."

She thrashed harder against me, thrusting her palms against my chest as she fought to get away. A flash of searing electricity shot from her touch, piercing through my chest. I gasped under its force, tightening my grip on her as a painful squeeze rocked through my bones.

"Let me go!" she shrieked, twisting her body enough to land a solid blow to my nose.

The bone cracked, causing the metallic tang of blood to run down the back of my throat as streams of it coated my face. I doubled over, tossing her to the ground with a curse.

"There's nowhere for you to go," I growled. Gritting my teeth, I snapped the bones back in place, letting the familiar wash of pain and anger overtake the foreign fluttering in my chest. "We're in The Underworld."

She landed with a thud on the rough pebbles, a whimper escaping her as she scrambled to stand. My eyes narrowed as I watched her body tense. Her gaze shot to the dark mountains behind me before combing over my body. Fear and something sweeter swirled between us as her eyes met mine.

"I'll keep you safe," I promised, slowly extending a hand. "Do you trust me?"

Because, for some reason, I trusted her. I knew without a doubt that she was the rightful Queen of The Underworld. It felt like lost fragments of my twisted soul had been returned. Like everything was as it should be.

"Why the fuck would I trust you?" she spat, before turning on her heel and heading straight toward the cursed waters of the Lethe.

PERSEPHONE

How the fuck did I get to The Underworld? The last thing I remembered was running through the forest—and then being drawn toward the cliff. The frost and shadows must have been whispers of death magic. And then I was falling.

The ground beneath my feet transitioned from black onyx to yellow citrine as I fled from the demon at my back. He was huge, the thin material of his tunic straining under all that muscle, and his eyes were a deep cerulean blue that seemed to peer into every part of my soul.

Faint traces of frost and pine still clung to me—his scent. Gods did I want to roll around in it, to forget every horrible thing that had happened in the last twenty-four hours and just lose myself to that gorgeous man.

But he wasn't a man at all. His allure, my body's response to his voice, his smell—all of it—was exactly why demons were so dangerous. Demeter may be the worst mother to ever live, but she was right about the threat of The Dark Faction.

They were beasts, vile creatures who had no respect for life. Monsters who grew stronger off the fear of their prey, and right now, I felt just like a rabbit being stalked by a wolf.

Sun glinted off the bright stones along the water's edge, illuminating the winding river in a sheen of yellow. In another life, I might have been able to appreciate its beauty, but right now, all I wanted was to reach the far shore and continue running for as long as possible.

I needed time to think, to regroup and form a plan. Lark hadn't sacrificed everything just for me to fall into the arms of a demon. I would find a way out of this mess and figure out how to get her out of Mother's claws.

"Stop!"

His voice reverberated through me, coaxing that dark, wicked part of myself to listen. Gods, he must be powerful. Only upper level demons were able to open the rift between realms. And it sounded like he was having no trouble keeping up with me, despite how depleted his magic stores must have been.

His presence alone made every inch of my skin tingle with electricity, the intensity growing as his thundering footsteps closed in.

Just a few more steps and I would reach the water.

"I said stop, little witch." This time his voice was a whisper, the heat of his breath fanning my ear as if he were speaking to a lover rather than his prey.

Before I could do anything but gasp, my feet were lifted from the ground. Dark shadows wrapped around my waist, yanking me backward. I thrashed against his magic, the water's edge rippling with the splash of stones I'd kicked.

I knew what he would do, what all demons did to their victims. He would use me to feed from, drinking in every drop of fear I could give him before handing me to The Night Children to use as a blood source. Or maybe he would sell me to someone else to use for breeding. Either way, I'd be *used*.

My lungs pulled in quick, shallow breaths as fear tightened

my throat. More shadows wrapped around my wrists and ankles, making it impossible for me to get away.

Black boots crunched over citrine gems, the toes of them coming into view as his shadows held me in place. Tears burned my eyes, borne of shame and anger and an overwhelming sense of failing. The shredded material of my dress was doused in red, my skin a macabre painting of shallow cuts and bruises.

"Look at me," the demon growled.

"Fuck off—"

A gasp pulled from my lips as his magic wrenched my wrists overhead, forcing my chest out. I fought for balance, but his shadows held me suspended, the toes of my boots just barely grazing the ground.

My chest heaved as I gritted my teeth against the pain. I was an unawakened witch, already captured and unable to access even a sliver of earth magic. In all actuality, I was probably going to die down here, but I needed to try. If not for my sake then for Lark's.

Being sure to take my time, I followed his command. My eyes lingered over thick thighs, the muscles beneath his pants just as sculpted as the chiseled planes of his chest. His arms were bands of muscles, the veins along his forearms standing out as his fingers flexed, maintaining control of the shadows that bound me.

I continued up—gods was he tall—to appreciate how his dark hair was cropped short along the sides, the longer pieces on top ending with a slight, stylish curl.

Forcing my chin up, I finally met his gaze. They looked like they'd been cut from the purest sapphires, the blues made even more alluring by the swirling flecks of midnight within. They held rage and power and a hard, commanding glint that showed he was someone accustomed to others bowing before him.

Every piece of him was perfection, as if an artist had glimpsed inside my mind and crafted him just for me.

Down girl. Why was it always the murderous ones that turned me on?

His lungs expanded around a large inhale, his lips twitching as if he knew exactly what I was feeling. As if he could *scent* me. With renewed horror, I realized he could.

Higher level demons of The Dark Faction were said to have descended from blood witches who once lived in The Realm of the Living. They were among the first group of followers to worship Hades, and in exchange he gifted them power from The Underworld.

There were great advantages, such as heightened senses: sight, smell, even the ability to heal. But death corrupts. Unlike earth magic, which sought to give, death magic demanded a sacrifice. It consumed, feeding on life like fire on gasoline.

Judging by the widening smirk across his face, it appeared my demon wasn't just physically strong, but magically as well, meaning he knew every dirty thought I'd just had about him.

Humiliation heated my face as I jerked against his shadows, but it only served to push my chest out further.

"No need for that, little witch. There's nothing to be ashamed of." He took a step closer as his eyes roved over my body. He cocked his head to the side. "Unless you enjoy the humiliation."

"What do you want from me?" I meant it to come out strong, but the words were little more than a whisper as my thighs clenched under his probing gaze.

"Many things," he said, his lips stretching into a wide grin. "But I wonder, what is it that *you* want?"

I opened my mouth to tell him exactly what I wanted, but a thick band of shadows wrapped between my lips, gagging me, before I could. With a twitch of his fingers, his shadows were moving, tracing soft patterns down my suspended arms.

My breathing hitched as their caresses drifted lower, trailing along my ribs, grazing the tops of my aching breasts. A shiver rocked through me as I arched into his phantom touch, my eyes fluttering closed as I willed them to explore more, unable to resist the pull toward him.

The pads of his fingers came to my jaw, tilting my face up to his. "You look so beautiful, gagged and bound before me."

I whimpered.

"Do the other witches know what a dirty girl you are?" He dragged his nose up the slope of my neck, the tip of his tongue licking the soft spot along my collarbone. "What would they think if they saw you right now, trembling with need for me?"

Shame burned through me, only increasing the delicious heat growing low in my belly.

Sex wasn't foreign to me, but my dalliances had been short and fairly basic. I doubted the word 'basic' was ever used to describe the demon before me. No… sex with him was guaranteed to be life altering—something I would never recover from.

With a snap of his fingers, the gag was removed, only to be replaced with the pad of his thumb dragging down my bottom lip. My tongue lashed out of its own volition, capturing the tip as my lips closed around him.

He tasted like frost and darkness. Like the coldest, purest parts of night had condensed into the epitome of wickedness.

"You *do* look delicious, little witch." His low chuckle jerked me back to reality. "And so eager for a taste of me."

I snapped my teeth closed, attempting to bite him, but he'd already stepped back. Looking me over with renewed interest, he circled me, completely ignoring the livid glare I shot his way. After a long moment, he spoke.

"That is the river Lethe. One drink and every memory you've ever had would have been wiped clean. These lands aren't safe. We need to leave as soon as possible, which would be a lot easier if you weren't attempting to throw yourself into a cursed river."

My eyes widened as my gaze flicked to the yellow shores.

Gods, if one drop of that water had entered my mouth I would've turned into a shell of a person. And this demon holding me in the grips of his shadow magic... had saved me.

"Why?" I asked, keeping my voice steady as I looked for any flicker of deceit on his beautiful face. "Even if my mind was turned to mush, you still could have fed from me. It would have been easier."

"Yes," he answered, tilting his head to the side. His knuckles drifted over the laces of my corset, the fraying tethers barely managing to keep the panels closed. "I could have taken you the moment I saw you running through the forest."

A question was poised on the tip of my tongue, ready to demand answers, but his fingers dipped beneath the ties and pulled, snapping the remaining threads of my corset with a swift yank.

My breasts heaved as what remained of the corset fell to the ground, leaving me in nothing but tatters of my destroyed gown and the golden chain around my neck. A tingling had started in my fingers from being suspended for so long, and my back ached from the angle I was forced into, but my nipples hardened all the same, the thin material doing little to conceal me from his hungry stare.

It's just demon magic, I told myself, stifling a moan as his shadows teased.

"Would you have liked that?" Shadows were replaced by his hands, pinching and twisting my nipples before he pressed a kiss to the sore tips through the thin fabric. I whimpered under his touch, embarrassed that I'd been reduced to nothing but a demon's plaything. I felt his lips twitch into a knowing smile.

"I think you would have." His hand drifted down as he trailed kisses along my neck, his fingers slipping under the hem of my dress. "I think you wanted me to catch you. I think you would've enjoyed every moment of me spreading your legs and fucking you for all to see."

Heat pooled between my thighs under the soft caress of his voice, so at odds with his sinful words. I squeezed my thighs together, attempting to hide just how much this game of his turned me on, but his dark shadows pulled them apart, allowing his fingers to slide between me.

"Such a dirty girl," he praised as his fingers slipped inside.

I moaned as my heart raced, the frantic tempo thundering in my ears. I should be fighting, doing everything I could to escape. This was the most frightened I'd ever been, the most desperate and humiliated... but I'd never felt more alive.

Undulating my hips, I ground my body against his palm, moaning as I found the friction I'd been craving. He let me fuck his fingers, bouncing on him as his shadows held me spread for him to see. Tendrils of darkness pinched and teased my nipples as more of his darkness wrapped around my neck, filling my mouth.

It felt like he was everywhere. A third finger joined the others, stretching me as I teetered on the edge of explosion. "Just like that, little witch."

My whimpers were muffled by the shadows thrusting down my throat. My pussy clenched his fingers as I swallowed around the fullness in my mouth, but he withdrew before I found release.

A dark chuckle heated my ear as he stepped back. "And here I was thinking I'd have to kill you after the wedding."

My eyes snapped open. Ice flooded my veins, clashing with the need to come.

"Don't worry," he said, pressing one last kiss to my forehead. "You might just have what it takes to survive the binding cere- mony and become what you were always meant to be."

I swallowed around the lump in my throat, pushing the want humming in my body down to meet his gaze.

"And what am I meant to be?"

His blue eyes darkened as he brought his fingers still slick with my desire to his mouth. I watched as he licked them clean, his gaze never leaving mine.

"Queen of The Underworld."

11

PERSEPHONE

THE WARMTH OF DESIRE COURSING THROUGH MY VEINS MOMENTS ago cooled as dread settled like a weight in the pit of my stomach.

"Queen of The Underworld," I repeated, my voice pitching at the ridiculousness of it. This had to be a joke. "As in the wife of Hades, the God of Death?"

The demon's eyes narrowed, his spine stiffening. "Technically, Thanatos is the God of Death. I'm the—"

"You," I said, cutting him off as the reality of my situation sank in. The tingling in my fingers had grown painful as I remained suspended in the demon's shadows, spurring on my anger. Demons were known to lie to get their way, but Queen of The Underworld was quite the tale. He might be powerful, but it seemed he was little more than a dog sniffing out his next bounty. If he truly was taking me to Hades, it would be to deliver me as his next play thing.

I was to be sold. Again. Despite the demon's claim, I was probably being carted off to someone at Hades's court of monsters. According to Mother, young women were often taken and forced to give birth to little witch-demon hybrids to swell The Dark Faction's numbers.

"You're what? A worthless demon fetching a shiny new toy for his master?" An incredulous laugh spilled from my lips as I leaned into my temper, allowing it to overcome my rising panic. "You're just like them, telling me what I have to do with my life."

"You say demon like it's a bad thing," he cooed, but his eyes were blazing. "Demons are very much like the witches in The Realm of the Living, the same source of magic, only linked to a different realm."

Ignoring the bite against my skin, I turned my wrists, gripping the shadows binding me as I glared. "Death should never be a source. It's dangerous, unruly—"

"As is life magic," he cut in. "If one doesn't know how to wield it properly. Death magic is powerful, but with a balance, all can be restored. You'll see."

"I won't do it," I seethed, injecting as much venom as I could. The pads of my fingers started to heat, to tingle and prick as if a live current was running through me. I gripped the shadows tighter, pulling myself up instead of just dangling there, and letting him see the truth burning in my eyes. "Whoever it is you're bringing me to, I'll *never* marry a demon."

His nostrils flared, a retort poised on his tongue, but his mouth snapped shut as he stumbled back, dropping to his knees.

I felt it, too. Scalding heat sparked around us, the force of it snapping the dark bindings holding me in place. My knees and palms dug into the sharp edges of citrine stones as I crashed to the floor, the new cuts causing blood to coat their pristine surfaces in red as I pushed to a stand.

The fresh wounds stung, my fingers were still slightly numb, and my body had already been stretched to its limits, but somehow the demon's shadow bindings had failed.

We stared at each other for a heartbeat, both disbelieving the turn of events. His eyes were wide with disbelief as he panted for air. A hand came to his chest, rubbing a spot just to the left of his sternum as if he'd been struck.

Our impasse lasted only a breath, before his narrowed blue eyes looked up at me through thick lashes and pieces of his dark hair that had fallen forward.

Whatever energy had broken his bonds was humming in the air. I was more aware of him—the flicker of shadows surrounding him, the faint traces of heat coming from his body. If the startled look flashing in his eyes was any indication, he felt it too. Whatever this was, it had changed something important between us.

Thunder boomed in the distance, snapping my attention to the foreboding mountains behind him. He followed my gaze, watching as thick, gray clouds billowed out from the distant peaks. I could just make out winged silhouettes taking to the sky, like hundreds of bats.

"The Night Children," he breathed, getting to his feet.

My mouth ran dry as I mimicked his motions, silently weighing my options. With a pissed off demon in front of me, the Lethe to one side, and the swarm of growing monsters to the other, it was safe to say I was thoroughly fucked.

Seeing no other option, I turned and fled, throwing what remained of my strength into my legs as I raced toward The Night Children, hoping to reach the mountains before they reached me. If I was quick enough, I might be able to find shelter.

I managed all of three steps before the temperature around me dropped and his swirling shadows seized me once again. They wrap around my forearms, weaving my hands together in front of me before doing the same with my legs.

I crumpled to the ground like a captured hare, the frosted

stones cold against my tear-streaked cheeks. Rough hands seized me in the next breath, lifting me like I weighed nothing.

"Let me go, you stupid demon!" I shrieked between sobs, knowing full well that I'd just wasted my last chance. I would never escape this place and Lark… she'd suffer at the hands of my mother and Cyrus for the rest of her life.

Cradling me in his arms, he stalked toward the Lethe, keeping close but veering west along its banks.

Another tendril of darkness wrapped around my neck, forcing my chin up to meet his enraged glare.

"My name is Aidoneus, little witch. I don't care if you hate me, or if every moment of your time spent in The Underworld is a living hell. You *will* go to The Dark Palace and bind your magic to The Underworld on your twenty-first birthday."

"If I refuse?" I said, finding a sliver of remaining defiance as I willed my body to stop trembling.

That cold, calculated gaze of his flickered with something akin to excitement as he noted the determination burning in my eyes. His lips quirked up at the edges before he tossed me over his shoulder, muttering something unintelligible beneath his breath.

A wave of fatigue crested over me as Aidoneus quieted, leaching what little strength I had left as he picked up the pace. Each step carried us further away from the monsters at our backs, only to take me closer to the one waiting for me at the end.

"Sleep now. If all goes well, we'll be at The Dark Palace when you wake."

Fear twisted my stomach, the adrenaline flooding my veins begging me to fight, but it was no match for the dark power dragging me down.

"You spelled me," I whispered on the verge of sleep.

He nodded. "Those in The Dark Faction, 'demons' as you call us, are just as skilled in spells as witches in your world.

There is much you don't understand, little witch, but you will in time."

A dozen questions rose to my lips, but the fog invading my mind grew thicker. Denser. Unable to fight any longer, I relented and let the darkness take me.

Hades

THANATOS WAS RIGHT. I COULDN'T RISK TELLING PERSEPHONE anything further about her role of restoring balance between the realms. I couldn't even call her by her true name without taking the chance that she'd do something irritatingly reckless. Not until she was protected behind my seat of power at The Dark Palace.

At least she was safe for now. My little witch was sound asleep over my shoulder, the rhythm of her gentle snoring surprisingly endearing. I tried in vain to conjure my wings again and again. Flying over the Lethe with her asleep would have been a lot quicker and safer than running along its shores, but most of my powers still evaded me.

Thank fuck I retained control over shadows, but the longer my powers were suppressed, the more I suspected this was the result of something more sinister than death magic. It almost felt like someone or something had cast a binding spell. Hecate would know. She'd be able to reverse any curse willed upon me, but I needed to reach her first.

Another reason to return home as soon as possible—that and the savior of our realms slung across my shoulder.

Persephone's heart-shaped lips had dropped into a sexy little pout when shock flashed across her face at the mention of being my betrothed—right before those emerald eyes of hers burned with rebellion.

I knew Demeter had poisoned her against me. That bitch

had been spreading lies about The Underworld since the moment she realized her daughter was the one promised to me. I'd thought it was misplaced love at first, a mother's need to keep her daughter safe, but after seeing what those witches did to her in The Black Forest... I'd make sure every last one of them would suffer.

12

HADES

The citrine stones of the Lethe began to transition into blood-red garnets as Persephone shifted in my arms. Her curls bounced as I jogged, but her eyes remained closed, her cheek resting against my chest. She would've looked peaceful if it weren't for the shadow bindings along her wrists and forearms. I'd undone the ones along her legs, but her hands would remain bound until I could be sure it was safe—that I was safe.

Whatever happened back in The Darklands hadn't been from a lapse of control of my magic. Persephone had broken my bindings somehow. And then there was that sharp lash of electricity that had rocked through my chest, sparking from the tips of her fingers when she'd shoved me away. I could feel the ramifications even now. Like I'd been struck by lightning, the searing heat still burning what remained of my blackened heart.

It hurt, but it hadn't been the familiar pain I'd grown accustomed to. This was warmth. Life forcing its way into my frozen shell of a body.

Part of me remembered what it was like to have warm blood racing through my veins. To feel the brush of a blade keenly.

The heat of a kiss like it was the only thing my soul needed to survive. Death magic had stripped that from me.

Now, I was cold. Forever chasing the memory of what it meant to be alive. I wouldn't find it. Not with the darkness leeching my soul—or was it humanity it chewed away at?

Death magic would continue to siphon the very best parts of my being, wearing my already precarious position as God of The Underworld down. I knew Hypnos and The Night Children were eager for my fall from grace. The Darklands of the North were waiting for time to run out so they could strike.

Hypnos didn't care if the realms faltered. Those in The Dark Faction who followed him and his band of blood-sucking creatures would continue even in the chaos of total destruction, trusting in Zeus to create more lifeforms for them to feast on.

Unfortunately, they were right. All the Olympians had sided with Hypnos. They were excited at the prospect of creating a version of humanity that would be more docile. More loyal to the gods of old.

But I didn't need prayers. All souls came to me one way or another. There was a time when I enjoyed death. When the ice of my soul was impenetrable and my dark shadows were merciless extensions of my will. I'd ruled over a land of torment. Reveled in the bitter cold of a world trapped in the grasp of my magic.

I'd run The Underworld as if it were my very own playground, unable to comprehend what empathy was. It wasn't until life began flourishing in The Realm of the Living that my ruthlessness was tempered.

Zeus and the others had created humans to weaken me. In a way, I guess they had. I knew what it meant to feel. Of how satisfying it was to punish the wicked, watching their blood splatter across the stones of Tartarus, while the innocents were left to thrive.

And now, I held the key to restoring balance in my arms.

Despite my better judgment, I glanced down, marveling at the way Persephone's lashes grazed her freckled cheeks. Not for the first time, I wondered if my little witch had any idea how powerful she was. Judging by the startled look when she'd broken through my shadows, I would guess not.

The yellow gem stones were shifting into a deep red, indicating the Lethe was coming to an end. Concentrating once more, I tried to call on the force of my shadows but something or someone was preventing me from moving freely in my own realm. I was left with nothing but wisps of darkness and lower level curses at my fingertips.

Gritting my teeth, I increased my speed along the river as the clear waters started to cloud and heat, becoming a mixture of molten rock swirling with the blood of the punished.

The Phlegethon had begun.

The river of fire would grow, increasing in heat and intensity as it angled west, descending into the heart of Tartarus. We needed to cross the bridge before we descended too deeply into the abyss. My monsters would be there, standing guard over the forsaken prisoners, but I'd have to risk it. Without my wings, this was our only option.

The main obstacle would be after when we came upon the frozen river bleeding through the desolate kingdom of Cocytus. The icy plains would test my little witch, but the only alternative would be passing through the heart of Tartarus, and circling around the Phlegethon toward the river Styx.

No, we would be forced to head toward Cocytus and the Mountains of Mourning, and hope my magic was returned to me.

Agonized cries rose up from the smoldering pit in the distance, like music to my ears. The monsters trapped in Tartarus, those tortured in The Valley of Torment, deserved every moment of suffering.

Inhaling deeply, I let their fear revitalize me, their unanswered pleas of mercy acting as a soothing balm for my aching soul. Tartarus was one of my favorite places in The Underworld. I was able to maim and kill, to slice and gouge as much as I wanted, knowing that every slab of skin and bones that came under my knife had earned its place.

Persephone shifted in my arms as the air grew hot around us. Her head rolled to the side, exposing the sleek curve of her neck.

I very much doubted my little witch would understand the beauty of Tartarus. There were monsters in her world just as there were in mine. The only difference was that the shrouds of righteousness the living wore were stripped from their heads the moment they entered my realm.

I should know. I was the god of monsters. The worst of them all.

She'd called me a demon, as if I were little more than a common errand boy, but I was the beast she feared, the one who would lay claim to her in every way.

But to do that, I needed her to agree to be my wife.

Thanatos had been right. I couldn't risk her fleeing again. Too much was at stake. Persephone wouldn't come with me willingly, that much was clear. I needed to hide my true identity until our souls were bound.

She would hate me when this was over. My little witch would curse and scream, she would fight me for every inch of freedom, and she would lose.

13

PERSEPHONE

Everything hurt. My muscles were aching, dozens of lingering stings coated my body, and there was this hazy warning brewing in my mind that the reprieve of sleep wasn't something I wanted to give up.

The scent of sulfur and brimstone singed my nostrils, banishing the comforting darkness further as distant crackling and sputtering of what sounded like fire rumbled around me. The rhythmic crunching of stones was synced with my body's subtle swaying, and I realized the warmth surrounding me was emanating from two strong arms holding me against a firm chest.

My eyes snapped open, muscles tensing as the events of the last day and a half came rushing back.

The first thing I saw was a river of fire outlined in garnets. Steam swirled high in the sky, the white tendrils stark against the impenetrable black clouds. Cracks had formed along the riverbank, the red gems glowing with smoking embers. My heartbeat raced as I traced the path of the river, finding the land rising as the blood-red waters descended. A sheen of sweat broke across my brow as I gazed upon lava flowing down jagged cliffs, the molten rock forming beautifully grotesque waterfalls ending in pools of red.

This was the Phlegethon.

I heard the agonized screams before I realized that the large maroon lumps floating in the pools at the bases of the burning waterfalls weren't stones, but people forced to endure their skin and muscles melting away until only bones were left.

Dizziness washed over me as I watched a freshly burned body crawl out from the blood-red lava, transfixed by the macabre scene playing out before me.

Bony hands clawed their way up the shore, held together with fibrous cartilage as they sank into garnet stones for purchase. The skeletal arms flexed, heaving a torso out behind them as layers of muscle started to build. When the poor creature's knees landed on solid ground, the top layer of skin and hair having only just regrown, the ground shifted, throwing it backward.

Its echoing wails screamed into the blackened sky as the molten rock swallowed them once more.

"Don't feel sorry for them." Aidoneus's voice cut through the horrific spell, the vibration of his chest against my body reminding me this wasn't a nightmare I'd concocted but my reality. Swallowing against the dryness of my throat, I glanced up to find his piercing blue eyes pinned on mine. "The pool is the beginning of The Valley of Torment. It stretches for miles, growing darker and deeper, until it reaches the bronze gates of Tartarus. Every soul sentenced has earned its fate."

"I can't imagine what they could've done to warrant an eternity of burning to death."

"No, I don't think you could," Aidoneus said, the vehemence of his voice momentarily stilling my tongue. His eyes flashed black, the sudden change pulling a gasp from my lips. He blinked, releasing me from his gaze, before looking ahead. "Believe me, the atrocities they committed fit the punishment. As far as I'm concerned, eternity isn't long enough."

A subtle buzzing started between us. The places where my body was curled against his pricked with electricity, reminding me of how he had rendered my body into a wet, trembling mess within minutes of capturing me. Despite the current anger simmering in his gaze, I found that I wanted to lean further into him.

Gods above, I must really have lost it, because I wanted to press my cheek against his chest and breath in his scent of frost and darkness. Did he feel the mounting energy between us the way I did? Clearly, I was delusional with exhaustion because I allowed the tips of my fingers to trail up the hard planes of his chest, tentatively exploring.

Jolts of power pricked beneath my touch, delivering a rush of warmth through my body. Aidoneus sucked in a sharp breath, his steady footsteps faltering as I pressed my palms flat. Heat coiled at the apex of my thighs, the metal of my necklace cool against the fire blazing through my body.

I was far too aware of how little I was wearing, of how his gaze took in my flushed skin and peaked nipples, but I couldn't find the strength to break whatever this was.

"Put me down," I breathed, alarmed at my body's yearning to give in to him.

The rocking of our bodies slowed as Aidoneus came to a stop. His discerning gaze saw far too much as he eased me to the ground, which was all the more reason to put distance between us.

The warmth of the garnet stones immediately heated the soles of my boots, causing me to shift on the balls of my feet. Wiping the sheen of sweat off my brow with the back of my hand, I desperately tried to reason with myself.

It didn't matter that Aidoneus was covered head-to-toe in muscle, or that, for some reason, I'd felt more rested asleep in his arms for a few hours than I had in years.

This was a demon for gods' sake—one who had captured and transported me through the realms. Based on the way he fed off fear, he'd probably aided The Dark Faction in countless attacks against The Realm of the Living.

I'd been wrong about him only being a bounty hunter. Aidoneus was far too controlled for that, and his ability to cast such potent spells meant he had to be higher. He'd also navigated through The Underworld with ease. I'd guess he held a very high rank. Maybe even one of The Dark Palace's guards.

I had been a fool to try to escape. Aidoneus wasn't the person I needed to run from. I needed to bide my time and learn all I could from him until I could find a way to return to The Realm of the Living and save Lark.

"I thought you were taking me to The Dark Palace to wed your master."

His eyes narrowed as the pulse in his jaw ticked, but he nodded. "The Dark Palace *is* our destination."

"Then why are we headed into the endless abyss of Tartarus?" I lifted my chin, shifting quicker on my feet as the heat rising from the ground became uncomfortable.

Aidoneus noticed my fidgeting, and for a moment it looked like he might pick me up again. I might have let him, but then he took a deep breath and trudged past me without looking back.

"There's no crossing the Lethe, little witch. Not unless you can fly."

Unable to contest that fact, I stalked after him, doing my best to ignore the way his thighs and ass shifted while he scaled the gemstone cliffs.

Eyes up here, Rae.

Sweat coated my body as I jogged to keep pace with him.

Not for the first time, I wished I would've kept my mouth shut about wanting to be put down.

So, I was attracted to him. He had felt it, too. I was sure of it. A part of me wondered if my reaction wasn't some type of spell because whatever the power was between us, it appeared to be affecting me a lot more than him.

"Couldn't we find a way around instead of walking willingly into the worst part of The Underworld?" The muscles in my legs burned as the ground ascended sharply. My curls were frizzing around my head and my skin was slick with sweat. I was panting by the time he slowed enough for me to reach him.

"We won't be getting close to the gory parts," Aidoneus said with a glance over his shoulder. "There's a bridge over the Phlegethon. It will carry us across the fires below and into the land of Cocytus."

"Cocytus?" I repeated, my brows drawing together. "The River of Tears?"

Aidoneus nodded, guiding me away from the cliffside. Garnets still littered the path, but much of it was now covered by blackened, volcanic ash.

"That's one name mortals use for it, along with The River of Wailing or The River of Lamentation. Its shores sprout from the pit of Tartarus opposite to the Phlegethon. A great portion of it is actually more lake than river, which is where we need to go."

Swinging my arms, I did my best to move quicker, both to keep up with Aidoneus and to quell the fire beneath my boots. Sweat coated my body, and the thin, white material of my gown was practically translucent now and matted to my skin.

"Could you slow down?" I called, hiking up the tattered ends of my dress. I was jogging along the path toward Tartarus, nearly naked, and trying to catch up to a demon. How had I ended up here?

"No."

My mouth fell open as my burning feet stumbled at his

reproach. I knew he heard me trip, but his body never broke stride.

"In fact, you need to move quicker. We must time our crossing or things will get unnecessarily complicated."

"This isn't complicated already?" I grumbled, my thighs burning as I pushed up the sharp slope. The soles of my boots were being warped by the heat, portions of them melting away with each step I took. The air grew thick with humidity and ash the higher we climbed, making it difficult to breathe.

"I guess strolling through Tartarus is just another day for a demon like you," I seethed, as I ripped away a tattered piece of my gown to make a make-shift mask. "It's probably a nice day off from all of the killing you do."

His shoulders tensed, but his gait slowed.

"Nothing to say?" I baited, needing to focus on anything other than the blisters starting to form on the balls of my feet. "Were you there when the Green Coven was attacked? Did you help turn their entire village into ash? Or was that your master, Hades's, doing?"

"Hurry up." Aidoneus's voice was low and laced with an unspoken threat.

A scornful scoff scraped my throat as I managed to tie the thin material around the back of my head. It didn't offer much protection from the ash singeing my nose and throat, but it was something.

"You demons are all the same. Soulless, vile monsters who find joy in murdering hundreds of innocents—"

My toe caught on a jutting garnet, sending me tumbling forward.

Aidoneus caught me before I could crash into the smoldering earth, lifting me up before so much as a finger was harmed.

My mouth fell open as his arms wrapped around me, holding me close. I stared up at him, unable to speak. Aidoneus stared back at my wide-eyed gaze, looking nearly as stunned as I was.

"You saved—"

"Your clumsiness has delayed us long enough," he growled, cutting me off.

Then we were moving.

14

PERSEPHONE

THE WORLD STREAKED BY IN FLASHES OF RED, ORANGE, AND BLACK as we climbed higher. It was stifling, like running through a blazing oven, but my mind was stuck on why Aidoneus had protected me.

I wouldn't have died, but it definitely would've been painful enough to power him up. He had no doubt gotten a good blast of fear from me just tripping, but he'd caught me before one edge of the hot gemstones connected with my skin.

Demons exploited any and every chance for their next hit. Not only did they incite chaos and death, but they enjoyed the suffering of their victims. That was why the covens in The Realm of the Living were adamant about finding a way to prevent them from crossing into our world.

Regardless of being a demon of The Dark Faction, despite everything I'd been taught, Aidoneus had *prevented* pain.

I dared a glance up at him, aware of every place our bodies touched as he continued up along the mountain filled with bright embers and blackened ash. Beads of sweat linked together, trickling down my neck and chest, but the thin layer of shadows surrounding us kept the worst of the heat at bay.

"Does the heat bother you?"

He lifted a brow but shook his head. *Interesting.* I should just let it go and allow us to continue in silence, but holding my tongue was never a strong suit of mine.

"You're using your magic to keep the heat away from me," I said, not posing it as a question but the stiffening of his posture confirmed it. Narrowing my eyes, I asked, "Why?"

"You're sweating," he replied dryly. "My shadows are hardly doing anything."

"But they are doing *something*," I insisted, needing answers. Everything about him was the opposite of what I'd been expecting. I was drawn to him, something inside of me urging me to relax into his body and *trust* him, but demons couldn't be trusted. "Why would you go out of your way to be kind to me?"

"Maybe I'm not," he replied evenly, but I swore something flashed in his eyes. "Maybe I'm aware of our close proximity and am trying to keep things as fresh as possible."

My mouth fell open the same time I flushed scarlet. "Excuse me for not being courteous and taking a shower before I was abducted and carted across The Underworld."

"Apology accepted, little witch." He was definitely smirking.

"I didn't—that wasn't," but his smile only grew. Deciding on a threatening glare, I crossed my arms.

After a moment of silence, Aidoneus offered me an olive branch. "If all goes well, we will have fresh water to bathe in tonight."

I waited for him to explain further, but he took one glance at the winding river of fire beneath us and increased his speed.

"You're really hustling up this mountain. Does the bridge close at a certain time?" *Nice Rae. Way to put him at ease.* Ignoring the blush staining my cheeks, I cleared my throat and tried again. "It's only that you said we had to time our crossing or things would get complicated. Is it a fire thing?"

"It's a monster thing," he grunted.

"Oh. What type of monster?"

"One I'd rather not run into," he said, clearly wishing to continue in silence.

Fully aware that there was no chance of reaching the top of this mountain on my own, but also unable to quell my damned pride, I lifted my chin. "All the more reason to tell me about it so I can be prepared."

A startled laugh split his lips in a disbelieving smile. "Prepared for what? You're an unawakened, unarmed earth witch on the edge of Tartarus. As you've mentioned, the fires of Hell are my territory."

Shoulders slumping, I deflated as I realized just how powerless I was here. A part of me had thought I'd be able to make it out of The Underworld, to track down a point of connection between the realms and escape... but how was I supposed to do that when I couldn't even walk without Aidoneus's help?

I hated relying on others... but even more, I hated that I wasn't strong enough to stand on my own.

My fingers wrapped around the fire opal dangling from my neck. Lark would've known what to do. She always did. She was brave and fearless where I was scared, always ready to find the solution. And I had left her to her fate, knowing just how ruthless my mother could be.

"You're right," I said, my voice hollow even to my ears. I felt Aidoneus glance down, but I was done with talking.

Drawing my arms around myself, I curled inward, allowing the small, splintered pieces of my heart the comfort they were seeking from my demon's embrace. I knew it was wrong, but a part of me liked that Aidoneus was a demon. He wouldn't judge me for my lack of earth magic because he didn't care how strong or weak I was as long as he completed his mission. I knew The Dark Palace bit was a lie, but I think I might have gone with him anyway. If Lark were free, I might have stayed here.

I *would* find a way out of this mess for Lark, to make sure she and her sister were free from Mother, but for now, I just wanted to sleep. Ignoring the hunger pains in my stomach and the way my entire body was sore, I closed my eyes against the world and welcomed oblivion.

THERE WAS NO WAY TO TELL TIME. THIS CLOSE TO TARTARUS, THE sky was always black. It felt like hours had passed before we stopped at the edge of a cliff with the bronze walls of Tartarus glimmering in the distance. They stretched high, obscuring vast portions of the hellscape before us, but the prisoners' tortured screams reverberated through the ash-filled skies.

Most of The Valley of Torment was covered in fire, blood, or bodies, but there was a small, shining piece of refuge among the barbaric landscape: a crystal clear pool surrounded by flourishing fruit trees at the base of an overhanging stone ledge. Plump figs and juicy plums dangled close to the water's surface, the sight alone enough to have my mouth watering.

A flash of movement in the center of the pristine pool caught my eye. A figure was submerged chin-deep in the water, his neck straining as he arched in a futile attempt to reach the fruit. A gust of wind caught the branches just before his lips closed, blowing them out of reach. He dipped his chin, looking as if he might drink from the pool, but the water receded before he could wet his lips.

"Tantalus," I breathed, realizing just who the unfortunate soul was. No pity came, though. I'd heard the stories. Tantalus had killed his own son Pelops, slicing his body into bite-sized pieces. Infanticide was vile enough to earn him his fate, but Tantalus then tried to trick the gods by serving them his son's body in a stew.

His cry of hunger turned into a flinch as pebbles from the

overhanging stone ledge trickled down. A large slab was poised right over his head, leaving no doubt that it would kill him if it did fall, but it looked as if the worst of the tremors had stopped.

"It will never break," Aidoneus's chest rumbled beneath my fingers, his blue eyes searching for something in my face.

"Good," I said, letting my disgust bleed through. I hadn't understood when we'd first hovered the periphery of Tartarus, but Aidoneus had been right. For some, eternity wasn't long enough. "He deserves to suffer."

His lips twitched as something like approval flashed in his eyes before he looked away, fixing on a crumbling arch in the near distance. It was thin, barely wide enough for two people side-by-side with pieces of it chipped along the edges. Crafted from the same porous black stone littering the mountainside, it stretched across the churning fires of the Phlegethon far below before disappearing into dark clouds and billowing smoke on the far end.

"Tell me that isn't the bridge to Cocytus?"

Aidoneus gave a tight nod as he transversed the last ridge. A landing of sorts was set before us, the volcanic stone tapering into the beginning of the bridge. My heart raced, my fingers unconsciously curling into the material over Aidoneus's chest for support. His grip around my thighs and shoulders tightened, but when I dared a glance up, he was focused on the swirling clouds above.

"The monster that guards this bridge is ancient," he breathed.

Following his gaze, I joined his search in scrutinizing the sky.

"Her claws and tail are lethal, but that's not what makes her dangerous. It's her ability to wield a soul's greatest fears against itself that causes trespassers to surrender to death willingly."

My breathing hitched as Aidoneus's shoulders tensed. I liked the way he held me closer as we stepped out onto the open ledge, grateful that I wasn't alone as a feeling of dread slid down my spine.

"What type of monster can do that?" I whispered, my palm pressing flat against his chest. My pulse was racing, the echo of it thundering in my ears, but I felt nothing beneath my fingers. A hollowness rang under my palm, over the place Aidoneus's heart should've been. He had been running for hours while carrying me, he'd gotten up halfway across The Underworld, but his body remained cool to the touch. And his chest was as still as the dead.

Brows furrowing, I looked to him with questions poised on the tip of my tongue. "How—"

An ear-splitting screech exploded through the darkness. The beast had a woman's appearance from the waist up, but in place of hair was a cobra's scaled hood. Thick, leathery wings stretch wide, and sharp talons curled where her hands would've been. Rather than legs, a thick, barbed tail stretched behind her reptilian body. Skin was replaced with a fine layer of scales, the finer scales flashing with a faint iridescent sheen as the light of the fires below reflected across her hide.

Gods Above. I knew what that was—who she was.

The blood drained from my face as I clutched the fabric of Aidoneus's tunic, wishing there was a way to sink into his protection like a physical shield. "Is that…"

He shifted me in his grasp, his entire body tensed and primed for battle as he tracked the monster overhead. "That is Kampe."

15

HADES

"THERE'S A CHANCE SHE HASN'T SEEN US," MY LITTLE WITCH SAID, her face as white as a wraith's. "Tell the demon you're delivering me to that you lost me."

I shot her a glare.

"Or that I died. We could run—"

Kampe let loose another great screech as her blood-red eyes locked onto us. I felt my little witch draw into me, her fingers curling into the material of my tunic, directly over my chest—before a bolt of electricity pierced my heart.

It was like the finest blade had slipped between my ribs and punctured the useless organ. It had to have been Kampe. She'd somehow lashed out with her barbed tail or razor sharp talons, but the monster swooped over us, circling from above once more. She was still warning us to turn back or suffer her wrath.

There had been no attack. So, why was my entire body quivering in pain?

"Aidoneus," my little witch warned.

Panic dripped from her voice, her body intuitively seeking mine for protection. There was a strange fluttering in my stomach as her small fists clenched tighter. It shouldn't have mattered. Plenty of women had done the same in the past centuries, running to me for protection. It had never mattered, but I could *feel* her. My Persephone.

Another lash of agony ripped through me, the force of it sending me to my knees.

Time seemed to slow as I fell, unable to stop myself. Persephone tumbled from my grasp, rolling a few paces ahead as I was left writhing in pain, immobile under her power. Clawing at the blast of magic seizing me, I ripped my tunic, my lungs pulling in sharp, ragged breaths.

A blast of agonizing warmth rocked through me, the sudden change like needles pricking through every inch of my body. It felt as if the useless, withered muscle trapped beneath my ribs squeezed, forcing a rush of stagnant blood through my frozen veins.

Disbelieving, I stared wide-eyed at my hands, gawking as they shifted from a sickly, pale sheen to that of an almost rosy hue.

Another squeeze. Another rush of warmth. And blistering torture.

My heart was beating. I hadn't felt anything other than coldness in centuries—not until my little witch. And now I was doused in flames, rendered immobile, leaving Persephone to face Kampe alone.

The third beat of my heart rippled through me as I fought through the torment I was drowning in and fixed my gaze on her. She was poised on the volcanic bridge just ahead, uninjured from what I could see, but on her hands and knees. The thin material over she face had fallen away, her cheeks streaked and stained with ash. Her entire body was frozen as Kampe screeched—and then dove straight for us.

Persephone shouted something but I couldn't hear. Couldn't do anything other than crawl as whatever power she wielded worked through my body, forcing deadened tissue to resurrect.

I willed my body to move, my muscles to respond, but even with all my strength and magic, I only gained inches. It was like my bones and tendons and every fiber of my being were being sculpted anew, rendering me helpless.

A fierce look of determination flashed in her eyes, a realization that I wouldn't reach her before Kampe did.

"Run back to me," I tried to shout, but it came out as a groan.

Balling her fists, she turned back to the flying beast and squared her shoulders. Gods be cursed, Persephone was half starved and unawakened, and still she meant to challenge Kampe, a powerful serpent hybrid on her own.

I saw the moment Persephone succumbed to Kampe's cursed gaze. I watched, unable to reach her as her back arched, her head thrown back and lips parted around a silent scream.

16

PERSEPHONE

MY FINGERS TRAILED OVER YELLOW DANDELION BLOSSOMS, enjoying the soft brush of their petals under my touch before I plucked a few of the larger leaves from the stalk for tea. It wasn't enough to kill the plant. Not even close. Dandelions were strong. They'd developed the ability to survive and grow just about anywhere. Rocky terrain or the lush fields, frost or heat, they always managed to persevere. Other witches my age liked roses or lilies, both of which were fine, but they didn't have the resilience that dandelions did.

I looked at the field of bright yellow blossoms surrounding me with a proud smile. I wouldn't be nine for another few months, the age in which my mother's powers started to manifest, but I had just brought an entire field back to life.

This had to make Mother proud. When I was younger, she would tell me tales of how I was meant to be the savior of us all. My magic was going to be strong enough to lead us out of the war with The Dark Faction and into a period of peace.

Those stores had stopped last spring. I wasn't sure what I did wrong, but it must have been something terrible, because it had been the first time Mother hit me. It had only been the back of her hand. The shock of it had hurt more than the cut across my lip, but things had only gotten worse from there.

Demeter was the strongest earth witch ever known, and as her daughter, I was expected to match her power. Staring at the field of swaying dandelions, I allowed myself to smile. This would prove I wasn't worthless. Mother would see this and be pleased... and maybe she'd go back to loving me.

"What did I tell you about sneaking off, Korae?"

I jumped at Mother's voice, the shrill note causing my breath to catch in my lungs. Ignoring my racing heart and the shakiness of my limbs, I turned to face her with a tentative smile.

"The forest was calling me," I started, launching into my explanation before her anger escalated. "Everything was coated in a sheet of frost. Most of the plants were already dead, but I brought the rest of them back to life."

Mother stilled, her eyes widening as she took in the hundreds of dandelions swaying softly in the early spring breeze. The surprise in her eyes caused my heart to flutter—for the seeds of hope to sprout. I felt tired and my legs were a little weak, but this proved that I wasn't a lost cause.

The delicate dream of her acceptance was banished the moment her hard gaze fixed on me. It was a look I knew all too well. One I dreaded, because I knew what it meant.

My smile faltered as I took a step back, raising my hands slowly. "I only want to be like you. I thought practicing—"

"You *thought*," Mother mimicked, the harshness in her voice causing me to flinch. She took a step toward me, and I quelled the urge to run. It wouldn't do any good. She would find me, either way. And when she did, she would make my punishment that much worse. "Thinking is beyond your abilities, daughter. Your job is to do what I tell you to do."

Dropping my gaze to her feet, I nodded. My hands were folded, my shoulders bowed as the familiar prick of tears burned my eyes. I couldn't let them fall. Tears were a weakness. And Mother *hated* weakness.

I felt like a mouse caught in the coil of a snake as Mother circled, her venomous gaze paralyzing before she delivered the killing strike.

"Did you take your tea this morning?" She brushed a strand of my red curls back from my face, the deceptively soft touch causing me to tremble.

"Yes, Mother."

"Look at me," she commanded, her ice-blue eyes reading every flicker of emotion across my face. I did my best to seal it away, to withdraw into myself, but it was no use. It was like she had the ability to peer into my mind. "Did you drink all of it?"

My face fell, the tears I'd worked so hard to contain breaking free. "I spilled only a little bit."

Her lip curled in disgust a moment before I felt the sting of her palm across my cheek. My head jerked to the side, but her fingers pinched my chin, forcing me to look up at her.

"You stupid, useless girl. Can't even obey a simple task without messing it up." She let my chin go, causing me to stumble back. With a long sigh, she turned to the side, her fingers massaging her temple. "It's my own fault, really. I should have accounted for you not being able to follow a basic rule, even if it is for your own good."

I knew better than to speak, but I couldn't stop my frustration from bubbling over. "No, it's not."

Mother's spine stiffened, the simple gesture causing my heart to race, the force of its beating almost painful. Sweat broke out across my brow as she slowly turned to face me, but I clenched my fists, needing to say what I've been thinking about for the past few months.

"I feel sleepy after I drink the tea. And weak, like I'm inside a bubble. Everything feels distant. The trees, the flowers, the earth, but today I sensed the forest."

She was still looking at me with those cold eyes, her lips pinched in a harsh line, but she hadn't silenced me yet. I let that bolster my resolve and continued.

"Don't you see, Mother? This could be the answer to our problems. Maybe if I stop drinking it—"

I caught the quick flick of her fingers before torturous vines erupted from the ground. Barbs dug into my skin as they wrapped around my forearms and legs, slicing into muscle as they anchored me in place. Mother was careful with her placement, the vines always in areas that could be easily hidden. Only Ruby had seen the crisscrossing scars and thought to question them.

Traitorous tears fell as cries shook my chest. I was stupid to have hoped for anything other than pain from her.

Her knuckles connected with my stomach, the blow strong enough to send me toppling to the ground, but her vines caught me, holding me up for her next hit. I bit the inside of my cheek to stifle a whimper, concentrating on the metallic taste as each strike washed over me.

"This is for your own good." Another blow caught me in the ribs, forcing the breath from my lungs. Something cracked and the cries I'd been holding back broke free.

"Stupid. Worthless thing. Why do you make me do this?" she panted, her eyes alight with unhinged rage and unabashed glee. "You know I don't like punishing you, but you never learn."

She backhanded my face as her vines vanished. I crashed to the floor; my palms braced on the blood-splattered ground as she stood over me. The yellows of the dandelions were speckled in red as I coughed, each quake of my chest staining their perfect blossoms.

"You are nothing more than a burden. A mistake I wish I could undo. Look at me when I'm talking to you."

Her boot caught me in the stomach, forcing me to roll on my

side. My arms came around my middle, trying my best to protect my throbbing body as I groaned.

"You're alone, Korae. Nobody wants you here." Mother sank to her knees beside me, gathering my aching body to her. She cradled my head in her lap, brushing strands of hair back from my brow as she summoned currents of her earth magic to soothe some of the pain. She couldn't heal me, but each beating was finished with her holding me, as if she wasn't the one who had caused this.

"Shh, it will all be over soon."

I blinked and I was no longer a child. My wounds were healed, and the bright blossoms of dandelions were replaced by a thick pine forest ending in a dramatic cliff. Its edge was a few paces away with nothing but the open sky beyond.

"You can end this," Mother promised, appearing at my back. "It will be quick. Just one step and you can rest."

I didn't move, but somehow I was standing at the edge with stones crumbling beneath my toes. A gentle breeze beckoned me forward. Soft clouds lined the horizon, looking as if they'd be a gentle place to lay my head among the infinite expanse, one I could get lost in forever.

Wanting so badly for the exhaustion to end, I leaned forward, but a brush of comforting warmth rising from the ground stilled my movement.

Shaking my head, I looked down to find a single dandelion stretching toward me. Its thin stalk wrapped around my ankle.

"All of your suffering would be over." Mother whispered in my ear, but my gaze stayed locked on the small flower.

It was a simple thing. Fragile. It could be broken without a second thought. Many people would consider it worthless. A nuisance. Something to get rid of. But I could feel its roots digging deep into the earth, the entirety of its being focused solely on tugging me back from the cliff's edge.

Its leaves thickened, the roots burrowing deeper as it wound further up my calf, desperate to hold me to this place. This one weed was holding me to this life, tethering its existence to mine.

I reached my hand toward it, my fingers a breath away from the outstretched blossom shining up at me.

A sharp lash of agony shot through me as the scent of my mother's magic filled the air.

"No," I breathed, watching as the yellow petals wilted. Tears fell along my cheeks as the last tendrils of warmth from the dandelion's touch faded. Chest heaving, I took a large step back from the cliff and turned to face my mother.

"Just because something is small does not mean it's insignificant."

Her sneer twisted, transforming into rows of fangs. The golden locks of her hair shifted into black, melding together to form a scaled hood.

A deep voice reached me through the haze, warning me to run, but all I could focus on was the red eyes staring into mine. A beastly screech pierced the air as the she-dragon dove, her talons outstretched and aiming right for me.

17

PERSEPHONE

ELECTRICITY BUZZED AROUND ME, THE SOFT CURLS OF MY HAIR rising toward Kampe as the air charged. Before I knew what was happening, the energy condensed into a searing heat and burst outward.

There was nothing visible, no blasts of flames or bolts of lightning, but the she-dragon recoiled as if I'd struck her. Her great wings struggled against the ash filled sky, each beat sending waves of hot, stifling air cresting over me as she fought for balance. Despite one of her wings being bent, she managed to pull her body up into the black clouds circling overhead, offering me a moment of reprieve.

Sulfur stung my nose and mouth as my mind fought to remember where I was. Sweat coated every inch of my body, the thin material of my gown clinging to my heaving breasts like a second skin with the fire opal hot against my chest. Obsidian stone lay beneath my fingers and knees stretching over a giant chasm with a river of fire beneath.

I was in The Underworld on the edge of Tartarus, dragged here by...

"Persephone," a low voice rasped, the sound like something

between a groan and a plea, but it cut through the haze of my mind.

My eyes widened as they landed on Aidoneus. He was struggling to stand, his lungs heaving.

His face was flushed, sweat beading on his brow as his entire body trembled. But he wasn't plagued by the cursed powers of Kampe. It wasn't fear that gripped him. I didn't think there was much in this world or any other realm that could frighten Aidoneus. This was *pain*.

Far too aware of the plunging drop, I stood, attempting to locate the source of whatever magic held Aidoneus in its grasp. He was a powerful demon, one at home in this part of The Underworld. He'd shown no signs of his body weakening from lack of food or water as mine had, nothing to hint at even a moment of discomfort. Until now. Whatever was affecting him was a force to be reckoned with.

"Enough," he growled, fighting through the unseen spell. He shifted forward on his knees, the black material of his tunic parting to expose the network of tattoos inked across his chest. There were intricate lines and ancient text, but one caught my eye: an up-side down torch placed directly above his heart.

"No," I breathed as my stomach clenched. My entire body tensed as if preparing for a fight, already sensing the danger before my mind caught up. That mark was a symbol for Hades, God of The Underworld. Witches whispered often about the one who bore it. He was the demon responsible for the devastation in The Realm of The Living. Dozens of villages, hundreds of innocent lives, all cut short by his hand. The only demon respected enough by Hades to be branded with his emblem: The Hound of Hell, Hades's general.

A ringing in my ears started as all sound fell away.

No. No. No. The word played on repeat in my mind.

Bile burned the back of my throat as I forced myself to meet Aidoneus's gaze. I'd let him hold me. I had even found a sense of peace as he carried me through The Underworld. I should have been trying to kill him the moment I laid eyes on him, but I'd been seeking *comfort* from this monster.

The bridge shook as the she-dragon shrieked overhead, the beating of her leathery wings showing that whatever power affected her moments ago had worn off. She was regrouping, and it was only a matter of time before she attacked again.

"Stay by me," Aidoneus commanded as he forced his way to his feet.

I was running out of time. Desperate for an escape, I glanced to the far side of the bridge, unable to see anything past the dense fog. Towering, snow-capped mountains were visible just beyond, confirming Cocytus was on the other side—A land of ice and heartbreak. It was suicide for someone like me to enter its borders. I was barely clothed with no food or supplies, but this was the furthest I'd been out of Aidoneus's grasp. I'd been too much of a coward before, but I wouldn't be able to live with myself if I wasted this chance to escape the Hound of Hell.

"Don't get any ideas, little witch."

A gasp left my lips as I snapped my attention back to Aidoneus, finding his cerulean blue eyes trained on me. Whatever magic had been present moments ago was gone now, and he looked all the stronger for it. His hooded gaze stared down at me through dark curls that had fallen over his face. His pupils dilated as he inhaled deeply, drinking in my fear and panic as if it were his favorite wine.

"It is taking all my will to keep my power in check," he said as unabashed desire burned in his gaze. I felt like I was a doe being sized up by a ravenous wolf, and for some gods forsaken reason, I *liked* it. "A demon like me enjoys the chase. And you're not ready for what happens when I catch you."

"I can handle more than you realize," I said, lifting my chin. I knew I should have kept my mouth shut, but despite realizing who he was and all the horrible shit he'd done, the fluttering in my chest and the spooling of heat low in my belly didn't slow.

Aidoneus's lips twisted into a wicked smirk causing my breathing to hitch. The fires blazing beneath us cast shadows across the hard planes of his chest, highlighting every dip of his muscles. His pants hung low on his hips, the tattoos across his chest dipping below his waistband. Savoring what he did to me, he took a step forward.

"There's nowhere in this world or any other you can go that I won't follow."

Blood rushed to my cheeks at the vehemence dripping from every word. Mirroring him, I took a step back, ash making the stone bridge slick.

"Stop looking at me like that," I snapped, hating myself for *not* hating him. Despite knowing he was a monster, the villain of my nightmares, a murderer of innocents, my traitorous body wanted him. Even worse, Aidoneus could tell.

"Like what?" His teasing gaze dipped to where my thighs clench, his nostrils flaring as slickness built.

"Like I'm your next meal." I was proud of the bite to my words, but it couldn't conceal the way my breasts heaved as he prowled forward.

"I have no doubt you'll thoroughly enjoy being my next meal, little witch. You're probably imagining it right now."

I shook my head, not trusting myself to speak. He grinned.

"Can you imagine it? What it would feel like to have my tongue buried deep in your sweet pussy? I wonder what sounds you'll make as I feast on you, tasting and licking until you're writhing against my face as I fucked you with my tongue."

A whimper escaped me as my breath quickened, every nerve in my body tingling with the need to let him take me.

"You'll be begging me for more, Persephone," he promised. "And I'll give it to you, until there's no doubt that you're mine."

My eyes dipped to his wicked mouth, imagining all the ways he could make good on his threat.

"You mean Hades's," I breathed.

Aidoneus froze, all the emotions flashing across his face moments ago vanishing.

"You're bringing me to Hades. I thought you were making it up, but you really are delivering me to The God of The Underworld, aren't you?" I swallowed as his lips pressed thin, not bothering to deny it. "I'll be his. Not yours."

Kampe screeched again, causing me to jump and break eye contact with Aidoneus. I looked up, finding her great, scaled body arching high overhead, before cresting into a sharp dive.

Damn it.

Aidoneus may be the left hand of Hades, but I needed him if I were to have any chance of surviving Cocytus and escaping The Underworld.

Against my better judgment, I dashed toward him, closing the space between us in a matter of moments. Aidoneus was ready, catching me in his arms as my fingers splayed across his chest.

A gasp tore from my lips as our bodies connected, the sound echoed by Aidoneus as heat flared beneath my fingertips. Electricity pricked as power surged between us, linking our souls together.

I could feel everything.

All of him.

Like the sparks of our individual flames had joined, transforming into a raging bonfire. But where my body felt hot, his was cool, the two opposing sensations clashing with one another.

Magic streamed from my fingertips, forcing some of the frozen pieces of his being to thaw. It felt like shards of crystals were in his veins, slicing and sluggish as his frozen heart contracted.

Firm hands grabbed my shoulders, pressing me back just enough for my hands to leave his chest. His full lips were parted, eyes searching my own for the answers to a riddle neither of us knew.

Before either of us could speak, he spun me behind him. Black-tipped talons slashed the spot I was moments ago, tearing out chunks of the bridge. Kampe rose, circling once more as she prepared for her next strike.

Stones crumbled at Aidoneus's feet, fissures spiraling outward as he stepped forward. Keeping one hand on my back, he lifted the other as he muttered a spell. I could feel his magic working as if the tendrils of it were still swirling in my body. He'd constructed a shield, a wall of his magic clashing with Kampe moments later. Though my eyes were fixed on the failing bridge beneath us, I sensed each burst of power cutting through the dark sky, sinking into the she-dragon's scaled hide. Just as I could feel Kampe tumbling through clouds, only to rise again.

It wasn't enough. With a curse, Aidoneus lifted both hands to the sky, stepping further in front of me as he gritted his teeth and sent pulse after pulse of magic.

The moment his touch fell away from me, my legs buckled. It felt like I'd been running for days, a soul-deep fatigue that leeched every ounce of motivation from my being. I watched as he took another step forward, the deep cadence of his voice continuing as he did everything possible to defend against Kampe's rage. I wanted to stay by him, but I couldn't stand, couldn't do anything but breathe through the unassailable weariness pulling me under.

Aidoneus sent a blast of magic toward her as she dove. It clipped her wing, changing the trajectory of her dive toward me. I somehow found the strength to roll, only just avoiding Kampe's large talons, as Aidoneus sent another blast toward her.

Cracks formed around the gash in the bridge, splintering outward and under my trembling fingers. I should be concerned that the fissures were growing. I *was*, but it was like a murky film had been cast over me. Adrenaline flooded my veins, the sound of my frantic heart beating in my ears nearly deafening. I needed to move, but a vast emptiness had opened, numbing every instinct screaming at me to run.

"Get up!" Aidoneus shouted in between spells. "We need to reach the other side of the bridge before the entire thing collapses."

His words stoked a small spark within my mind, but it was caged, surrounded by rings of icy apathy. My shoulders rounded, my body bowing forward as I watched the rock fracture beneath my palms, splintering toward my knees.

"Little witch," Aidoneus pleaded as he battled Kampe a few paces ahead, but his voice was like a whisper on the wind. "You need to move."

I glanced to the edge, seeing the blood-red fires of the Phlegethon beneath me. The monstrous river appeared small from this high up. Peaceful, almost. I wondered if it would hurt when my body crashed into it. I wondered if the scorching steam swirling up from its cursed waters would kill me first.

"Persephone!"

That name pierced through some of the fog. I shook my head, fighting to draw my gaze up against the bone-deep exhaustion overtaking me.

"That's it, Persephone. Listen to my voice."

Aidoneus was racing toward me, great shadows stretching out behind him, like the ghost of wings. My brows furrowed as I tried to focus on his face, but everything was blurry. Several small pieces of the bridge broke off beneath my fingers, the obsidian shards starting their long fall.

"Aidoneus," I breathed, terror flaring deep in my soul as I stared up into his eyes.

He reached out, his hand inches from mine—before black talons pierced through his stomach. Blood welled from the wounds as Kampe snatched him from the bridge, his eyes widened in disbelief as he was hoisted up.

I screamed, scrambling forward on my hands and knees as I watched him being swallowed by the dark, churning clouds overhead. With my gaze searching the ash-filled sky, I didn't realize the bridge had collapsed until I was already falling.

18

HADES

My brows furrowed as I tried to understand why Persephone was growing smaller, drifting further away. Then, the searing pain across my middle hit, lashing through my stomach.

Gods dammit, Kampe.

Twisting, I forced her talons to slice further into my gut as I arched my spine to face her.

I'm not sure what my little witch did, but I felt *life* humming in my veins, the loud pounding of my heart. The fact that my magic felt more present was also proof that she'd undone some of the curse that had bound me since returning to The Underworld. I could still feel something subduing my magic, like a faint dusting of snow, but with Persephone's power coursing through my veins, I was able to summon my true form.

Ram horns spiraled back from my head and black wings larger than Kampe's shimmered into place as my pupils expanded. I allowed the tips of my fingers to grow into claws, gripping Kampe's shoulders as I forced her to look at me.

It's me, Kampe. Hades.

Kampe's wings faltered, her reptilian eyes going wide as I spoke into her mind.

Master? But you don't smell like yourself.

She hovered amid the black clouds, eyes narrowed as if this were a trick. Any other time I would have just killed her and let her body regenerate, but this close to Persephone's awakening, my powers were limited. I couldn't risk burning through more magic when we were so close to setting everything right.

Still, I couldn't have rumors spreading about my weakened state.

I'm aware. My little witch's doing. I added just enough inflection to make it seem as if I'd been thoroughly enjoying myself.

Kampe studied me. *The girl?*

I nodded, gritting my teeth at the nerve of her questioning me.

Her forked tongue lashed out, searching for a lie. She found none.

My apologies, Master, she said, retracting her talons. I gritted my teeth as they withdrew, blood spilling from the gashes, but Persephone's life magic rose to the surface, sealing the wounds in seconds.

Your witch is the one responsible for your current state? Kampe hovered there, her head cocked to the side as I held her stare.

"She is," I answered, knowing Kampe had scented the life magic on me. I narrowed my gaze, daring her to question me further. She may be obeying orders for now, but I couldn't risk showing vulnerability. My wings rhythmically pumped as I sized her up, noting the way her talons were still slick with my blood.

Best go catch your witch before the Phlegethon claims her. With that, Kampe turned toward The Valley of Torment, leaving me a moment before Persephone's screams pierced the air.

My newly beating heart nearly stopped as I snapped my wings against my sides and dove.

A flash of red curls among the tumbling black rock caught my eye. I veered toward her, burning through more of her magic and mine as I cut through shadows to reach her. Her body was limp as she fell, rendered unconscious.

She'd gifted too much of herself, my brave little witch. I doubted she even knew what she was doing. I hadn't realized what was happening until our life threads awoke beneath her touch. They were eager for the bond, drawing the two of us together.

My arms came around her, securing her close to my chest and I slowed our fall, before reversing it. I took to the skies, my ebony wings pumping as I angled our path toward Cocytus.

If my true power had returned to me, I'd be able to fold through shadows and appear at The Dark Palace in an instant, but I could already feel the warmth in my body cooling as I funneled magic into maintaining my true form.

I had no doubt Kampe was watching, along with a horde of prisoners in Tartarus. Not much changed here. The spectacle Persephone and I made was sure to garner attention. Her presence, a living witch among dead, cursed souls was no doubt already circulating. Hades and his witch. I couldn't afford having anyone think they could challenge me. Not now. Not when I was so close to having everything.

As much as it pained me to admit, I *was* vulnerable, more than I had ever been before, but appearances were ninety percent of the battle. If I appeared strong, then I was. No one would risk their lives by testing me as long as I maintained the fear I'd worked millennia to cultivate.

Looking as if I were enjoying the dark recesses of my kingdom rather than being forced to endure it, I set a leisurely pace as I crested The Mountains of Mourning, gliding toward the land of Cocytus, until the fog thickened around us, ensuring we'd be safe from prying eyes.

Few could navigate passage through the mountains. They

were caught in the middle of Tartarus and Cocytus, between fire and ice. Dense fog paired with the billowing clouds overhead meant it was nearly impossible to pass, but I was familiar with the terrain, allowing my mind to wander as my body navigated the mountain pass by memory.

My mind drifted to our current predicament, hoping that Persephone's magic was strong enough to hold off whatever binding spell had been placed on me until we were safe.

Someone had placed a curse on me. And I knew exactly who was responsible. My magic should've taken us to The Dark Palace, but I'd been grounded on the banks of the Lethe, just outside The Darklands of the North. Each time I attempted to access my magic, it felt like a thin layer of dust was separating it from me—or a very fine layer of sand. This had to be Hypnos's doing.

The God of Sleep hadn't made his dislike of me a secret, but he was nothing if not self-preserving. An open attack would never work. He'd incur not only my wrath, but all those loyal to me. But *cursing* me allowed him to test the limits of my magic. Had I been at my full power, I doubted I would've noticed the attempt. As it were, I'd been torn through space and deposited on his doorstep.

He must not have expected it to work. That was the only reason I could think of why he wasn't waiting there with an army of Night Children at his back.

Returning to The Dark Palace was vital, not only for my survival, but for my little witch's too. The Dark Palace was my seat of power. If I could return before Hypnos thought to mobilize, we'd be safe. It was a direct link to The Underworld. As long as I remained there, most of my magic would be accessible.

If luck was on my side, Thanatos would be preparing forces to defend against a possible attack. I should be helping to prepare, slaughtering each and every threat to my people, but none of that could happen until my little witch and I passed through Cocytus and into the Asphodel Plains where The Dark Palace resided.

Persephone's body gave a shudder as an icy blast rose from the frozen valley before us, whipping at her tattered dress. Her nipples hardened, her slightly upturned nose growing pink against the wind's onslaught.

The beating of my heart lurched as I stared, awed by my little witch's beauty. Sweat and ash coated her, smeared through her tangled red curls and across her forehead, but gods did I want nothing more than to have a taste of her sweet lips.

She had broken through Kampe's compulsion, resisting the urge to take her own life. I'd never seen it done before. Persephone was a fighter, a queen in the making. I was embarrassed to admit, I hadn't seen it at first. I'd thought this union would have been swift and then over, another sacrifice I would make for my realm.

But now. Now, I *craved* her. Yearned to inhale her subtle scent of vanilla and wildflowers every day for the rest of my existence. To sink my cock into her pussy so deep that I'd brand her body and soul as mine, forever.

My Persephone.

Demeter thought changing her fate's-given name would keep her from her destiny, but my little witch was too stubborn for that. She had responded to her true name, if not consciously, then by instinct.

I would show her why we needed to be, convince her to stay by my side long after I had bound our life threads and secured my realm. But first, we needed to survive Cocytus.

The bitter cold wouldn't affect me, even with Persephone's life magic flowing through my veins. I made this world, the primal magic channeled from my being, but my little witch had no such protection. She needed clothes, food, and water.

I clutched her closer as I angled downward, thinking a bath for my little witch might not be such a bad idea either. Luckily, I knew just where to go.

1 9

HADES

"I'VE GOT YOU, LITTLE WITCH," I SAID, PRESSING A KISS TO HER brow as we landed along a cluster of rocks in the foothills of the Mountains of Mourning. Obsidian rock made up much of the range, great pockets throughout forming an extensive network of caves caught in between the chilled air gusting up from Cocytus and the vast flows of magma deep beneath the surface, their rivers stemming from Tartarus.

Persephone's green eyes blinked open, still glazed with sleep just as I allowed my wings to fade from view. Her small hands balled against my chest, gripping the shredded pieces of my tunic. It was just a brush of her knuckles against my skin, but a shock of electricity shot through me.

She gasped, jerking back and nearly toppling from my hold.

"Put me down," she snapped, pushing against me and causing another pulse of power to leave her palms.

I stumbled back under the force of her magic, gritting my teeth against the heat searing through my veins. The life magic burned as it forced the stagnant parts of myself to come alive. It was mending, healing all that had been dead, but every part of me that was resurrected felt like another bundle of raw, blistered nerves freshly awakened.

She landed on her ass, scrambling to her knees as she drew to the edge of the ledge. Rubbing against the throbbing of my chest, I watched as she took in our surroundings, like a doe caged by a wolf. There were only a few feet in either direction with the cave's entrance at her back before land fell away with the sharp mountain sides.

"Still thinking about running, little witch?"

Her rich green eyes snapped to mine, her chin lifting as she squared her shoulders. "Where are we?"

I tilted my head to the side, my hungry gaze trailing the curves of her body. Her nipples were hard and ready to be sucked, and I could glimpse the thin layer of fabric between her thighs, barely concealed by what remained of her dress. She was thin, as if she'd been forced to skip meals often, but that would change as soon as we reached The Dark Palace. I intended to dote on my future wife, ensuring she never felt the pangs of hunger again.

Persephone's body was incredible. Fucking perfect. But nothing compared to the way her fists clenched or the fight in her eyes that suggested she'd rather skin me alive than accept my help.

"We're at an in-between of sorts."

Her brows furrowed, showing a flicker of uncertainty. "Tartarus is behind us while Cocytus is ahead, but you'll need fresh clothes if you plan on maintaining that life thread of yours."

Her eyes narrowed, but I caught the sound of her stomach grumbling as I took a step forward.

"Food and water are also inside," I continued, striding ahead.

She stepped to the side as if I'd toss her over my shoulder. Pausing, I leaned into her, letting a smirk twist the edges of my lips as I inhaled deeply. Her pulse quickened as I gently lifted my hand, savoring the way her breathing grew shallow as my thumb swept across the blush staining her cheek.

"You will join me inside, little witch." She licked her lips, eyes staring up into mine as if horrified at her body's reaction. My pupils dilated as I scented her arousal, like the sweetest vanilla. "If not for food, then for the hot springs."

She swallowed as fear and excitement warred within her. "Hot springs?"

Persephone

UNABLE TO LOOK AWAY FROM AIDONEUS'S CERULEAN GAZE, I WAS almost too exhausted to remember why I hated him. Every inch of me hurt. It went beyond a physical pain, as if whatever Kampe had put me through had tapped into my life-force. If the fates inspected my thread at this very moment, I wouldn't be surprised if it was tattered and frayed along the edges.

I was seconds away from collapsing, wanting nothing more than to find myself nestled in Aidoneus's arms. His arrogant smirk was irritating, and I cringed inwardly at all the suffering he'd caused, but gods did my body want to give in, to follow him into the caves and yield to his whispered promises.

"Hot springs?" I heard myself ask, my voice sounding breathy and a little desperate.

Aidoneus's eyes swirled with mischief as he took a step back, and I hated the way I was left colder for it.

"Yes. You're in desperate need of a bath."

Scowling, I shoved past him and stalked toward the darkness of the cave. *Arrogant bastard.*

"Not all of us can fall from a bridge over a boiling river of blood and fire and look as perfect as you."

"You think I'm perfect?"

I shot him a glare. Ignoring his radiant smile as he fell into step beside me, the two of us entered the cave together.

"I was being sarcastic," I muttered as I stepped further into the cave, following the sounds of bubbling water. The heat was the first thing I noticed. Gooseflesh pricked along my skin as my bare arms and legs started to thaw. I wrapped my arms around me, rubbing out the subtle pricks the rapid temperature change caused. Gods above, did it feel good.

"Sarcasm isn't your strong suit, little witch. It sounds far too close to flattery."

"You wish," I scoffed, but I was realistic enough to be grateful that Aidoneus had brought me here. I doubted he needed much in the way of clothes or even food for that matter. No... this— whatever this was—had all been for me.

I'd expected the cave to be pitch black, but the obsidian walls were mixed with vibrant reds. The cave was more of a cavern, stretching far overhead with spots opened to the skies beyond. It allowed for faint traces of light to filter down, still dim but I was able to make out a worn path.

I was about to start down it when the fine hairs on the back of my neck rose. Aidoneus stepped behind me, the warmth of his chest heating my back as he closed the distance between us. My spine stiffened, my lungs hardly daring to breathe as he leaned down, his lips pressing the whisper of a kiss to the soft spot beneath my ear.

"My *wishes* involve you stripped bare on your knees before me, little witch."

"You're disgusting." I meant to sound repulsed, but my words were more breath than bite. Aidoneus's lips tilted into a smile as he no doubt scented what his words did to me.

"That wicked mouth of yours would be wrapped around my cock, tears spilling across your cheeks. Your lips would be pink and swollen, sore from my abuse, but you would hollow your cheeks, taking all of me as I used you."

I stopped breathing, my thighs clenching as I fought to remain standing. He pressed another, deceptively soft kiss further down my neck. I tilted my head, allowing him better access.

"And when I'm done fucking your mouth, I would have you on your back, legs spread wide as I licked you from ass to that sweet pussy of yours, feasting until you screamed my name."

I whimpered as his fingers brushed against my hip. It was only a whisper of what his touch could be, but it blazed through me.

"Only then, once your body was limp with pleasure, your thighs slick with desire, would I sink my cock into your sweet heat. And you'd enjoy every second of it, Persephone."

Persephone.

My gaze snapped to him, my chest tightening at the sound of that name, joining the warmth coiling between my thighs. "Why do you keep calling me that? My name is Korae."

"No, little witch. It's not."

20

PERSEPHONE

AIDONEUS'S GENTLENESS WAS WORSE THAN ANYTHING ELSE. I could hear the sincerity ringing through his words, see the adamant clarity shining through his eyes that what he said was the truth.

"Your true name is Persephone, The Destroyer. You're not a meek, naive maiden as your mother's chosen name suggests, nor were you ever meant to be. Your destiny is written by the fates, woven together with the Lord of The Underworld's to establish a lasting balance between life and death."

"Restore balance? With what power?"

Aidoneus lifted a brow as if waiting for me to answer my own question.

"Even if I did, even if what you said was true and the fates designated my name, why would my mother change it?"

"To keep you hidden," Aidoneus answered, holding me. He shook his head a moment later against something he saw in my eyes and turned down the path.

"Hidden from what?" I asked as I chased after him, the two of us coming to a fork in the road. One tunnel was nearly black, smelling of sulfur and something rotting, but the other had a faint shimmer along the cave walls, a reflection of water with the promise of fresh springs in the distance.

Aidoneus continued down the bright path, the sounds of bubbling water growing the further we went.

"Aidoneus," I grumbled, reaching for his arm as the path opened to a wide chamber.

Steam swirled up from simmering pools of waters, dancing with the flashing light of Tartarus reflected in the dark clouds.. I blinked up, seeing the small opening far above. Portions of the springs were covered in vast columns of rock crafted from the steady drip of water from the ceiling overhead. They connected in places, forming towering structures, while others were left still climbing toward each other. It was beautiful in a harsh sort of way, though I supposed all things in The Underworld were like that.

Pulling my gaze from the marvels around me, I focused on Aidoneus, needing an answer. We weren't allowed to delve into what being part of The Dark Faction actually meant, but every witch in my coven knew to fear them.

"Earth witches are taught only to hide from your kind. From The Dark Faction. Mother wouldn't need to change my name to justify that."

"Yes," Aidoneus mused, slipping the remains of his tunic down his shoulders.

My eyes widened despite myself, taking in the sculpted chest and torso decorated in tattoos. *Now was not the time to get distracted, Rae—or was it Persephone?* I drew in a deep breath, forcing myself to focus as he spoke.

"It's convenient she's made The Dark Faction evil, despite Hecate supporting all of her magically inclined family."

"Don't claim to know what the Goddess of Witches condones."

"Or what? I'd be just like all the witches in your coven?"

My cheeks flared a bright red as embarrassment washed

over me. Because he was right. It wasn't like Mother had met Hecate. "The High Matriarch communicates with Hecate on behalf of the coven."

"Sure she does," Aidoneus said, rolling his eyes. "I'm sure convincing the elders that demons were responsible for all that is going wrong in The Realm of the Living was easy with witches believing that."

My brows furrowed at his flippant tone as he turned and walked toward the nearest pool. He acted as if the death magic ravaging our world wasn't his doing. And that Hecate somehow accepted those in The Dark Faction despite them having bound their souls to The Underworld.

"I've seen the destruction unchecked death magic—your magic—has on the world above," I seethed, following close behind. "You can't mean to tell me that's been a lie."

Aidoneus spun, the speed at which he moved causing me to stumble into him. There was another zap where our bodies touched, the sensation both painful and frighteningly good, like the scrape of teeth before a kiss. All thoughts left me as my breathing deepened, his masculine scent of frost and darkness spurring my body on.

I wanted him to lean further down, to press his lips to my mouth the way he'd teased my neck earlier. I wanted to forget about all the reasons I couldn't want him. To know exactly what it would feel like if Aidoneus kissed lower, sucking and nipping as he went. I hated everything he stood for. Everything he'd done in his long, terrible existence, but that selfish, stupid part of my heart yearned for him anyway.

Aidoneus's eyes grew hooded, looking at me as if he could hear every filthy thought I'd had. I licked my lips, salivating for a taste of him. His gaze dipped to the small movement, and I wondered if he was imaging what my mouth would look like filled with his cock.

"You were meant to be raised in The Underworld, Persephone." His voice was low, strained, as if took every bit of will power he had to hold himself in place.

A denial was poised on the tip of my tongue, but he silenced me with a shake of his head. "You were meant to know kindness and unconditional love among the women of The Elysian Fields until the eve of your twenty-first year. At which point, you would take your rightful place as Queen of The Underworld."

I stared into Aidoneus's eyes, needing to see his unguarded expression as I asked the next question. Because if what he said was true, my entire life had been a lie.

"My mother uprooted our entire coven because of an attack from The Dark Faction ten years ago."

He shook his head. "There was no attack from The Underworld."

"There was," I insisted even as my knees weakened and my heart raced. "The High Matriarch before my mother was killed. All of us were taken into hiding, cut off from the source of our power in The Crystal City. You're saying all of it was staged to keep *me* from Hades?"

"Demeter always had plans to take the High Matriarch position, but yes. I believe hiding your power was her main concern."

Silence resonated between us. My chest heaved as he held my gaze, the sound of my blood whooshing in my ears. Mother sacrificed her comfort, the good of the coven, she'd slaughtered our High Matriarch... for me? I was both horrified and strangely touched.

Despite the years of verbal abuse that had spiraled into physical abuse, the endless hours of neglect, even gifting me to Cyrus as if I were nothing more than an animal to trade and barter, could some small part of her actually care about me?

It was foolish to hope, but I replayed the night Lark and I ran, searching my memory for any evidence that Demeter might not have been a part of what Cyrus had planned. Everything had been based on what we'd heard Cyrus say, and whoever was in the room with him—the woman wearing the thin bracelet with the teardrop diamond dangling from it.

I desperately wished I could talk to Lark right now. My mother was a horrible person. I wasn't deluded enough to think otherwise. She'd kidnapped Lark's sister and kept Lark as a servant—a prisoner—for years. But maybe she didn't want me dead. Subdued and compliant but not quite dead. And I had repaid her years of keeping me hidden from The Dark Faction by running right into the arms of a demon.

The demon. The Hound of Hades, the very one who intended to return me to his master. Because as much as I had wanted to believe becoming Queen of The Underworld was a weak ploy to get me to come with him willingly, it was becoming alarmingly clear that there was more going on that I understood.

I already felt the prick of tears at the corners of my eyes as my gaze locked with his. "If my mother hadn't hidden me, I would've what? Been offered up to Hades on a silver platter the moment I was awakened?"

Aidoneus tilted his head to the side, brows pinching as if he couldn't understand why I was angry. "On your twentieth birthday, the courtship would've begun, ending with your bonding on the day of your awakening a year later."

My hands fisted at my sides. "You still have every intention of delivering me to The Dark Palace?"

"Yes." His blue eyes were open. Honest. And I loathed him all the more for it.

I wasn't sure what I'd expected him to say or why I thought things might've changed since first entering The Underworld, but that single word felt like a spear through my chest. The force of it caused me to flinch as if I'd been physically struck. Fighting to gain control of the threatening tears, I dipped my head, not wanting Aidoneus to see.

His two fingers grazed the underside of my chin, tipping my head up until my eyes locked with his. The gesture was so tender, conveying the type of intimacy that I'd always craved but never conquered. "Come, Persephone. You need to wash and rest."

My world had flipped upside down. Again. By his own admission, Aidoneus was the bad guy, and my mother had been trying to keep me safe in her own way. Finding a way back to The Realm of the Living had always been the plan for Lark's sake, but it felt more urgent now. Like if I didn't find a way back soon, I'd end up giving into Aidoneus in more ways than one.

I followed his gaze to the clear pool beside us, the gentle bubbles breaking over the surface. The way he spoke to me felt like we'd known each other for years. It felt like he was talking directly to the broken, lonely parts of myself that I kept hidden from everyone. It had to be some type of dark magic because every part of me wanted to give into him. To believe he would keep me safe regardless of the promise he'd just confirmed that he intended to deliver me to Hades.

Even with all the evidence set before me, when Aidoneus draped his arm around my waist and led me forward, I didn't resist.

The pool was big enough to fit four or five people easily, but I knew the two of us would still somehow feel...crowded. The edges were more red than black and smoothed over time. There were hard planes of the shiny stone among the columns of sediment, reflecting the inviting waters of the pool back at us from half-a-dozen surfaces. Steam rose as we crept toward it, beckoning me to ignore all remaining shreds of decorum and sink into the waters.

And why shouldn't I?

First, Mother insisted I be Cyrus's whore. Next, I was supposedly betrothed to the evilest being in The Underworld. I hadn't spoken vows of loyalty to Hades or any other person for that matter. Nor would I.

Aidoneus claimed balance needed to be restored and that I was somehow an integral part of that, but demons lied. This was a tale as old as time. A demon scheming a soul. If the ultimate wielder of death magic sought to balance his destructive magic, he wouldn't destroy my world every chance he got. He also wouldn't bother with an essentially powerless witch.

But Aidoneus had acted like that wasn't the case, either.

Glancing down at Aidoneus's extended hand, I thought back to each time we'd touched. *Something* had caused the spike of electricity between us. It had felt different than the subtle bursts of life magic I'd sensed before. Every flicker of my power had been after sex, but even a subtle brush of our skin felt much stronger. It probably had something to do with his magic, the seducing powers of a demon were always hard to pinpoint, but if it were, in fact, *my* power, I would do everything I could to help it grow.

Including playing the good little witch in Aidoneus's story.

Squaring my shoulders, I met his heated gaze unflinchingly and placed my hand in his. He led us past the first few pools to the larger one in the back.

"You seem like you've been here before," I said, marveling at the black and red crystal making up the cavern.

Aidoneus's lips quirked into a lopsided grin as he tossed his ripped tunic to the floor. "I've been here a time or two. Lucky for you, I know which paths are safe."

"I would imagine there are a lot of things that are deadly in The Underworld," I said.

"Most things," he nodded as his fingers worked the ties of his pants. "But this mountain pass in particular has tunnels leading to all sorts of places, most of which aren't as comforting as The Realm of the Living."

"The tunnels lead to other realms?" I heard myself ask, but

my attention was fixed on the way Aidoneus's thumbs dug beneath his waistband, slowly sliding the fabric down to reveal more of those delicious tattoos.

"Are you enjoying the show, little witch?" His voice was low, but my pet name came out more rasp than words.

"Yes," I breathed. My cheeks heated, but I stood my ground, glancing up to find his pupils blown wide.

"Good," he smirked, sliding the rest of his pants down.

My gaze dipped, taking in his powerful frame before staring at his cock already half hard and reaching to mid-thigh. Gods above, the size of that thing was alarming. It was more likely to split me in two than deliver any pleasure. Maybe I didn't need a bath after all.

"Don't underestimate yourself," he said, gripping the base and giving his length a stroke. I licked my lips as I watched a bead of come appear at the tip, wondering what it would taste like. He groaned. "I'm going to watch as you come undone around my cock, delighting in the way you scream my name."

"I think you're getting ahead of yourself," I said, forcing my gaze up, even as my breasts heaved and my pulse raced, but I couldn't stop my thighs from clenching or the slickness gathering between them, none of which went unnoticed by Aidoneus.

"I plan on fucking you into oblivion, little witch. Over and over until you can't tell when one orgasm ends and the next begins. Until you understand that all of you—your mind, body, and your beautiful fucking soul—belong to me."

21

PERSEPHONE

THE SPACE BETWEEN US GREW CHARGED, THE AIR ALREADY humming with magic. Shadows swirled toward me, leaving whispers of kisses along my arms, trailing up my legs. I fought back a moan as they teased between my thighs, wanting nothing more than to give in to him. A simple brush of our skin already sent shock waves through me. I could only imaging how explosive the power between us would be if we fucked.

With my breathing heavy, I met Aidoneus's black gaze, his pupils completely eclipsing the blue. There was no doubt in my mind he would make good on his threats. If I did this, if I took one more step with the demon before me, he would own me.

"Stop denying yourself what you want," Aidoneus rumbled as his shadows slipped beneath the thin fabric.

Gods above, I *did* want this.

And why shouldn't I take what I wanted? It would be *my* decision. I would give myself to Aidoneus not because I was forced to or because the fates deemed it so. This wouldn't be like taking a lover to spite my mother or even to get a glimpse of my powers. This was about giving myself permission to make a choice and not feel guilty about it.

I'd worry about my conscience tomorrow, but right now, I intended to have a night full of uninhibited sex, free from judgment and shame.

Swallowing against the dryness in my mouth, I stepped forward.

Hades

PERSEPHONE MIGHT DENY WANTING ME, BUT I COULD SEE THE WAY her nipples harden beneath the scraps of her dress, just begging for my lips around them. She'd clenched her thighs together, but there was no hiding the scent of her arousal, like the sweetest vanilla. Her entire body was trembling, weeping for my cock to split her in two.

I had no doubt it would happen soon, but my little witch wasn't ready for that yet. She still thought I was only Aidoneus. If she knew I was the Lord of The Underworld, the Dark God she feared, she'd never look at me again.

Last week it wouldn't have mattered to me. Persephone was only a means to an end, a link to the life magic my realm so desperately needed. I'd intended to catch her, bond her, and fuck her before turning her loose. It wasn't enough to convince her to pledge her magic to me, I needed her thread woven with mine, something only complete by a vow freely given and a good fuck.

But that was before she had pressed her small hands against my chest and forced my heart to beat again. Now, she was in my head, her magic coursing through my veins, like the most addictive drug. She had invaded every cell in my body, branding me as hers forever, and I intend to do the same.

"Did you mean it?" She asked, the slight wobble to her voice giving her away, but she stepped forward despite her trembling legs, her fingers toying with the fabric along her shoulders.

I tilted my head to the side as my shadows swirled around us, waiting for her to continue.

"About me belonging to you."

"More than you know."

Her pulse skipped, and I watched as determination solidified in her features. Persephone lifted her chin, her green eyes never wavering from mine as she pushed the sleeves off her shoulders, one and then the other, until the material pooled at her feet. She stepped out of her clothes until only the golden chain and opal around her neck remained.

Persephone's red curls fanned out around her, matching the small tuft of hair between her already slick thighs. Her body was thin, the swell of her hips narrow, but there was a decent layer of muscle coating her frame. I intended to thicken her up as soon as we were home. Even so, every inch of her was fucking perfect. A goddess built for me to ravage.

A flush started over her body, her chest and cheeks rosy with the heat of blood thumping beneath her fair skin.

"All of it," I said, eyeing the fire opal around her neck. I wasn't sure if it was responsible for the spike of power between us, but I didn't want to take the chance of anything preventing me from touching Persephone as I pleased.

Her eyes snapped to mine, burning with defiance, but she obeyed. Carefully setting the necklace on top of her rags, she started across the slick stone floors toward the water's edge, swaying her hips as she went.

"Do you know what you're playing at, little witch?"

She bent down, facing me as she sat on the edge of the pool, letting her legs dangle in the pristine water. Daring to meet my heated gaze with a fire of her own, Persephone took her time studying my body, perusing as if *she* were the seductress.

And maybe she was. I already felt the limits of my self-control faltering as she stared, her tongue licking her pouty bottom lip.

"If you lick your lips one more time while staring at my cock, I will shove it down your throat until you gag."

Her eyes widened as her gaze met mine, but I didn't miss the sweet hint of vanilla spiking in the air.

"My little witch would like that, wouldn't she? My hands fisted in her hair, her lips bruised and swollen as I fucked her face?"

I let my smirk show as I stepped into the pool. The warm mineral water was already thawing the soreness clinging to my muscles, but I knew my little witch felt the hardship of the journey much more than I did. She would need tending to in more ways than one, and I couldn't think of a single thing I wanted more than to care for her.

"Yes," she breathed as I crossed the small pool toward her. Placing a hand on either side of her hips, my palms flat against the rock, I dragged my nose up the column of her neck.

She arched into my touch as I pressed gentle kisses along her throat, my fingers trailing up her spine.

"So needy," I rumbled as my other hand found her breast, teasing the peaked tip. A gasp fell from her lips as I pinched the sensitive bud, and I took advantage of the needy sound, capturing her mouth with mine. Our lips clashed, my tongue sweeping out as I tangled my fingers in the curls along the base of her neck and tugged. She opened further for me, those small, breathy sounds shifting to uninhibited moans as I claimed her.

She met me stroke for stroke, her tongue lashing against mine as I kneaded her breast, pinching the nipple between my fingers. Another gasp came from her pretty lips, but she leaned into the touch, silently begging for more. It seemed my Persephone liked her pleasure tempered with a bit of pain.

I broke the kiss only to gather her sore nipple in my mouth, soothing the pinch with my tongue.

She held my head to her, her legs spreading for me to step between them. I allowed myself one moment to bask in the feel of her thighs wrapped around me, my cock poised at her entrance, before I grabbed her ass, and lifted her off the edge.

Her arms came around my neck as we sank into the warm water, a moan escaping her perfect mouth for an entirely different reason.

"It's the minerals in the water," I breathed against her neck, tasting her lips one more time before gently unwrapping her legs from around me. Mustering every thread of control I could find, I turned her so that she was sitting across my lap, my cock straining against the outside of her thigh.

Confusion and hurt flashed across her face, her cheeks heating. I captured her chin in my fingers before she could look away.

"I have every intention of finishing what we started, Persephone. When I fuck you, I plan on taking my time. I want to watch you come apart as I bury myself in you. I plan on tasting every moan out of your lips as you bounce on my cock, watching you take every inch I give you like the good girl you are."

She swallowed as I tilted her chin up, capturing her lips with mine.

"But that's not what you need right now."

I could feel the exhaustion gnawing away at her, like the last flickers of a dying candle. I wanted nothing more than to bend Persephone over the edge of the pool and fuck her until morning, but despite how good that would feel for a moment, it would drain what little energy she had left.

"The water has healing properties," I said, gathering handfuls of the enchanted water and running it through her hair. She seemed to realize I was right, because she settled against me a moment later.

That small display of trust stirred something in my chest. This was a different type of vulnerability, one that left her body and soul open for me in a far more intimate way.

22

PERSEPHONE

"THERE'S NO NEED FOR SOAP OR OILS," AIDONEUS CONTINUED, HIS strong fingers working out the soreness of my muscles. Gods, it felt nearly as good as his lips on mine. I'd been ready to give him everything only moments ago and had been hurt by his refusal, but Aidoneus worshiped my body with his hands, erasing the horrors of the last day as I came alive beneath his touch.

Sinking into him, I closed my eyes, allowing my cheek to rest against his chest as his hands roved over my back. They worked lower, one exploring the curves of my ass as the other traced patterns along my thighs.

Shifting my back against his chest, I parted my legs for him, wanting his touch everywhere. He'd been right about me needing rest, but I already felt better than I had a few minutes ago.

"The water will restore you to peak health," Aidoneus breathed.

My breathing deepened as his fingers trailed up, his knuckles grazing my entrance. His other hand wrapped around me, fingers splayed against my stomach, hindering me from grinding further into his touch.

"Such a needy little witch," he purred, stroking me harder. I whimpered against his restraint, needing friction. He cupped my pussy, his palm grinding into my clit as his fingers pushed inside. "Is this what you want?"

I moaned around the stretch, my eyes falling closed as he pumped, only to withdraw in the next breath. Before I could complain, Aidoneus lifted us from the pool, sitting us on the edge of the heated springs. He lifted me as if he owned me. As if he would move and position my body however and whenever he pleased.

"Eyes open, Persephone." His breath fanned my ear.

My eyes fluttered open, staring across the steaming pool to a large obsidian wall, the smooth sheet of rock reflecting us as clearly as a mirror.

"I want you to watch as your demon makes you come."

I turned my neck to look up at him, but he gripped my chin, making me watch our reflections as his other hand trailed down the inside of my thigh. The pads of his fingers wrapped around my knee, lifting my leg up and over his before doing the same to the other side.

My skin flushed. I wasn't sure if it was from desire or shame, but then Aidoneus was there, lips kissing along the curve of my neck as his gaze held mine in our reflection.

"Look at you spread wide for me." I whimpered as he ran his knuckles along my slit, revealing just how turned on I was. "If you look away, I stop."

He angled his knees, spreading me wider, exposing all of me. Swallowing, I kept my eyes open, fixed on where his fingers ran the length of me, teasing and taunting until I was panting with need.

"Aidoneus," I pleaded, reaching between my legs, trying to gain some relief, only for him to capture my hand and pin it on the curve of my stomach.

"Are you desperate for me, little witch?" he whispered as he slid two fingers between my slick heat until his palm ground against my clit.

My head fell back against his chest as I met each thrust, riding his fingers. Every nerve ending stood poised as that coil drew tighter. Aidoneus kept me trapped just before release, teetering on the edge of a blade in the best and worst way possible.

"Beg me," he commanded as his pace increased.

"Please, Aidoneus," I breathed, my body shaking as I shamelessly ground my ass against his hard cock at my back. The hunger in his eyes was just as ravenous as my own. I would beg if he wanted me to, but we both knew I wasn't the only desperate one.

He released my hand with a growl only to wrap his fingers around my neck. Firm pressure tilted my head up, stretching my body as he added a third finger inside. My heart raced, thundering in my ears as his grip on my throat started to tighten, his fingers fucking my pussy ruthlessly. Steam rose around us, the gentle bubbling water, the only other sounds besides the needy breaths escaping me, until those too were cut off.

"You look so beautiful panting and wet for me."

He met my gaze in the reflection, my vision starting to spot from the lack of oxygen. My hand came up, grasping his forearm, but I didn't push him away. Didn't ask him to stop.

A wicked, knowing smile stretched across his face. "I could end your life right now, if I wished."

My pussy clenched, that mounting pressure low in my belly growing painful. Gods, I must be fucking crazy putting my life at the mercy of a demon. But I'd never felt more alive.

Shame mingled with the need for release, the warning emotions swirling together, taking me higher as Aidoneus worked my pussy. My vision clouded, all sounds falling away just as his fingers curled.

"Come for me, Persephone."

I exploded, electricity igniting every inch of my body. Oxygen rushed back as he released my neck, holding me in place as the orgasm tore through me. Normally, I got a glimpse of power, a small tingling in my fingers or palms, but this was explosive.

I was weightless, like Aidoneus might have killed me and I was now floating outside of my body in an endless state of bliss. If this was what sinning got me, if *this* was the hell others warned of, I would gladly burn for eternity.

I vaguely recalled Aidoneus's gentle hands washing me before carrying me toward a narrow alcove in the back. It was semi enclosed with towering slabs of obsidian set around a modest sized bed. There was a low table in the corner set before a small pool with a lone cup and sheathed dagger set upon it. Soft blankets were tucked around me, my eyes closing for the briefest of seconds before Aidoneus was there holding a cup of fresh water to my lips.

Still coming down, I let the water spill across my tongue, surprised by the slightly citrus notes. Each sip eased the hunger gnawing in my belly, soothing the remaining soreness in my muscles.

"Is this your home?" I asked, sitting up to take the cup from his hands. My gaze dipped to his naked body, unable to prevent myself from looking at the impressive length still ready to go. I took another sip of the enchanted waters, knowing that if I were going to survive *that*, I would need all the help I could get.

He shook his head, a smirk teasing the edge of his lips. "I stop here occasionally, but the passages beneath the mountains can be dangerous."

My brows drew together, meeting his gaze as I recalled what he'd mentioned earlier. "You never answered where they led to."

He knelt before me, lifting the cup to my lips once more. "Many places. Some to other parts of The Underworld, and yes, there is one that leads to The Realm of the Living despite its smell of death."

My eyes widened and I fought to keep my breathing even. "The path we turned away from earlier?"

I could have sworn his eyes narrowed at my question, but he was standing before I could be sure, placing the empty cup on the table.

"Rest, little witch," Aidoneus said, and I felt the familiar weight of sleep settle over me.

I hadn't realized I'd closed my eyes again, but I must have, because the bed dipped as Aidoneus slipped in behind me.

No, I thought. He'd all but confirmed I was yards away from returning home. From being able to save Lark and demand answers from Mother. I needed to stay awake.

The electricity humming through my body sparked. I focused on the heat, containing the tendrils threatening to snake out and holding them to me. A warmth settled in my chest as the weight of Aidoneus's sleep spell was pushed to the edges.

He draped an arm around my waist, resting his head on the pillow beside me.

"Sleep now, my demon." I uttered the words in little more than a whisper, but felt the hovering spell shift its attention from me to him.

I waited until his breathing evened out and his body was lax against mine. It felt nice to be held. To be wanted. A part of me desperately wished to stay here, to pretend that this wasn't a fleeting feeling, but Aidoneus still had every intention of delivering me to The Dark Palace.

If he wasn't lying and Hades really did think I was the key to fixing something with his magic, I didn't want to be around when The God of The Underworld realized I was the weakest witch in the Earth Coven.

And Lark was still trapped with Cyrus.

Slipping out from under his arm, I allowed myself one look back at him. Damp, dark curls were brushed back from his face, the tattoos over his perfect frame somehow less intimidating than when he was awake. Everything about him seemed... peaceful, so at odds with what I thought a demon would be.

"Goodbye, demon," I whispered, before retrieving my dress and necklace and fleeing down the path.

Hades

I knew something wasn't right the moment I laid down. Somehow, Persephone had been able to deflect the effect of the spell and shift its attention to me. I was aware of the way she slipped out from under me, felt her weighted stare at the edge of the alcove as she wavered between staying and running.

And fuck if I didn't hope she would stay.

But my little witch ran.

Her scent was still heavy in the air when I shook off the last of the spell. She couldn't have gone far, but if she made it to the cave. If she was too focused on returning to The Realm of the Living to see the dangers around her—

No. I wouldn't let that happen.

Calling on my shadows, I flitted through the tunnels, tracking her scent. Vanilla and wildflowers clashed with the pungent smell of rotting flesh as I turned down the forked path.

Persephone's screams echoed up ahead, jolting something in my chest.

Burning through more of the little magic I had left, I folded into the shadows, appearing at the mouth of the cave a moment later.

Massive, blood-red stones littered the cave, evidence of a time when a golden-haired hero had banished the hydra back to my world. Columns that had stood the test of time for thousands of years had been reduced to rubble, blocking the narrow path wrapping around the lake. A crumbling gate stood at the far end, guarding the stairway leading up. The passage would, indeed, lead to The Realm of the Living if one was able to reach it.

The once pristine lake set before the gate was now a sickly black, poisoned by the acidic blood of the hydra that inhabited its depths. The water was choppy, the surface of the lake having been disturbed from tumbling rocks.

Dread curled in my stomach as I spotted Persephone stumbling over sharp rubble blocking the path. Blood coated her hands and knees, the bright red mixing with the darker shades of the stone.

Midnight waters churned as the spindles of the hydra's back peaked through the surface, sending ripples outward as the creature stalked toward her, scenting a lurking prey. She didn't notice. Persephone was so focused on escaping me, she didn't see the danger heading straight for her.

"Don't move," I breathed.

Persephone's gaze snapped to mine with a retort poised on her lips. I shook my head, sending my shadows out to shroud her. One wrapped around her mouth before she could utter a word just as the scaled head of the hydra lifted from the water.

23

HADES

Large, clouded eyes peered over the black waters as the serpentine neck rose. Spikes fanned out around its head, framed by eight grotesque stumps. The other heads had been hacked away and cauterized the last time the hydra faced an opponent, leaving ragged clumps of blackened flesh behind. But the center head was immortal. It took centuries for it to reform after Hercules buried it, but the creature had regenerated, returning to its home in between our realms.

Persephone froze, her fear coatings the air in thick clouds as the hydra's forked tongue lashed out between sharp fangs. Its dark blue scales shimmered in the dim light of the cave as it scented the air, the mangled necks twitching in turn as its nostrils flared. The hydra had terrible eyesight, but its sense of smell would prove difficult to out maneuver. Especially with Persephone's blood swirling in the air.

Realizing a moment too late, my shadows circled the cuts along Persephone's knees and palms, but it was like chum to a ravenous shark. The hydra hadn't fed in centuries.

Its body tensed, the thick muscles in its reptilian neck coiling before it struck.

Persephone screamed, throwing her hands up as I dove through darkness to reach her. My arms wrapped around her waist, spinning us until she was safe behind me. The hydra's fangs were inches away from my chest, slicing through the thick blanket of shadows I'd cast.

I wove spell after spell to slow it down, using Persephone's fear to bolster my power, burning through the reserves of magic I had left. If I was at my full power, I would've been able to escape unscathed. But this was going to hurt.

"Don't touch the water," I said over my shoulder as bands of night wrapped around the creature's neck, squeezing. "It's acidic."

"The blood," Persephone breathed, her voice shaking. Her fingers dug into my shoulders as one of the bands of shadow around the hydra's neck snapped.

A pulse of electricity shot through me, burning through the chill that had begun to creep over my body once more. Magic.

But it wasn't the power of frost and darkness that I'd mastered, this power felt like life. Like pain and emotion and blazing fire taken from the surface of the sun.

I drew on it, allowing it to act through me as I raised my hands. Words fell from my lips as I wove spells, guiding them with my fingers, but it was Persephone who called the ripple of power to the forefront.

A blast of sunlight illuminated the cave, blinding the hydra as its terrible shriek reverberated off the walls. The hydra dove, attempting to escape the brightness. The rocks beneath our feet wobbled, some tumbling toward the deadly water as the entire cave shook. The Hydra's tail thrashed against the black water, the spray of acid slicing through my shadows and finding their mark in my skin.

"Hold on!" I shouted over the Hydra's cries, relieved a moment later as I felt Persephone's arms wrap around my torso. I turned away from the monstrous creature only long enough to gather her in my arms before I called on the darkness once more and fled.

Persephone

IT FELT LIKE I WAS BEING SQUEEZED BETWEEN TWO THICK BLOCKS of ice. The surrounding darkness was indefinite. There was no way out. No breath in my lungs to even scream.

My chest expanded as the world opened before me. The shadows that had been holding me up fell away, causing me to stumble to the floor. The black-red stone of the enchanted pools Aidoneus had first taken me to were beneath me, the gentle reflection of bubbling waters shimmering along the dark walls.

The cuts along my knees and palms stung as I pushed to stand, taking in the vast network of pools ahead. They were larger than the ones we had been at and far deeper judging by the way the light turquoise waters transitioned to a dark blue at the centers.

"Get dressed," Aidoneus barked as the hydra screeched in the distance. He tossed a clump of clothes at me as I turned to face him. I stumbled back as I caught them, shooting him a glare over the mound.

His eyes narrowed as he stalked forward, the pupils expanding to fully eclipse the white of his eyes. "You should think twice about testing me right now, Persephone. You could've *died*."

The break in his voice drew me up short, rattling something deep in my chest. Shadows spooled around him as if Aidoneus wore nothing but a robe of night. My heart shuddered as I realized that was all that covered him. He hadn't bothered to dress before coming for me.

"I didn't ask you to save me."

"You would never have to," he growled, but it sounded like a vow, one given to the fates. When he spoke next, it was little more than a whisper. "I heard you scream, and I wasn't there."

"I slipped," I said, looking down as I shifted the clothes, needing an escape from the anguish in his eyes.

"A lot worse would've happened had you fallen." His palms closed over mine. "But your magic saved us."

My gaze snapped to his, finding nothing but honesty in his eyes. "The light?"

He nodded. "And judging by the lack of blood scenting the air, I'd guess your cuts have healed, too."

"How?" I asked, glancing to my knees and finding the skin whole and unharmed. The sting along my palms was also gone. I wanted so badly to have magic worthy of an earth witch, but to possess magic powerful enough to stop the hydra's attack? That seemed like a dream.

"The real question is why you've been cut off from your magic for this long." Aidoneus tilted his head to the side, studying me. "You've always been powerful, Persephone. The fates have deemed it so. You're the promised one meant to save our worlds. A child of earth. The bringer of life. You *are* Persephone, The Destroyer. You were always meant to be feared."

24

HADES

PERSEPHONE LOOKED SO FUCKING GOOD DRESSED IN MY CLOTHES. The pants were baggy and the shirt reached her knees, but gods did I love the way my scent clung to her. She'd been quiet after the hydra, contemplative and lost in her mind.

"I'll have to carry you," I said as we approached the mouth of the cave. Her full pink lips turned down into a pout and a crease formed between her brows. Unable to help myself, I cupped her face, loving the way her green eyes widened at my touch.

I'd hoped to allow her time to rest before venturing into the frigid kingdom of Cocytus. I had such fun playing with my little witch before she ran. I had pushed her last night, taking things too far without warning her first, but my little witch rose to the occasion. When I'd had my hand wrapped around her neck, she had yielded so beautifully to me. Letting me hold her life thread in the palm of my hand as my fingers fucked her sweet heat.

Her breathing hitched as I dragged my thumb down the center of her bottom lip.

"I can walk," she said, batting my hand away, but we both knew her boots were useless. Scorched and half-melted from Tartarus, they were more hazard than help.

"We're flying for most of it," I continued conversationally.

"Flying?" Persephone eyed me a moment longer before realizing just how high up we were. "You flew us?"

I lifted an incredulous brow. "How else did you think you survived falling from a bridge over the Phlegethon?"

Her cheeks flushed a deep scarlet, the blush making my cock twitch.

Gods below, I hadn't felt this much in years. Not only had I enjoyed every moment of her writhing beneath my touch, but the delicious sounds spilling from her lips as my fingers stretched her had stoked a fire within my heart. I wanted to imprint the feel of her body clenching around my fingers, ingrain the sound of her moans, and the sweet scent of her pleasure on my soul forever.

Holding her gaze, I let my wings unfurl, allowing her a glimpse of the monster beneath.

A foreign twisting in my stomach had unease pricking along my spine. This would all end the moment Persephone learned who I was. She would find out soon enough. If my little witch was honest with herself, a part of her knew something was wrong the moment she saw the tattoo of the upside down torch over my chest.

With my true form hidden, mortals gazing upon me had convinced themselves that I was a trusted general to Hades. It made them too uncomfortable to think that I could move among them so easily. I had resented the attention those in The Realm of the Living bestowed on my brother for centuries, but now it seemed they'd provided me the perfect cover.

"You have wings," she breathed. I didn't miss the note of awe in her voice as she stepped toward me, her green eyes widening as the leathery hide of my wings stretched.

"What? No demon comments?" I quipped, waiting for her to recoil. But she only stepped closer, the pad of her finger tracing the veins to the sensitive patch of skin behind my shoulders.

A growl ripped through my chest as I caught her hand, gritting my teeth against the primal urge to bend her over right now. But my little witch would never forgive me. Not without her knowing who she was giving herself to. I would have to wait until our bonding if I intended to keep her. And I *would* keep her.

"Sorry," she squeaked, not daring to move.

Forcing a breath in through my nose, I released her hand, but she stayed frozen in place, her gaze fixed on mine.

"My wings are sensitive."

"Oh," she breathed, pulling her bottom lips between her teeth.

I leaned forward, dragging my nose up the column of her neck. "So fucking sweet, little witch. Like vanilla."

Her breathing hitched as I pressed a kiss at the edge of her jaw. Her hands trailed up my chest, exploring the curve of my shoulders, before teasing the same spot.

"I'll teach you all the ways I like my wings played with," I said through gritted teeth. Gripping her hips, I pressed her against me, grinding my hard cock against her center. "Just as you will show me exactly how you like your pussy eaten and fucked."

"Do you have to talk like that?" she asked as she ground against me.

"You seem to enjoy it."

She stilled, drawing back to shoot me a glare before crossing her arms over her chest. "Aren't you supposed to be flying us somewhere?"

Instead of pressing the matter, I gathered her in my arms and launched into the dark skies above.

I would keep my identity a secret a little longer. There would be no turning back once our threads were secured. Despite how badly I craved her, nothing could jeopardize the safety of my realm, not even Persephone. But a growing part of myself wondered if that was still true. Billions of souls hung in the balance... and yet, if there was a choice to be made, I didn't think I could give my little witch up.

25

PERSEPHONE

AIDONEUS HAD THE FILTHIEST MOUTH. AND GODS DID I LOVE IT. He said things that made me feel desired to the point that I could almost believe he cared. If I didn't think too long on who he was or where he was taking me, I let myself envision a future where I could really be his. Where someone could actually love me. Not that I would want that person—demon—to be him. But the possibility of having a *choice* in my future would be nice.

I didn't ask to be the daughter of Demeter. To be used by her and Cyrus until I was nothing but a shell of a soul, cracked and hollowed. I didn't want to be Queen of The Underworld or to restore some cosmic balance when I wasn't the one who fucked it up in the first place. Maybe that made me selfish, but I wanted at least a facade of free will.

All I was asking for was the freedom to fuck up my life the way *I* wanted to. My life wouldn't be perfect or heroic. There wouldn't be any songs written about me or great legends to commemorate my name... but the book of my life would be written *by me*, the pages filled with failures and successes, adventures and heartbreaks of my own device.

Ironically, Aidoneus was the first being that had shown me glimpses of what that would look like.

Tilting my head, I glanced up, marveling at how his great wings beat. The air had grown cold, the smell of embers and ash replaced by frost tinged with brine. It wasn't like the sweet scent of snow that clung to Aidoneus. This was a numbness borne of pain.

Another gust of frigid air lashed against us. Thankful for Aidoneus's oversized clothes, I curled further into his chest. The rhythm of his steady heartbeat acted as a soothing lullaby and I latched onto it, anchoring myself to his strength, knowing that I had very little left of my own.

Aidoneus said I was powerful. He'd called me Persephone, The Destroyer.

Lark would've loved that title. She was always ready to test boundaries, breaking rules every chance she got, even if it was only playing with her forbidden magic.

My fingers brushed against the opal necklace as memories of our time together surfaced. We had spent every chance we got testing the boundaries of her persuasion. It usually involved me saying something ridiculous to a boy or sneaking an extra pastry from the kitchens. Nothing big. But the mere act of Lark using magic and me practicing breaking it were both actions that weren't tolerated in the Earth Coven.

We were supposed to escape the Earth Coven together, but now I realized we'd never stood a chance. Mother had imprisoned her sister. I hadn't known Lark *had* a sister.

It explained why she hadn't run, why we never made it further than the edge of the forest when we'd scouted for an escape route. But why not tell me?

I wondered how Mother was punishing her now. I never saw a bruise on Lark's body, but that didn't mean Mother hadn't found ways to torture her. Or worse, take out her anger on Lark's sister.

Gods above, Lark had been with us for four years. Disgust twisted my stomach as I realized Mother must have been holding her sister as a hostage all this time. I hoped to the gods that Demeter hadn't been aware Cyrus intended to kill me, that some sliver of my mother might actually care about me, but she'd been perfectly fine selling my body and magic to him.

But selling isn't quite the right word. What did Cyrus have to gain from bonding me? As far as the coven knew, I was a witch with minimal powers. Sure, I was the daughter of the great High Matriarch, but there was no way I'd take over the coven one day.

Or maybe Mother knew about my magic—the possibility of it, at least. Maybe everything Aidoneus had said was true.

I swallowed against the flush creeping up my neck as I thought about the blast of power that had stilled the hydra's attack, and then to the magic that had hummed in my veins when Aidoneus had made me come. It was single-handedly the best orgasm I'd ever had. Magic had seared through me, touching every inch of my soul. The fatigue gnawing away at me from our time in Tartarus had gone. I wasn't sure if it was my magic or the enchanted waters, but my body felt rejuvenated.

Release magic was the only type of magic I'd been able to access. I had always hoped it would be the key to unlocking more of my magic, but nothing had ever happened... until I came to The Underworld.

Mind whirling, I searched my memory for every instance there was a flicker of energy between Aidoneus and me. When his shadow bindings failed on the shores of the Lethe, the small pricks when we had climbed through The Valley of Torment, along the bridge when Kampe appeared. And again, when I raced toward him, seeking refuge in his arms as the she-dragon gave chase.

Each time I was afraid.

Could all that magic really have come from me? A part of me knew the answer, but I wouldn't allow myself to believe it.

Cold whipped around us, bringing with it high pitched wails of souls trapped in agony. Daring to look over Aidoneus's arm wrapped around me, I peered below, finding a barren land of ice and snow stretching before us: Cocytus.

"Their cries will only get louder as we draw near," Aidoneus said, answering my unspoken question. "There's no hope among the souls banished to Cocytus. They are traitors forced to wander alone forever."

I gave a small nod, spying a winding river in the far distance, but my mind was elsewhere, searching for answers to questions I wasn't prepared to ask. Focusing on the warmth inside my chest, I called on my magic. Pricks of electricity tingled along my fingers, the faint shimmer dulling within moments and leaving me weaker for it.

"Sleep, Persephone," Aidoneus whispered. "There are miles left to travel, and you'll need your strength."

Knowing there was nothing more to be done, I closed my eyes, trusting my demon to keep me safe.

Hades

The icy tundra of Cocytus stretched before us. Darkness consumed everything, leaving only frigid planes in its wake. It was always night here, the unnatural clouds born of misery and regret blotting out most of the faint light from above.

Shards of ice and rock littered the otherwise barren land-scape, peaking out beneath vast snow banks and leafless trees. The Cocytus river was the only glimmer of color. Its slow moving waters composed of ice and tears lapped against sapphire stones that gave off a faint glow, drawing wandering souls toward its edge.

These were not like the souls in The Asphodel Plains or even those in Tartarus. These spirits were traitors of the worst kind. Deception and betrayal consumed their lives while they'd been in the Realm of the Living. All had willingly led innocents down trails of lies. And so, they too must wander aimlessly, following the frigid blue river on a path downward, spiraling toward the desolate center.

The souls believed the pit would offer them a reprieve, a place to rest their weary, wounded bodies, but that too was a false hope.

In truth, they were meandering toward the lowest point of The Underworld, even lower than Tartarus, with nothing but a frozen lake waiting for them. Most of the lost and broken souls swarmed its edges, but the worst of them were sentenced to infinite torment within its icy waters.

Another cold gust barreled toward us, causing Persephone to bury her face into the warmth of my chest, even in sleep. Her small body shivered, igniting an irresistible urge to protect her from all that was to come. To save her from a life tethered to me.

I angled for the northern bank of the icy river as the control over my magic and wings started to wane. Fear gripped my chest as I crested lower. Our realms wouldn't be safe until we were bound, wed, and Persephone had come into her powers, but the balance could begin to shift in the right direction if any one of those things occurred.

I had planned on forcing her to marry me the first night I'd caught her, but we'd ended up in Hypnos's territory without a way to return to The Dark Palace. I had no doubt that Thanatos and Hecate were looking for us. They were the ones to suggest beginning the process of weaving out threads right away. And fuck if I didn't want to make Persephone my wife in every way possible.

Her eyelids fluttered, her pouty pink lips now tinged in blue. She had no idea the monster she feared most was the very one that she'd submitted to last night. The one she would have given everything to. Despite all that I'd told her, she trusted me to keep her safe.

Her hand clutched at my chest, drawing her body closer to mine. Electricity pricked beneath her touch, the small sparks sending waves of heat pulling through my body. I wanted to be better for her. To earn her affections and have her give herself willingly to me—to Hades.

But I wasn't a hero. I wasn't noble or self-sacrificing. I was selfish and greedy. I'd coveted many things in my long life, but nothing like I did Persephone.

My realm was harsh. Cocytus being a prime example of that, but this wretched kingdom was a brutal reality my little witch needed to endure if she was to rise to her full potential. If she was to take her rightful place as my queen.

"I'm sorry," I breathed, pressing a kiss to her brow. The moment she woke, I intended to deceive, to lie, to tell her whatever she wanted to hear to ensure our threads were woven together. To bind my Persephone to me forever.

26

PERSEPHONE

THE SCENT OF SWEET FROST AND DARKNESS ENGULFED ME, clashing with the stinging wind lashing through my cocoon of warmth. I whimpered, curling further as I sank into the meager heat Aidoneus's body offered me.

My palm splayed against hard, smooth muscle, the pads of my fingers tingling. The gentle thudding of his heartbeat skipped, the rhythm jumping under my touch. Half asleep, I allowed my fingers to explore, heeding the spark that begged me to follow.

"Don't." A warm palm captured my wandering fingers as the chest I was pressed against rumbled.

My eyes flutter open, finding Aidoneus's deep blue gaze boring into mine. I'd undone the top buttons of his tunic, exposing the hard planes and swirling tattoos along his chest. A sheet of midnight clouds was cast overhead, but I could just make out the various symbols spanning outwards toward his shoulders. And the particular symbol my fingers were poised over.

The upside down torch.

"Sorry," I breathed, glancing up at him. Blinking the sleep

from my eyes, I realized we'd landed. Snow covered everything except for the luminescent river to our left and the rocky path Aidoneus followed. There were clumps of trees, but the thin branches offered next to nothing in terms of shelter.

A powerful gust reared up, forcing me to tug at the thick material covering me. My brows furrowed as I noted the extra layers, eyes widening as I looked back toward the thin material covering Aidoneus's body.

"Is this your coat?"

"It was the only way I could stop you from shivering," he said, unable to look me in the eyes.

"But what about you?" I asked. "How are you not frozen?"

Vast sheets of ice coated the surface of the slow moving river composed of brilliant blue stones. Endless snow and rough paths woven through barren trees made up the rest of the landscape, spiraling downward toward a pit at the valley's center. Stumbling, lost souls all headed in the same direction. We'd reached Cocytus.

Distraught souls wailed endlessly, their infinite tears running down the expanse of their decrepit bodies to join the valley of ice around them. Some looked much the same as those in The Realm of the Living, but others were little more than ghosts. Shades destined to wander these cursed shores forever.

"I am a part of The Underworld," Aidoneus said with a shrug, the simple gesture somehow softening his sharp features. "The cold doesn't bother me."

"Is it a demon thing?" I asked, my gaze falling to the tattoo over his heart once more. It must have been spelled, because I wanted to press my palms flat against his chest and feel the beating of his heart again. I craved to taste him, to lick the edges of the very tattoos meant as a warning to stay far away from him.

Gods above, what was happening to me?

"As much as I enjoy your touch, it's best if you keep your

hands to yourself. At least until you can master control over your gifts. When life magic is extended beyond your stores, it will pull from your own thread."

My eyes widened. "The only magic I've displayed was when your fingers were inside of me."

Aidoneus's lips quirked in a cocky grin as my cheeks heated.

"That was a beautiful start to our adventures together, but your power far outshines the boundaries of release magic."

"I'm not awakened," I said, refusing to believe it despite the evidence before me. "This can't be my power."

"Many witches display low level power before their awakening, as you know. The stronger the witch, the earlier the magic will be present."

My mother's voice echoed in my ear, never letting me forget she was only ten years old when the first rose bush bloomed under her touch. But there were never any signs of my own magic.

Aidoneus's eyes narrowed, his brows furrowing as he studied my face. "To wield magic that powerful before your awakening, you must have been young when your magic first manifested."

"No," I whispered, but the word didn't feel quite right. Flashes of the nightmare from the bridge on Tartarus flitted through my mind, each one more confusing than the last. "The nightmare Kampe forced me to see... I think it was a memory. At least, part of it."

"What was it?"

"I was able to do magic in the dream—nightmare from Kampe. I must have been eight or nine years old, but I brought an entire field of dandelions back to life after it had been decimated by death magic."

Aidoneus's grip tightened around me, tugging me closer. It was the support I didn't realize I needed and would've never thought to ask for, but it soothed the churning of my mind enough to continue.

"Mother knew." I swallowed against the dryness of my throat, my stomach clenching. "I thought she'd be proud, but she was so angry."

"She was threatened," Aidoneus corrected, his voice taking on a hard edge. "And desperate."

"For what?" I countered. "I've always been an embarrassment, the weak, useless daughter of the great Demeter. Having magic would have fixed all of that."

"Or it would've stripped Demeter of her chance to discredit you. A witch of your power could easily sway the coven, usurping her position."

"I never would've done that," I muttered.

"Demeter isn't one to leave her power up to chance," Aidoneus said, the words dripping with hatred.

"How could I not know I had access to magic?" I asked, watching his face for a response. I wasn't sure what I was hoping for. For him to be deceiving me? For this all to have been a ploy by a wicked demon to claim what little life magic I could impart?

But then why save me from the Lethe? Why go through all of this if I was just another witch destined to die on her awakening unless Aidoneus had been telling the truth from the beginning.

"There are ways for a witch's powers to be suppressed. The bigger issue is getting you to The Dark Palace in time for the bonding ceremony and making sure you have access to your powers."

My eyes snapped to his, disbelief coating my words. "You still intend for me to wed Hades?"

His shrewd gaze met mine, drawing me in close as if he would give the answer I wished for. But wishes were often left unanswered.

"Yes."

27

PERSEPHONE

THE BEATING OF MY HEART FALTERED AS THE WORD HOVERED between us.

"You intend for me to be Hades's whore," I snapped, feeling like he'd just wedged a knife in my chest.

"Queen," he corrected, eyes narrowing. "You'll never be forced to do anything, and enjoying sex doesn't make you a whore, Persephone. You will be bound—"

"So, I'm to be *your* whore?" I interrupted, fighting back the sting of tears. "All of those things you said to me, about making me yours, that was all lies?"

Aidoneus's jaw ticked, but he didn't answer.

"Put me down," I breathed, not daring to meet his eyes. "I can walk."

He didn't slow, trudging on through a small cluster of trees with icicles clinging to bare branches. "The cold would freeze you in minutes."

"Then it will be a few minutes without having to feel your hands on me."

His steps faltered, fingers flexing around my thighs and shoulders for a moment longer, before he swung my legs down.

He made sure my worn boots touched the brown stone first, before stepping back.

The wind instantly leeched the heat from my body, despite the extra layers, causing my knees to shake. Aidoneus looked as if he might pick me up again, but the fierce, stubborn glare I fixed him with had him stilling.

"Only step on the stones. The snow banks can be a lot deeper than they appear."

I started forward, but he grabbed my wrist.

"Stay close, little witch. Most of the souls here are too absorbed in their own torment to notice us, but there are some who are more aware. Their bitterness and rage have replaced their humanity. I've not been able to carry their souls to the Lethe as I should have, so they remain here."

Something about what he said raised the small hairs on the back of my neck, but then he looked down, his thumb brushing against my cheek. And I nearly forgot to breathe. "You wouldn't want to end up on the wrong side of a wraith."

I batted his hand away, ignoring the blush of warmth it left along my skin. "I'll take my chances."

He lifted a brow, the edge of his lips twitching. My fists clenched in the fabric of his tunic, hating how he looked perfectly content among the darkness with only a pair of pants and a thin top on.

We had been gallivanting across The Underworld without food or water and there was barely a hair out of place on him. Meanwhile, my body was shaking from the frigid air of this gods forsaken valley. My dress was little more than rags, the only piece of civility remaining being my opal necklace, and I was being forced deeper into The Underworld—every step taking me further away from saving Lark—by a gods damned demon intent on delivering me to Hades, the Royal Demon, himself.

It didn't help that Aidoneus's dark magic was doing things to me, stirring warmth in places that shouldn't be affected by the way his cerulean eyes seemed to burn as they looked at me, or the way his defined muscles across his chest and thighs shifted as he moved. It definitely didn't help that he could scent the arousal from my traitorous body even as my mind screamed for the chance to kill him. And it *really* didn't help that he was standing there in the snow before me looking as if he thought my hatred of him was somehow cute.

Clutching the layers of clothes, I pushed past him, continuing along the rocky path beside the river. Shards of ice hung low among the branches, causing me to stoop more than once to avoid their sharp tips.

The sounds of lamentation were deafening, clashing with the distant thundering of water on rocks. Ignoring the numbness in my toes, I followed the path of the river, searching for a source of the sound.

My foot slipped as I leapt to the next stone, sending me toppling toward the stretch of sleet bordering the river. Aidoneus was behind me in a flash, the warmth of his palms on my waist a welcomed reprieve from the cold, but he withdrew as soon as I was steady, stepping between me and the souls along the river. It was a simple gesture. He probably hadn't realized he'd put himself between me and the distraught souls, but the fluttering in my chest wished he did.

"The Cocytus river falls thousands of feet into a frozen lake where the worst of the traitors are held. The Algea preside over it."

"The Algea?" I asked, following his line of sight. I searched among the wailing souls, their bodies so dense now that it was difficult to see beyond. Luckily, the river diverged from the stone path, putting some much wanted distance between us and the horde.

"Three sisters: Lupe, Akhos, and Ania," Aidoneus said. "Responsible for distress, grief, and sorrow."

The blue water had picked up speed, sheets of ice breaking into shards as they approached a cliff in the distance. Squinting through the icicle covered branches around us, I focused on the varying shades of white, realizing that the ground stopped abruptly. A vast pit was waiting in the center. Caves spotted the far side with rough, narrow paths traversing the steep cliffs.

Most of the wandering souls followed the blue-stoned river over the cliff, their ghost-like bodies tumbling down until they were swallowed up by ice and snow.

My body shivered uncontrollably as I traced the path we were on to the edge of the pit. "I don't see a path around it."

Aidoneus hovered nearby, two of his fingers lifting the tip of my chin until I was forced to meet his eyes. Unable to help myself, I pressed further into his touch.

"We're not going around it, little witch."

The gentleness of his voice sounded like we were out for a stroll in the woods, as if we were speaking of far more intimate things. My fingers pricked with the urge to reach out and stroke his chest. There was a buzzing in my veins as the electricity stirring between become nearly tangible.

"In order to enter the safety of The Asphodel Plains and reach The Dark Palace, we first must venture beneath Cocytus to connect to the caves."

"Caves that lead to The Dark Palace?"

"Yes."

I stared at the tattoo of the upside down torch on Aidoneus's chest. He was Hades's general, one that would succeed in his quest to deliver me to The God of The Underworld.

As much as I yearned for a chance to live a life of freedom, I knew I wouldn't abandon the souls in need. If my life and magic were needed to save the countless souls above from being rendered into blackened husks, I would die willingly.

The crystal around my neck heated, my fingers grazing the opal stone, seeking guidance. My thoughts sharpened, my pulse quickening as I realized I couldn't leave Lark to her fate. I couldn't let my mother terrorize her sister, and the dozens of other sisters or loved ones she held captive.

Last night was a mistake. I had let myself lose sight of who Aidoneus really was. What we'd done clearly hadn't meant anything to him, seeing as how he still had every intention of delivering me to Hades. And for what? Because I was supposedly the key to saving our realms?

Suddenly, it all seemed so foolish.

If we passed beneath Cocytus and into The Asphodel Plains, I'd be doomed. Now was my only chance to escape. To set things right with Lark before my fate was written.

I let the pad of my finger drag against the ink along his chest, pressing closer to the warmth his body offered. "Are they the same caves we just left? The ones with the hydra?"

Aidoneus searched my face. "Their paths connect. Just as various paths stretch across all kingdoms of The Underworld and to The Realm of the Living and The Aboveworld."

"I hadn't realized how vast they were," I breathed, trying to focus on the small heat at the tips of my fingers—heat generated by my magic. Focusing on stoking the small embers, I willed my power to grow, searching for a connection to the earth that might help me discover a way out of this.

An intricate network of roots answered my call, like a torch put to kindling. Hundreds of pathways illuminated under my magic, each with a different feel. I focused on the one that led up, the vibrations in the air reminiscent of the small tavern at the edge of the forest that I'd frequented with Lark.

"Is this where Orpheus came to rescue Eurydice?" The question left my lips before I thought better of it, but Lark's tales of a heartbroken musician rose from the back of my mind. The blacks of Hades's eyes expanded as a whisper of wings showed at his back.

I looked away, studying the gleaming icicles clinging to the branches around us. It would have been beautiful were it not for the endless suffering all around. I couldn't defeat the hydra, but I could climb out of the same cave Orpheus had.

"It's only that Cocytus seems like the type of place Orpheus would've been, what with saving his wife only to turn around and watch her vanish right before his eyes."

"He was told not to look back until she was secured in The Realm of The Living. He disobeyed."

I narrowed my eyes at Aidoneus's clipped tone. "He was worried."

"He should have trusted in his wife's abilities," Aidoneus bit back. "And yes, the passage he took is among those beneath Cocytus, but don't get any ideas. We won't be anywhere near there."

I schooled a neutral expression on my face, acting as if he hadn't seen right through me. "I suppose there are just the two passages linking my realm with yours?"

"On the contrary, there are many ways a soul can cross. Most involve death, but if one of the living wished to venture into The Underworld without cutting their life thread, they'd have limited options: The spring in the Mountains of Mourning is now tainted with Hydra venom, as you know." His lips twitched as he noticed the glare I shot him. "The Cave of Taenarum is the one Orpheus took, and is, indeed, below us. The last is a descending staircase along the banks of the Acheron River. There was another in The Darklands of the North centuries ago. Hypnos claims a rockslide has closed it off for good, but I'm not so sure."

Great. Each passage sounded more horrible and out of reach than the last. I went to rest my head against his chest, but my necklace flared again, tapping into the embers of life magic I was still connected to in the earth yards below us.

"We didn't take any of those paths when you kidnapped me," I breathed, gripping the fire opal.

"No. We didn't. But if you were to seek a way into The Underworld on your own, you'd have to risk a crossing like any other mortal."

I swallowed against the sudden dryness in my throat.

"It's best if you stick by me. We are a few yards away from the edge of the pit where the path zigzags through caves until we reach the floor. If you step off the stone path, you risk falling through feet of snow and winding up in the middle of the network of caves below us."

This just keeps getting better and better.

"Don't worry, little witch. Your demon will keep you safe."

Scowling, I tore my body away from his, standing beneath the icy tree at the edge of a large stone.

I was an earth witch—with powers. Strong powers. The soil was meant to speak to me, guide and aid me when necessary. I could already feel the caves beneath my feet. Magic had helped when Lark and I were running from Cyrus. It should be the same for The Underworld, right?

Aidoneus stood before me, content at watching me struggle to decide my next move. I loathed the slight tilt to his head and the small grin playing at the edge of his lips. As if I were nothing more than a toddler throwing a tantrum.

"There's nowhere for you to go, Persephone," he said, leaning toward me.

I pressed my back against the trunk of the tree, a few of the icicles clinging against one another.

"Are you quite finished, little witch?" He twirled a loose curl around his finger, waiting for me to ask for his help.

"Not even close, demon."

I let Aidoneus see all the hate in my eyes as I called on my magic, the embers heating me from the inside. His eyes widened, taking in my power and the infinite defiance burning in my eyes, before I broke off an icicle overhead and thrust it into his chest.

2 8

HADES

PERSEPHONE WOULD BE THE DEATH OF ME. I PULLED THE SPIKE OF ice from my chest, tossing the blood-coated tip among the trees as she leapt from the stone path, and sunk beneath the snow.

I was wondering when she'd try to escape. My little witch didn't like being told what to do. But the look of fierce determination in her eyes as she thrust the shard into my chest... fuck if it didn't make my cock hard just thinking about it.

Fear would've stilled most mortals' hands. Would have had them clinging on to me, begging me to find a way out of Cocytus for them, but I should've known Persephone's pride wouldn't let her fold, not when I had laid out the possibility of an escape so prettily before her.

Last night was incredible. Even facing off against the hydra. Watching her tap into her magic while drinking in her fear was delectable. I wondered how delicious her pussy would be.

I'd only allowed myself a quick taste of her on the banks of the Lethe. I hadn't allowed myself anything further, not trusting I would be able to mask my true form once I had lapped at her sweet heat. Even with my fingers buried in her, my body had hummed with the force of her magic bleeding into the air around us. Every nerve ending in my numbed soul had awakened, much like how she forced my withered heart to beat again. The forgotten emotions of desire, passion, lust—all had flooded into me as her pussy clenched around my fingers, her breathy moans singing through my ears like a most cherished ballad.

My little witch had begged for release—for me—and yet she still stabbed me.

And then jumped.

A startled shriek followed her descent as she went, further and further into the deepest part of my realm. She thought she was running, thwarting my plans, but she was surpassing every milestone I'd laid out.

Persephone had been trained from a young age to think she was weak, but here she was, trusting in her abilities to find a path out of this hell.

It was mad to risk so much with so little information at her fingertips, but you must be a little mad to rule a kingdom of tortured souls. Pride raced through me as I heard a faint thud followed by a curse. There was silence for only a moment, and then my little witch was moving.

Persephone

THAT WAS TERRIFYING AND DEFINITELY ONE OF THE STUPIDEST things I had ever done. My body was chilled and disoriented from the rapid descent. Unable to see, I felt the ground beneath my knees, using my palms to push the snow out, until I had a small circle of space to breathe.

I glanced up, expecting to see a tunnel from above, only to find the snow had closed over. My vision spotted as I realized I had just buried myself alive. The frantic beating of my heart was ringing in my ears, a sharp pain in my chest growing as I fought for breath. It felt like I didn't have enough air. Like my lungs were trying to expand, but my ribs had suddenly become too small. Caging them. Just as I was caged beneath the hopelessness of Cocytus.

No. I can't give up now.

Forcing my fingers to unfurl, I stayed on my hands and knees, pressing my palms against the luminescent blue stone.

At first nothing happened. But I concentrated on the feel of the smooth sapphires beneath each pad of my fingers, tapping them in a rhythm until the vise gripping my sternum eased and my mind calmed.

A faint brush of power sparked. It wasn't warm like the earth in The Realm of the Living, but it didn't feel hostile, either. More like a subtle curiosity.

Instead of drawing my magic forward, I took a deep breath and opened myself to an exchange of power. It was the difference between fighting the ebbing of the ocean's waves and allowing the water to carry you back to shore a little at a time. Gentle strokes synchronized with the natural rhythm of the waves were far easier than plowing through the churning of the water.

An ember caught, the flash of heat expanding over my palms. I blinked my eyes open, grinning as I saw the faint shimmer of light coating my hands. A shiver rocked through me as my magic coursed through my body, repairing all damage done by the fall and the cold before settling over me in a cloud of warmth.

Gods above. I'd done it. I was channeling life magic.

The opal along my neck pulsed. Lark would be so impressed. So relieved. This may be the craziest thing I had ever done, but I *was* doing it.

This power, this incredible magic, was coming from me. I choked down an incredulous laugh. Lark was going to be beside herself when she saw what I could do. I only hoped I wasn't too late to save her.

29

PERSEPHONE

SAPPHIRES AND SLEET CRUNCHED BENEATH MY WORN BOOTS, small puddles forming along the edges as my life magic burned bright through the layers of snow surrounding me. Slowly making progress, I followed my magic along an unforeseen path, looking for a cave entrance.

The earth of The Underworld helped when it could, like a subtle tugging deep within. I could also feel Aidoneus behind me, somehow remaining close despite me literally jumping to my possible death to get away from him.

That demon had seriously fucked with my mind.

It should have been easy to distance myself from sex and emotion. It had never been a problem before. The Earth Coven may have hated the idea of casual sex, and gods knew we were taught to hate ourselves for it, but Lark and I carved out our own morality code.

My worth wasn't defined by how many partners I took to bed. I wasn't used or dirty. I wasn't a ripped piece of cloth poorly stitched back together or a crumpled flower with its petals plucked and tossed to the floor.

My body was my own.

It was mine to do with what I pleased. Sex didn't condemn me. Allowing myself to believe the truth of those sentiments had dramatically altered my life for the better. It was freeing. I'd never let that self-confidence waver. And because of that, I'd never let the line between physical and emotional blur. Until Aidoneus.

There shouldn't have been anything to distance myself *from*. But he'd gotten under my skin. Limits didn't exist for Aidoneus. He took what he wanted, and he didn't once question himself. Power came naturally for him, that much was obvious, and I found myself reaching for my own power when he was near.

He made me want to push. To shatter the expectations that had been placed on me by my mother, by the coven, but also... by myself.

It had been so hard for me to accept that I had power. That the humming beneath my veins, the pricks of electricity at my fingertips—that such power could be *mine*.

I'd been told so often that I was worthless. Weak. Useless. That I was a burden who would never amount to anything... it was hard to believe there was a reality where I was powerful and strong—one where my life had *meaning*.

And yet, somehow, Aidoneus had believed in me.

Shaking my head against the onslaught of budding self-worth battling with years of learned helplessness, I lifted my hands and drew more of that fire to my palms.

Melted ice trickled down the sheet of snow covering me, but the bank in front of me felt weaker than the others. Less oppressive. The sapphires at my feet hummed. I followed their urging, calling more of the magic in my veins as I pushed forward.

The snow broke, the edges tumbling around my forearms as my palms melted through the last of it. I stepped out of my sleeted path into a large tunnel illuminated by the continuing, faint blue stones at its base.

Brine and frosted air reached me as I blinked against the gleaming blue light reflecting against the walls. It was both forbidding and comforting as the cries of the cursed souls echoed through the caves. Rumbling water pounded the ground further ahead. I was sure of it, just as I knew the icy pit of Cocytus was waiting for me, wanting me to make my way toward the hopeless shores like all the other wandering spirits.

A tingle caressed my spine, snapping my head back toward the wall of snow I'd just left. Aidoneus was drawing closer. I needed to move faster.

Letting out a shuddering breath that fogged in the chilled air, I jogged toward the light. Aidoneus said we needed to travel beneath the frozen lake to reach The Asphodel Plains, but I had no intention of going to The Dark Palace just yet. I would return to The Underworld and fulfill my duty, I swore to the gods I would, but only after Lark was safe. For now, I needed to focus on crossing the lake and getting through the caves on the other side to reach the staircase Orpheus took, all before my demon found me.

I let my desires fuel me, focusing every thought on finding the path to The Realm of the Living. And then simply... let go. My magic rose to the surface, keeping my body warm as the temperature plummeted around me. I'd never been particularly excited for my awakening, considering I anticipated dying, but for the first time, I wondered if I might have a chance at living beyond my twenty-first birthday. And what that would mean.

The tunnel linked up to others. Souls stumbled in, the crowd of them growing until I was surrounded by the dead. Aidoneus's warning about wraiths rang through my mind as I fell into step beside the meandering souls. Their boots and slippers had been rendered to scraps as they walked on bloodied feet, and there was a constant stream of tears tracking down their cheeks, staining their tatters of clothes in rivulets, but they continued mourning without sparing me a second glance.

For the most part, the souls were like people in my realm, but wraiths had been here centuries. They had little memory of what they'd once been, clinging only to their infinite bitterness and loss. It became exceedingly harder to keep my distance as more joined our steady progression downward.

"Sorry," I mumbled automatically as a woman with the same dark curls and hazel eyes as Lark bumped into me. Her shoulders and chest were slimy with years of spent tears, her black robes tattered and frayed at the edges. She blinked, her puffy, swollen eyes seeming to come out of a fog as her gaze met mine.

That couldn't be good.

Tilting my head down, I picked up my pace, weaving through the souls as quickly as I could. My magic flared brighter as panic gripped my chest. It took effort to reign in the heat pouring off me. Sweat beaded on my brow, and my pulse raced as more and more souls took notice of me, their anguished cries quieting as I raced past.

Frozen skin drawn tight over skeletal hands reached for me, tugging at my clothes, ripping at my hair. Losing all pretense of blending in, I reached for the warmth of my magic and sprinted for the growing light in the distance.

My lungs burned with each inhale of icy air, but I didn't slow. I couldn't. Too many had snapped out of whatever hell they'd been trapped in and had set their sights on me.

I willed my body to move faster as my boots slipped on bits of ice and sleet that coated the path. Somehow, the world grew colder—the atmosphere harsher—as my legs trembled. Fear spurred on my movements as I pushed my body to its limits. A metallic tang coated my lips as frosted breaths stung my lungs, the taste of blood rolling over my tongue. It was too cold. Even the air was painful to breathe. But the tunnel was opening, the sounds of the suffering obliterated by the thundering waterfall.

Water crashed into the sapphire pool below, causing the ground beneath my feet to vibrate. I tilted my neck up as I sprinted from the cave, watching horrified as bodies pitched over the edge from far above, their bones joining the bed of broken dreams and icy shards before me.

Nausea twisted my stomach as I looked at the abandoned souls trapped beneath the thick layers of ice, my gaze darting over them until I found one staring back at me.. My legs carried me forward, it's intelligent blood-red eyes locked with mine. I was so fixated on them that I didn't notice the sapphires beneath my feet shift into sheets of ice.

I slipped, palms crashing against ice as the force of my fall carried me further across the slick surface. The throng of souls trailing close behind slowed, stopping where blue stones met the cursed lake.

I was forgotten once more.

Thank the gods, because I'd slid a good deal. I had intended to avoid the risk of walking over ice and stick to the stone path as I searched for... something.

Shaking my head, I placed my palms against the ice, rolling to my knees as I concentrated on standing. I had to keep going. To keep moving... But why?

A suffocating wave of hopelessness descended on me as a sob tore through my chest. I hung my head, unable to look away from my feet. From the melted soles warped from climbing through the borderlands of Tartarus, and the too-long pants rolled up around them.

Aidoneus's pants.

My shoulders rounded as my chest shook. The light emanating from my palms dimmed as I realized I couldn't feel him. Aidoneus was too far away. He must have given up on me. It was easier to find another earth witch, one who would be grateful to be a queen.

I was always complaining. Always failing.

Aidoneus said the fates named me Persephone, The

Destroyer, but mother had it right. Korae was fitting. I was meant to be nameless and compliant.

And I'd failed at that, too. Misery sliced through my chest. It felt like I was being split open with a dagger, the sharp edge digging in only to be ripped a second later, leaving me gutted and bleeding.

My palms and knees burned, but not from fire. From ice. Blinking away the blurriness from my eyes, I realized my body had started to sink into the frozen lake, my magic melting layers as my tears added to them.

My stomach twisted as dark shapes shifted beneath my fingers. Dark wisps of hair undulated around a pale face, warped and frozen in a silent scream. The nose was blackened, bits of the cheeks and lips eroded into charred bits of what used to be skin, but it was the bloodshot eyes that were full of clarity —of awareness—that caused my pulse to race.

The dark eyes snapped to mine, startling a terrified gasp from me as they widened, its scream vibrating through the layers of ice to hum beneath my fingers. Then there was another voice, a warmer one that I wanted so badly to run to.

"Persephone!"

My name. That was my name, but I couldn't take my eyes away from the soul beneath me. Couldn't do anything but picture myself there with him as tears streamed down my face, solidifying as they joined the ice beneath my hands.

"Persephone, look out!"

The deep voice rocked through me, latching on to the dim embers still burning inside of me. It was small, a bit of kindling added to coals nearly gone, but the current of my magic caught.

A wash of darkness rolled over me, giving me the strength to shatter the fine layer of icy tears as I curled my fingers into fists. I gritted my teeth as I forced my boots to find purchase. My arms pushed as my knees lifted, and soon I was standing.

Gods above, there were souls everywhere, littering the ice. I should be afraid, but I felt numb, like I'd been disconnected from my body.

"Persephone!"

Aidoneus's voice was louder, cutting through the swarm of lamenting souls. I clung onto his voice, searching for its source. He was at the edge of the lake. Relief flickered through me, but his cerulean blue eyes were wide with abject horror.

My brows furrowed as I took a step toward him, only now beginning to understand that I must have been caught in the song of one of the Algea. But it didn't matter. My demon was here.

An unhinged shriek sounded from my left. Its clothes had long since gone, most of the skin and muscle as well, causing white bones to protrude where its fingers had once been, and the translucent face was contorted into a manic grin.

There was no recognition. No presence like the other souls held.

This was a wraith.

Great tendrils of night stretched from my right as the wraith launched its mangled body toward me, moving with supernatural speed. I turned to avoid the worst of it, but the bony tips slashed through my chest with ease, making contact a moment before shadows descended.

I could smell sweet frost and darkness in the air as I screamed, the red splattering of my blood steaming as it connected with the frozen lake. The wraith was reduced to powdered bone in the next breath, the ash dusting the pool of blood I knelt in.

My blood.

Then night closed around me. And I saw and heard no more.

3 0

HADES

USING THE FIRE IN MY VEINS PUT THERE BY PERSEPHONE'S LIFE magic, I flitted through shadows, bypassing the lake's edge as I darted toward a narrow break in the snow. It was slim, looking like nothing more than a split in the towering snowbanks, but it was the path that would take us to The Asphodel Plains—Persephone's only chance at survival.

Clutching her tighter as I moved through time and space, my fury rose as I gripped the blood-soaked tunic. It was saturated. Despite me tying it as tight as I dared without stopping her ability to breathe, the bony claw marks along her ribs kept bleeding.

My magic was death. It only took. Never gave. I could do nothing but get her to Hecate or Thanatos and pray the Goddess of Witches and God of Death knew a way to stop this.

I underestimated Persephone. I shouldn't have let her get so far away, but I'd thought last night had changed something between us. We were destined to be together. Couldn't she feel that? Sense how our threads yearned to be joined?

Apparently not, because she'd stabbed me and then jumped off a fucking cliff.

She fucking *ran*. I knew my little witch needed freedom. Gods below, I was the one who wanted her to have the confidence to take it, but she had nearly got herself killed trying to escape me.

I couldn't stand watching her fall to the Algea. The three of them swam through the darkest depths of the lake, singing songs of pain and sorrow. Of every type of anguish imaginable. Songs that obliterated the will to live. Most souls didn't make it past the edge of the tunnels, succumbing to their whispers immediately.

But Persephone had.

Of course, she had. My queen was brave. Even when the odds were stacked against her. Even with her fear held like a vice around her neck, she lifted her chin and found a way to keep breathing.

I'd thought her leaping and free falling through packed snow was her testing her independence. I would have let her stretch her legs as I hovered in their periphery. But only until she was ready to rejoin me.

The faint illumination by the lapis lazuli stones faded as I flitted through the tunnel, but I didn't need to see. I *was* darkness, folding between the plains of this world until the blue gems gave way to rich earth.

Tapping into the full might of my power as we crossed into The Asphodel Plains, I moved quicker, careful to not jostle Persephone. I didn't allow myself to think about how the scent of fresh soil was marred by the metallic tang of her blood or how she'd lost consciousness on the icy lake of Cocytus and hadn't woken.

I could only focus on the growing light as the tunnel tilted up.

Another jump, and we surfaced, the bright rays of The Underworld's sun heating her shaking body. Wilted grass and gnarled pomegranate trees stretched before us. The grove had been barren for years, leaving torturous branches with sparse leaves, but my gaze stayed focused on the gleaming golden spires in the distance: The Dark Palace.

A flash of feather-white wings appeared from the tallest balcony, his blond hair acting as a halo of light as he flew: Thanatos.

My jaw clenched. It appeared I wasn't the only one struggling with my magic. Thanatos was able to flit through light the way I could shadows. If flying was the quickest way to reach us, it meant there were far greater problems waiting for me here than I'd thought.

Inhaling deeply, I rolled out my shoulders, allowing my great, leathery wings to unfurl. The prick of my ram horns returned, and my vision sharpened as my essence rooted in The Asphodel Plains returned to me.

My wings beat, launching us into the sky as the force of my power whipped through the shuddering grove, branches cracking and splintering as I gave flight. I stared down at my little witch, brushing a red curl back from her face. The freckles splashed across her cheeks were stark against her pale complexion, the beating of her heart now quick and faint.

"This is not your fate." Pressing a kiss to her brow, I willed the fates to hear my promise to her. "You will be my queen, Persephone. My savior. Even if our realms fall and the gods curse us, I won't let you go. Not now. Not ever."

PERSEPHONE

It felt like I'd just swam through the roughest ocean, my weary limbs scraping the edge of a sandy bank only for a strong current to drag me under again. Everything hurt. Each breath sent lashes of pain through my chest. I could feel soft cotton beneath my fingers and a fluffed pillow supporting the weight of my head, but it was all I could do to remain on the periphery of consciousness.

Voices were muffled, the words blurring together until a familiar tenor reached me through the fog.

"It's Hypnos." Aidoneus's deep voice pitched, venom dripping from the name. "I'm sure of it. How else would I have been transported to the shores of the Lethe just outside of The Darklands of the North?"

"We can't attack unless there's proof," a softer, more melodic voice chimed in. "With death magic spiraling out of control, the other factions are looking for reasons to renounce you."

Aidoneus scoffed, and I swear the temperature in the room dropped a few degrees. "They would die before a rebellion ever took root."

"If it were as simple as that, we would've killed them ages

ago," the androgynous voice countered. "But Hypnos is vital for The Realm of the Living. Without sleep, the mortals will—"

"Lose all semblance of sanity," Aidoneus cut in. "I know, Thanatos, but I was blocked from my magic. I couldn't shift, couldn't travel through shadows. Persephone was plummeting to the fiery banks of the Phlegethon and the only reason I was able to call on a sliver of my true form was because she *accidentally* pushed life magic into me, weakening whatever curse had plagued me."

Footsteps echoed in the stretching silence, growing louder until the bed dipped. Sweet frost and darkness swirled around me as the faintest caress trailed across my cheek.

"She didn't even know she had magic." The concern in Aidoneus's voice had me wanting to reach for him, to assure him I was okay, but my body was too weak to respond. "Demeter must have been suppressing it somehow."

"The curse blocked you from me," Thanatos said. "I knew you were in The Underworld, but I couldn't sense where. Magic strong enough to break through that level of power would have manifested at a very young age. Twelve, thirteen at the latest."

"Eight, actually," Aidoneus answered, and I could practically see the proud tilt of his lips. "Persephone was only eight when she first displayed magic powerful enough to resurrect a field decimated by death magic."

A sharp intake of breath sounded from my left as Thanatos drew nearer. "So, she *is* the one. The earth witch promised to us."

"She is," Aidoneus rumbled. "And so much more."

"You really think Demeter would strip her only daughter of magic, of her woven destiny, to keep her from us?"

Aidoneus brushed back another wayward curl before answering.

"No. While Demeter is cruel enough and threatened enough to hide Persephone's destiny by uprooting her entire coven under the ploy of attacks from the Dark Faction, she is far too selfish to go through years of plotting simply to deny me Persephone. Killing her as a child would've been easier. We're missing something."

The other presence paced a few steps before stilling. "I've only been able to cross into The Realm of the Living when a soul is ready for reaping, but the earth coven has yet to change their location. From what I've glimpsed, the witch Persephone was with appears to be a servant of some kind—Lark, I believe her name was."

Lark. My ears pricked as my pulse picked up, willing my body to fight off the temptation of sleep.

"She's being held by the green witch named Cyrus, but I couldn't see much beyond the forest where the soul I collected was."

"Another witch?" Aidoneus asked.

"Yes," Thanatos answered, his voice low and even more dangerous for it. "Another claimed by her awakening."

Her awakening? Oh gods, he must mean Willow. But her birthday wasn't for another week. It couldn't have passed already, and she wouldn't have been claimed. She was far too strong for that.

"What does Hecate make of it?"

The mother-of-all-witches Hecate?

"She's furious," Thanatos said, the sounds of padded footsteps picking up as he resumed pacing. "Apparently, the witch was destined to further good relations between covens."

"Her crossing?"

"Just like the others. Nothing but wisps of a soul. She's been to the Lethe and is healing in the Elysian Fields. Hecate is tending to her, but she should be along—"

"Right now."

The weight overlying my body seemed to lessen as the feminine voice rang through the room. It was as if my magic was replenishing as she drew near. Gods above, she must really be the Hecate of legends, the Mother of Witchcraft. And she was here, helping *me*.

"Thanatos said the promised witch was stable but unable to wake."

I can hear you, I wanted to shout, but my lips didn't even twitch.

"It's been two days," Aidoneus growled as the weight on the edge of my bed lifted. There was a definite chill to the air, but the sounds of Hecate's soft footsteps didn't falter.

No wonder I felt like death. I was probably halfway to the grave if it had been two days, and I still couldn't open my eyes.

"Yes, and I've spent the last *three* stitching a shredded soul back together," the feminine voice clipped.

The bed dipped again, less so than before and the subtle scent of moonflower swirled around me. My magic tingled in my veins, rising to the surface as Hecate leaned forward. I felt the heat of her hand a moment before her palm pressed flat against my chest.

"Oh," Hecate breathed.

"*Oh?*" Aidoneus repeated, the drop in temperature causing the fine hairs on my arms to rise. "Oh what?"

"Keep that death magic in check. Persephone is awake." There was a beat of silence before the cold withdrew and Hecate continued. "The wraith that attacked her must have been cursed to never know a moment's rest, because though her body is still healing from the gouge marks created from its bones, her mind is very much present. I've no doubt she's heard everything you two have said. I hope you were gentlemen."

Heat built beneath her palm, seeping into my body right over my heart. Each beat pushed her magic through my vessels, the core of it circulating until the restlessness holding me hostage broke and my eyes fluttered open.

"There," Hecate said, her deep, green eyes finding mine. Her full lips were tilted into a kind smile, and her dark hair was half pinned back with a serpent pin, her long curls tumbling down. A golden tunic draped across her full figure, the silky material captivating as it caught the light from near-by torches along the walls. The white tattoo lining her forearm dimmed as the heat of her magic lessened, the snake winding through a crescent moon seeming to settle.

My gaze bounced to the minimalistic room behind her, the white curtains and dark walls shadowed by the hulking form poised over her shoulder. His blue eyes bored into mine, causing my heart to flutter.

"The energy you feel now is remnant from my power," Hecate said, pushing to a stand. "The crystal you've chosen to wear will maintain it for a few minutes longer before the fatigue of your mind catches up. But don't worry, you're safe here. Daddy Darkness wouldn't have it any other way."

"Daddy Darkness?" I breathed, gaze flashing to Aidoneus.

Aidoneus stiffened as the figure who must have been Thanatos failed to hide a chuckle. Thanatos was the complete opposite of Aidoneus, his bright crystal-blue eyes crinkling at the edges as elegant, feather white wings shook with his suppressed laughter. He was bright, all soft angles and androgynous features to Aidoneus's hard lines and shadows.

Thanatos nudged his shoulder, the force of it causing Aidoneus to take a step forward. "You've been called worse things."

Aidoneus only lifted a brow at Hecate, waiting for her to give him the all clear.

Crossing her arms over her chest, she held his gaze a moment longer, before rolling her eyes. "Go ahead, but I'm serious about keeping your death magic in check."

"It's not his fault," Thanatos chimed in.

"Isn't it?" Hecate pressed. "He should've anticipated Persephone would face challenges with her magic after learning what Demeter was doing to the witches in the Earth Coven."

"Yes but we couldn't have foreseen she'd know nothing—"

"Enough," Aidoneus rumbled, his voice low and cutting through their bickering with ease. Cautiously, he sat on the edge of the bed beside me. With a gentleness I didn't know he was capable of, Aidoneus helped me to a sitting position. My limbs were stiff and achy, but the worst of the pain had gone as I accepted his help. "I wish to be alone with my little witch."

"I think that wise," Hecate mused from the doorway with Thanatos at her back. "The two of you have many things to discuss."

HADES

SHE HAD BEEN AWAKE THE ENTIRE TIME, ABLE TO HEAR everything Thanatos and I discussed while her body remained paralyzed. There were too many secrets between us, too many lives relying on Persephone weaving her life thread with mine. I would need to force her if she refused me. It was the only logical option. Our two realms would continue to be ravaged, the souls in both subjected to the wrath of unconfined death magic. The stakes couldn't be higher... but there was a gnawing ache in my chest at the thought of her not *wanting* to be mine.

Shoving the barb of rejection aside, I made sure Persephone was strong enough to sit on her own, before folding my hands in my lap.

"How much did you hear?"

Her green eyes narrowed as she lifted her chin. "Enough to know there's a lot you haven't told me. Like Willow's soul being shredded."

Persephone's voice wavered on the last word, her bravado flickering as she no doubt pictured a witch she'd known her entire life undergoing such a thing, but if that was her greatest concern, she hadn't learned my true title. Good. I would have to tell her soon, but enough things were spiraling out of control at the moment without adding that into the mix.

"Hecate was able to patch her up," I said. "The Lethe will wipe any lingering memories from her time in The Realm of the Living, including the pain she felt."

Persephone flinched. The slight furrowing of her brow and far off look confirmed her mind was elsewhere when she dared to ask, "What has the power to shred a soul?"

"We don't know, though Hecate has her theories."

Her eyes snapped to mine. "That *was* the real Hecate?"

I nodded, head tilting to the side as Persephone's lips pressed thin.

"Why isn't she stopping this? Why didn't she help when The Dark Faction ravaged town after town, demons sucking the life from our world? Why is she in The Underworld in the first place?"

Her chest heaved, her freckled cheeks flushed, but there was a faint sheen of sweat across her brow, proof that the boost in energy from Hecate's magic would soon be spent.

"Hecate may be the mother of all witches, but her power isn't infinite. She will be reborn in time, like every other soul. While her power does grant certain exceptions, her life in The Realm of the Living ended."

Persephone swallowed, leaning back against the pillows. Her breaths were still too quick, the pulse along her neck beating too rapidly, but she nodded for me to continue.

"Do you know what it means for a witch to awaken?"

"They're blessed by Hecate and granted access to their magic once they swear fealty to a coven."

"And what of witches not in a coven? What about those who have been lost, or placed with humans, do they not also inherit their magic?"

Persephone's full lips pulled down into a frown. I lifted my hand, cupping her cheek as my thumb tracing the edges of her pout. Her eyes dipped to my fingers and fuck did I want to kiss her right then. To brand the taste of her into my soul.

"Witches are granted access to their full magic on their twenty-first year, just as Hecate was. If one chooses a coven, their power will be joined to that coven. Likewise, if she weaves her life thread with another's, the two will be linked in all ways."

Persephone's frown deepened, her conflicted gaze searching mine as she drew back. "Then why would Hecate take so many sacrifices? Why make us pledge to a coven at all?"

My spine stiffened, knowing this next bit of information would hurt her, but there was no way around it. She needed to understand how dire our situation was.

"No witch is forced to join with a coven." Her brows furrowed as confusion flashed in her eyes. "Hecate doesn't collect sacrifices, Persephone. What purpose would she have in killing her own children?"

Persephone shook her head, pushing the cotton sheet off as she stood on trembling legs.

"You need to rest," I said, coming to stand beside her. "You're running on the fumes of Hecate's healing magic. You're going to crash any moment—"

"No."

Persephone repeated the word over and over again as her hands tangled in her hair. She paced the length of the room and I let her, giving her time to work this out as I matched her stride, knowing that her entire worldview was shifting.

"Witches are dying. Willow's soul was shredded. *Shredded.* Because Hecate is angry with us for not stopping The Dark Faction. For not being strong enough. But… Hecate is here, in The Underworld."

She turned slowly, seeking answers to questions she wasn't ready for, but needed to know all the same.

"You're… friends?"

"Yes," I answered truthfully. "Hecate is like a sister to me."

She squared her shoulders, closing the distance between us until she placed her palm just over my beating heart. Heat warmed beneath her touch as her thread reached for mine. They were just brushing one another, but the contact was enough to open Persephone's mind to me. I could feel her trepidation, her distrust of me and The Underworld as a whole, but I could also sense her mounting realization growing like a looming wave on the horizon.

"Every time a witch dies on her awakening, her magic is returned to the coven. Is that true?"

"Partly," I answered, knowing she felt the truth of my words through our connected essence. "If they've pledged themselves to a coven, and die when their magic is bound to it, a small portion will be gifted to the remaining witches. But most of a witch's power is supposed to return to the realm upon her life thread being cut."

"Supposed to?"

I nodded, letting her fit the pieces into place.

"But their power is remaining with the coven... isn't it? Or with the witch's bound partner..."

Again, I nodded, watching as her throat bobbed.

"Mother encouraged all of us to bond with green witches before the awakening. She said it was the best chance we had at not being taken by Hecate, but as High Matriarch she..."

Persephone dropped her gaze from mine, her fingers slipping. Catching her hand, I pressed her palm into my chest, keeping our connection intact a little longer as I used my other hand to tilt her chin-up.

"As High Matriarch, Demeter will be gifted with the witch's magic first, and trusted to return it to the coven and the earth."

"And if she chose to keep that power for herself?"

"It would create a great imbalance, one only worsened when she chose to hide the earth witch intended to return life to The Underworld."

"Oh gods," Persephone breathed, shaking her head just before her legs buckled.

Persephone

AIDONEUS'S ARMS WERE AROUND ME BEFORE I EVEN CAME CLOSE to hitting the floor. He cradled me against the hard planes of his chest as he carried me back to the bed. My body was exhausted, my mind as well. It felt like I was a candle burning through the night only to discover my wick had been cut short. But even as he arranged the blankets and pillows around me just how I liked, I couldn't allow myself the reprieve of darkness just yet.

I'd know mother was selfish, her reputation and power coveted, but I'd wanted to believe she had protected me. That some small part of her had kept me safe for *my* sake... but it had all been for hers.

"I really was raised for the slaughter," I breathed. "Like a bird with its wings clipped, kept docile and caged until my death served a greater purpose than my life."

"No." The unwavering strength in Aidoneus's voice snapped my gaze to his. "You are not broken, Persephone."

"Aren't I?" A sob shook my chest as tears pricked my eyes. I hadn't meant to speak the thought out loud, but Aidoneus's eyes blazed, his pupils expanding until there was only a sliver of his sapphire irises.

"You escaped their cage, little witch. Your powers have already started to manifest on your own, but together, we'll be unstoppable."

The deep tenor of his voice soothed the storm of betrayal raging within my heart. He was right. I felt life magic humming in my veins, and Hecate herself had healed me. I was more powerful than I'd ever thought possible, and I hadn't gone through my awakening yet. Once I did, I would use that power to free Lark and then—

"Wait." My brows furrowed as I pinned Aidoneus under my stare. I could hear the pounding of my heartbeat in my ears, my tired body already processing what my mind was rushing to connect. "What do you mean by 'we'?"

He stood, spine stiff as the shadow of wings appeared at his back, but it was his eyes that demanded my attention—they were so dark. I couldn't see any of the cerulean blue and it looked like even the whites had started to recede.

I'd meant to sit up, intending on standing to face him, but my body wouldn't respond. It felt like I was weighed down, the last of my energy being sent to my racing thoughts.

Breaking our staring contest, my eyes darted from the bare walls surrounding me to the windows, most of their view blocked by heavy curtains. There was nothing personal, no items or decor to hint at where I was.

"Where are we?" The prickling sensation along the back of my neck warned me that I already knew the answer but didn't want to believe it.

I glanced at his chest, to the place where I knew the upside down torch was branded on his skin. Aidoneus was powerful, to be sure, but he was just a demon. He had only ever been a demon following orders, but what if he wasn't. What if he were someone else entirely...

At the hot springs—*gods above*. I'd offered him everything. *Everything.* Thinking I was making my own choice, claiming a morsel of control over my life, when really...

"Shh. Everything will be all right, little witch."

Shaking my head against the truth, I dared to look up, needing to be wrong.

His eyes were entirely black now, his wickedly beautiful wings unfurling behind him. A disarming smile tilted his lips as

I fought to remain conscious, captivatingly horrified as I watched great ram horns spiral into place.

He was the cause of my nightmares. The villain of my reality. The God of The Underworld. And I'd followed him right to my demise.

"Hades."

He leaned forward as my eyelids closed, my body succumbing to unconsciousness. The intoxicating scent of him swirling around me as his lips pressed a gentle kiss to the top of my head.

"Don't worry, Persephone. I've got you now, and I'm never letting you go."

33

PERSEPHONE

DARKNESS SHIFTED. I BLINKED AS I APPEARED ON A FRIGID LAKE with the bodies of witches from my coven frozen up to their necks in the ice surrounding me. Their cries created a cacophony of pain, rivulets of tears running down their cheeks to form small pillars of ice that had joined the larger block holding them in place. Others less fortunate were already below the ice, their bloodshot eyes darting frantically around with mouths frozen open in not so silent screams.

"I'm sorry," I muttered as my own tears started, recognizing far too many of their faces. They were the witches who had been claimed. The ones murdered by my mother. "I'm so sorry. I didn't know what she was doing."

"You didn't want to know," one argued. Icy dread slid down my spine as I slowly turned toward the sound of Willow's voice. Her rich brown eyes were now glazed over, opaque and unseeing, but she appeared to stare right into my soul. Her chest was split open, ribs and sternum cracked in three parts. It looked like she exploded from the inside out, the splintered ends of white bone angled toward me.

"Powerless little Korae, so desperate for mommy's approval.

She didn't see what was happening right in front of her." Blood trickled from the hole in her chest as Willow's mangled corpse took a disjointed step toward me. "You were supposed to be our next High Matriarch, our *queen*, but what type of queen runs away?"

"Cyrus was going to kill me—"

"Then you would have died like the rest of us!"

Willow lunged forward, the skin along her fingers lashing out, splitting the muscle over my chest to grind into my ribs. A scream ripped through my chest, scraping the back of my throat as the world turned.

There, at the edge of my blurry gaze was a man towering over me, cloaked in darkness.

"Time to wake up, Persephone."

My chest heaved, the thin cotton shift was matted to my body and slick with sweat. Reflexively, my hand wrapped around my chest, still feeling the sting of Willow's phantom claws.

Blinking the last dregs of terror from my eyes, I looked up. I must have been brought to a different room because everything had changed. The dark walls were illuminated by the morning light shining through high arching windows stretching on either side of the massive bed I was tucked into. The room opened, the obsidian stone floors warmed by spiraling rugs and embroidered furniture. Bookshelves lined the far wall with a large chair set before it. There was a dip worn into the cushion, as if the owner indulged in reading often, and a dark tunic tossed over the back of it. This must be Aidoneus's room.

No, not Aidoneus—Hades.

"What did you dream about?"

Glancing to the left, I found Hecate stilling in an ornate

wooden chair. A large volume of what appeared to be spells was open on the table before her, but her deep green eyes were fixed on mine.

"Willow." I swallowed against the burn of bile coating my throat as I peeled the remaining sheets off me. "She was dead but not, and she was angry. So angry with me."

"Splintered spirits tend to be angry," Hecate sighed as if the notion was something she was used to. "What you experienced was an echo. Her spirit was abused, and her life thread cut short. The ones responsible for her suffering are still in The Realm of the Living. You were the closest spirit she could reach. I took her to the Lethe as soon as she was stable enough, but I should have known pieces of her soul were wandering."

"Pieces of her soul?"

Hecate offered me an indulging smile that seemed to say, 'one step at a time', before coming to the edge of the bed.

"Let's get you dressed and ready for the day. Hades thought it best for the two of you to have some space, and I thought it would be nice to show you around."

Hades.

My stomach flipped as the events of yesterday returned. He'd lied to me.

"No," Hecate said, cutting off the track of my thoughts. "He didn't lie to you, only omitted the truth."

"Same thing," I muttered as I pushed from the sheets that still smelled of Hades's sweet frost and shadows. I swung my feet to the edge of the bed, the soft fluff of the carpet warming my toes as I stood. My legs wobbled, but Hecate was there to steady me.

"It is and it isn't. Would you have continued through The Underworld with him if you knew he was Hades?"

"Absolutely not. He's murdered thousands of people. Killed entire villages."

"Exactly why he didn't clarify who he was when you assumed he was just another demon." A frown settled across my lips as I let Hecate led me to the large armoire. "Your strength will return slowly over the next few days. You really pushed the limits of magic for an unawakened witch, but you'll be able to wield far greater power in just under two weeks."

I blinked, coming to a standstill, only half paying attention as Hecate rummaged through swaths of the finest gowns.

"Two weeks? My birthday isn't until next month."

Hecate plucked a floral gown out from the others. The sweetheart neckline was covered in lace flowers that cascaded down the floor length skirt. Dark vines with silver barbs wove through the rich green fabric, creating a gown that looked both casual enough for the day while still commanding attention.

"Your birthday is in thirteen days on Ostara." Hecate held the dress up to me, cocking her head to the side. "This will be perfect."

"Perfect for what? And how do you know my birthday?"

"I know you were born on the spring equinox just as I know you are the strongest earth witch to wield life magic in centuries. Yes, even stronger than your mother."

I'd opened my mouth to argue, but promptly closed it.

"You've been made to believe you were helpless your entire life because Demeter is a callus, power-hungry bitch who never wanted to have a child, and was never meant to raise one. She agreed to carry and give birth to you for a price, but make no mistake, Persephone, you were born of the gods."

A faint buzzing filled my ears as I leaned against the chair. "Are you saying Demeter isn't my mother? That it's not her blood that runs in my veins?"

"She was only ever meant to be a surrogate, a responsibility she took on for a very heavy sum of magic."

I followed Hecate in a daze as she led us toward a set of double doors with the gown draped over her arm. She pushed open the heavy double doors, stepping into the largest and most opulent wash room I'd ever seen. The vanity was huge, complete with a golden chair set before a diamond cut mirror. Various shades of rouge, charcoal, and jars of every size were present.

"Don't get me wrong," Hecate continued with a grunt as she stretched to place the dress on a hanger across from a small glass room—not room, shower. A wide spout tracked overhead, which looked like it would mimic getting caught in a summer rain. Hecate gestured toward it, trying to usher me inside. "Plenty of surrogates love the lives they grow, but Demeter only thought to keep you because of the power displayed at your birth."

I pinned her with a stare, hands resting on my hips as I refused to move another inch until she explained.

"The Crystal City was covered in wildflowers in a matter of moments after you arrived. Dandelions were everywhere, which Demeter hated. She only ever cultivated the most expensive and rare flowers. Even after ordering every one of them plucked and killed, dandelions still sprouted—a testament to the well of power that would one day be yours." Her smile faltered as her brows furrowed. "Hades didn't tell you?"

"No," I grumbled, crossing my arms. "As you've mentioned, we have a lot to catch up on, and yet he's chosen to avoid me."

She shrugged. "That's what he does when he's upset. Anger or avoidance. I've been telling him for centuries that it's not healthy but it's a little hard to explain empathy to a being whose heart has stopped. Thanks for fixing that, by the way. All my spells have failed."

"What do you mean his heart stopped? And how would I have fixed it?"

She lifted a brow.

"Right," I said, dropping my gaze to stare at my fingertips. "Unrivaled life magic."

"Yep."

"He didn't say anything..." I started to say, but my voice trailed off as I thought back on our time together.

"It's been centuries since he's felt anything besides rage or numbness. I doubt he understands half of what he's feeling." Hecate squeezed my hands, offering me a kind smile. "Now, *please*, go wash up so I can help get you dressed. We really need to get going if we're going to make it before midday."

I nodded as Hecate reached in, the sound of running water hitting the river stone floor moments later. She made it to the edge of the doorframe before I thought to ask.

"Where are we going?"

Her green eyes shimmered as her full lips tugged into a grin. "The Elysian Fields."

34

HADES

TUCKING MY WINGS IN CLOSE, I DROPPED THROUGH THE branches of the pomegranate trees, landing among gnarled roots and tufts of grass. The earth vibrated as Thanatos landed behind me. The ancient grove was my personal reprieve. I allowed souls to explore most of The Asphodel Plains, but this small piece of The Underworld was mine alone, making it the perfect place for Thanatos and me to talk.

And fuck if we didn't have a lot to talk about.

Persephone hated me. She'd looked at my black eyes and ram horns with my monstrous wings stretched wide behind me and trembled as if I were fear incarnate.

I'd been the villain in so many stories, the evil God of The Underworld for millennia. It hadn't bothered me before. So, why did the look of revulsion staring out at me through her fierce green eyes feel like my chest had been cleaved in two?

"Did you hear anything I said?"

Thanatos stepped over dead leaves to stand in front of me, his blond brow lifting as his pale pink lips pressed into a thin line. He was my opposite in every way from the white feathered wings to his outlook on life. Where I was the kill first, hunt for answers later type of person, Thanatos looked for peaceful alternatives. Ironic, seeing as how most souls in The Realm of the Living feared death, when its god was far kinder than me.

"I have thirteen days to get Persephone to weave her thread with mine—twelve actually, since we need to be joined *before* her awakening. And she fucking hates me."

Thanatos's brows furrowed, the frustration shifting into confusion. "And that... bothers you?"

"No," I snapped, the denial confirming the exact opposite.

He let out a low whistle as his eyes widened. "Hecate was right. Persephone really has gotten to you."

I glared.

"Not that it's your fault," he clarified. "She's powerful and the fates have woven her destiny with yours."

"I told her of her place at my side, and still she stabbed me."

"No," Thanatos laughed. "Really?"

"Yes," I practically growled. "With an icicle in Cocytus before jumping into a snow bank. She would rather sacrifice both our realms than bind her life to mine."

"Did she *say* that, or did you assume?"

My teeth clenched. "Her actions made it pretty clear."

"Maybe," Thanatos shrugged, the feathers of his wings rustling the leaves of the nearest tree. "But there could be things you're not seeing. When I collect souls from her realm, there are so many secrets between the living and the dead. Dozens of missed opportunities to reconcile. Times when a simple miscommunication set two souls on different paths when they could've carved out a happier one together if they'd only set pride aside and spoke to each other."

I drew my own leathery wings in close, fists clenching as I silently forced myself to consider his point. Persephone hadn't realized I was her fated partner because I'd purposely been evasive. Things may have started out different, but Persephone deserved more. She deserved everything.

"Gods below," Thanatos whispered, his light blue eyes peering into mine and seeing far more than I wanted him to. "You... *care*. She not only healed your physical heart, but Persephone has managed to bring back your ability to feel. I thought death magic had obliterated everything but your ruthlessness and temper. Hecate always said that love and hate were separated by a single conversation, but it's been centuries—"

"I'm aware," I snapped, hating the *vulnerability* of it all.

Thanatos's brows lifted at my rebuke, and I swear I saw the faint traces of a grin, but he had his features schooled into a neutral mask in the next heartbeat.

"Right, we'll circle back around to *that*. For now, we need to focus on our immediate problems. Another three souls have turned into wraiths, one of which followed you and Persephone through the tunnels and nearly reached The Asphodel Plains."

"Following Persephone's scent?" I asked as my magic rose to the surface. The dark power hummed beneath my fingertips, ready to feed. It was always hungry, ravenous in its need for destruction, but my little witch's power had tempered it some. It didn't feel as wild—still primal and not the least bit subdued, but harnessed.

Thanatos nodded. "It's driving the spirits crazy. She smells like..."

"Hope," I answered grimly, and gods below did I understand how that could drive a soul to the verge of breaking.

"They need to be taken to the Lethe before others turn. Without crossing the Lethe and traveling to the shores of Oceanus, the souls can't be reborn. They will be forced to wander The Underworld forever unless—"

"Unless we cross into Hypnos's territory." The pads of my fingers rubbed my temple as I searched for another way, but there wasn't one. "We'll have to risk it. My magic should be strong enough for the journey after spending time here."

Thanatos was skeptically silent.

"We don't have another choice. Letting wraiths wander would practically be announcing my control over death magic is fading. Hypnos has already succeeded in binding my magic once. We can't risk him realizing it. If you and Hecate hadn't been here to deflect, there wouldn't have been a Dark Palace for Persephone and me to return to."

"At least bring a few warriors with you. Morpheus has been spotted in nightmares."

My eyes snapped to him. "Morpheus hasn't had anything to do with his father's meddling before. What's changed?"

Thanatos shook his head, lips pressing into a grim line. "Those who have seen him deny any intervention. It could be he's merely curious about how his father's magic works, or..."

"Or he could sense the shift in power and is capitalizing on my weakness." I ran a hand through my hair, the longer curls drifting down over my forehead. "Invite them to the palace."

"To The Dark Palace?"

"What other palace would I mean?" I bit back.

"Only checking," Thanatos said, raising his hands in a sign of surrender.

With a sigh, I stared through overgrown branches of the pomegranate trees to the golden spires in the distance. Persephone was getting ready right now, waking up tangled in my sheets. She would take a shower next, hot water cascading over the curves of her body as she used my bath oils to wash and knead...

"Would it not be better to metaphorically draw lines in the sand?" Thanatos asked. "Hypnos has all but declared war. Though Morpheus hasn't acted against us, we must assume he'll follow in his father's footsteps."

"But we don't," I countered. "My father is locked in the deepest part of Tartarus, put there by myself and my siblings. Sometimes children learn what not to be from their parents."

Bright rays of the sun peered between heavy clouds, landing

on the stables alongside the palace—and the two women walking toward it. Hecate was clad in her typical golden tunic, but I could just make out a swath of deep green fabric that must be Persephone.

I needed to speak with her, and knew it was cowardly to run, but there was such a storm of emotions raging through me. The familiar tug of anger had started to feel more like hurt—or was that shame?

No, it was best Hecate showed Persephone around, introducing her to everything The Underworld had to offer. She may hate me, but I'd make sure Persephone fell in love with this realm and did everything in her power to protect it. Including binding herself to me.

"Invite Hypnos, The Night Children, even Morpheus—all the souls in The Asphodel Plains and The Elysian Fields to The Dark Palace. After we secure the wraiths to the Lethe, we have an engagement to celebrate."

35

PERSEPHONE

SPRAWLING GRASS AND LUSH GROVES STRETCHED TOWARD THE horizon as the sun climbed over distant mountains. Clusters of mushrooms clung to the thick trunks of trees with groups of flowering bushes as far as the eye could see. In the distance, quaint homes with thatched roofs lined the cobblestones streets. A gentle river ran alongside the cozy town, forming a small lake nestled between apple trees. The lively sound of giggling children drifted through the air as rowdy footfalls headed our way.

"Brace yourself," Hecate warned, but her eyes were alight with mirth. "The children of Elysian can be ruthless."

A throng of children clutching twine sacks raced through the trees, branches bowing as their elated screams reached us.

"Hecate! You're here! We've been waiting so long." A young child with dark braids and freckles broke away from the others, shooting into Hecate's open arms and nearly tackling her to the ground.

"I saw you yesterday, Phoebe," Hecate grinned, catching her with a laugh.

"But we've been up for hours planting seeds for Ostara, and you said you would help us."

"Ostara isn't for another thirteen days."

"Kassandra said we needed to plant the seeds today. It's going to be better for the season, and you know how she is with her predictions."

"I do," Hecate answered, looking toward the figure moving at the back of the cluster of children.

A stunning woman with wavy blond hair streaked with gray reaching past her elbows stepped forward. A dazzling smile tilted her lips, evidence of a lifetime of happy years lining her warm, brown eyes. She glanced from Hecate to me, bringing with her a calming presence. "I thought it would be a nice way to introduce you to the children, Lady Persephone."

I had stopped a few paces behind Hecate, always having been a little awkward around children. They were unpredictable, like mini wild cards. Nothing and everything scared them all at once. One wrong move could make them hate you forever. But there was no hiding now. The boisterous group had fallen silent, the lace bodice of my gown suddenly felt tight as all eyes turned to me.

"Hello." I waved a tentative hand, fighting the urge to flee. "Feel free to call me…"

My smile faltered as I struggled for an answer. I was no longer Korae. If my time here had taught me anything, it was that I had *never* been Korae. She was a lie made up by my mother—by Demeter.

It was time to reclaim a little of who I was meant to be.

"Please, call me Persephone."

Hecate beckoned me forward, her eyes alight with something that looked like pride. "This is Kassandra, mother to lost or forgotten children."

Kassandra dipped her head. "You've grown into a beautiful

young woman, My Lady. I would've been honored to have been able to call you daughter."

I inhaled sharply, my eyes darting to Hecate in a silent question. She nodded; her voice was soft when she next spoke.

"Kassandra was to be your chosen mother."

A sad smile ghosted across Kassandra's face. "To have seen the years in between would have been a privilege, but I am grateful for our time now."

A few of the children were openly gawking, tugging at the hem of Hecate's dress.

"It's true, children," Hecate said. "This is our Lady Persephone, Lord Hades's betrothed and your future queen."

My stomach flipped at the title, still not having resigned myself to that fate, but I forced a smile as their little faces beamed up at me.

"Perhaps all of you could show her how we celebrate Ostara in The Underworld?" Kassandra asked. "After all, it falls on Lady Persephone's birthday."

Cheers rang around us as excited little hands reached for me and led me through the trees. The edges of Kassandra's eyes crinkled as she fell into step behind us, leaving me no choice but to follow the cluster of little feet.

"We plant seeds on the eve of Ostara," Hecate clarified as the children ran ahead, sprinkling seeds as they went. "They represent the potential for growth and planning for the year ahead."

"It takes a lot to nurture a seed," Kassandra added, linking her arm through mine. I felt so overdressed with my gown while she wore a simple cotton dress, the hem splattered in mud, but I suppose that was why Hecate had selected it: to present *Lady* Persephone. "One must get their hands dirty, cultivate sturdy roots that run deep. Only when the stalk is established can the flowers bloom."

"Smooth, Kassandra," Hecate quipped, falling into step on

my other side. "But I think Persephone knows what's worth cultivating."

"Oh, I don't know," I said, my temper flaring as I realized who they were speaking of. "Some crops aren't worth the time or the effort. *Some* seeds prove to be a drain of resources rather than a fruitful investment."

Even as I spoke the words, I knew they weren't true. Hades may be a lying demon—*God*—but my betrothal wasn't about him. It was for the sake of our realms.

Hecate and Kassandra shared a worried glance, but I spoke before either got a chance.

"Even so, I understand even the most poisonous plants can provide nourishment to the field. Isn't that right, Kassandra?"

I glanced up when she didn't answer. Her face had paled, tension pulling along the edges of her lips.

"What is it?" I asked, following her line of sight to the horizon. Fields that were thriving moments ago were now coated in a swath of black.

"Excuse me, Lady Persephone," she breathed. Sparing only a panicked glance for Hecate, she rushed forward, moving quicker than should have been possible as she chased after the screaming children. There were flashes of light whenever she reached one, the field around us growing quieter with each one as Hecate and I rushed after her.

"It stopped advancing," Kassandra called as we pressed through the last of the branches, joining her at the edge of darkness.

"The children?" I asked, finding the field vacant except for the three of us.

"Returned to the temple," Kassandra breathed, her fierce gaze meeting mine. "I can call on my own magic when needed."

I nodded, wondering for a split second what it would've been like to have been raised by a mother like her, one willing to face off against death magic to save her children without a second thought.

Hecate's mouth was pressed into a thin line as she surveyed the damage. Frost clung to wilted leaves, the cold burning through trees as it leeched color from everything it touched. Trees and wildflowers were twisted into bitter frost and blackened remains. All the warmth of thriving flora and vegetation had been stripped away, leaving only the shell of a destroyed paradise.

This was death magic.

"It's never breached Elysian before," Kassandra muttered. "Especially not in our corner of it. This has always been our refuge, a place of unwavering safety."

"I'll inform Hades as soon as I rebuild the wards," Hecate said, raising her hands as the shadows began to stir. Energy hummed in the air. I could feel more than see the microscopic links of light forming around the edges of the deadly shadows.

"Wait," I called, stepping to her side. The buzz of energy dimmed but didn't slow as she continued to work. "What are you doing?"

"I'm walling off part of Elysium to keep the women and children safe." Hecate kept her eyes forward, molding a pulsating wall around the contours of blackened ground. "Death magic has weakened the ground here. Without wards, it could expand."

The slight tremble of her voice had my pulse racing. Hecate, goddess of witches, feared death magic. She sought to contain it just as witches of the earth coven had. But we weren't the ones responsible for this.

"Where's Hades?" I demanded. "Shouldn't he be here, cleaning up his mess?"

Kassandra's eyes widened, snapping to mine as if seeing me for the first time. "Lord Hades has done all he can to protect us, My Lady."

My brows furrowed, a frown tugging on my lips as I glanced between her and a focused Hecate. "But... he's the God of The Underworld. He wields death magic. He has for centuries. I've seen him murdering innocents in my realm, using power just like this."

With her penetrating gaze locked on mine, Kassandra slowly shook her head. "No, Lady Persephone. I'm not sure what you saw, but Lord Hades would never jeopardize innocent souls. He is the only god powerful enough to *consume* death magic. He's sacrificed pieces of his soul to keep the devastation from claiming our people, to *protect* souls in The Realm of the Living. Lord Hades has done everything in his power to maintain balance."

My stomach clenched as a wave of nausea rose. Because Kassandra had no reason to lie, and if she was telling the truth.

"Gods above, "I breathed.

"There are more than enough gods below," Hecate said, her palms taking on a soft glow as the power of her magic built. "But even gods have limits. Care to help?"

Swallowing against the bitter taste of bile, I shook my head and turned toward her. "Stop."

She lifted a brow my way, but her power didn't slow. "Didn't you hear what Kassandra just said?"

"Yes, and I'm sorry. I'm so sorry for everything, but I think I can fix it. If what I remember is true, I've done it before."

Hecate lowered her hands an inch, her deep green eyes lined with a golden ring of light. "Can you heal the earth?"

"Maybe," I said, noting the swirling tendrils of darkness.

"Yes or no, Persephone," Hecate snapped. "Expanding death magic isn't something to play around with. Can you stop it or not?"

"Not everything will return, but..." Taking a deep breath, I lifted my chin and met her hard gaze. "I can do this."

I tore my gaze from hers, looking toward the wilted leaves

and the blackened soil. Even now, they called to me—roots, I realized. Some were destroyed, but others, the ones with roots deep underground, were clinging to whispers of life.

"You can feel them," Hecate breathed, her hands falling as her eyes widened.

I nodded.

She hesitated only a moment longer before stepping back. "Five minutes. I don't want to chance it spreading, and your powers are still limited while you're unawakened. Don't drain yourself."

"I'll try not to," I said as my fingers heated. Electricity pulsed through my veins, seeming to swell from deep within me as I stepped forward, toeing the edge of black. My magic rose to the surface, pressure mounting as it was drawn toward the embers of life nestled beneath the earth.

Raising my hands, I took a deep breath, and let it out.

36

HADES

My shadows forced the last of the wraiths across the citrine stones littering the cave's floor toward the Lethe's cursed waters. My shadows wavered as the wraith thrashed. Gritting my teeth, I tucked my wings in close, and wrestled the death magic under control. It responded, tamed into compliance as my shadows dunked the wraith beneath the Lethe's surface. Its splintered soul stilled immediately.

Chest heaving, I leaned against the cave wall, the dark surrounding rock cool against my wings as I attempted to catch my breath. The strong current swirled around the quiet soul before carrying it deeper into the recesses of the cave. It would lead to Oceanus where the soul would be healed and eventually reborn. I hoped it made better choices in the next life.

"That bought us some time," Thanatos said, watching as the wisp of white disappeared into the blackness. "But others will turn soon enough. You don't need to wait for Persephone's awakening to start the bonding process."

My wings bristled as I wiped the back of my hand across my forehead, not liking how a thin sheen of sweat clung to my brow. I shouldn't be this tired after taking care of a few wraiths, but exhaustion spotted my vision.

I was already on edge having to set foot in The Darklands of the North and weak as the time to restore balance between the realms ran out. I didn't need Thanatos pushing me, especially not while we were trespassing on Hypnos's territory.

My jaw ticked. *Not* Hypnos's territory. The entirety of The Underworld was my domain. Hypnos served under *me*. At least, that was how it had worked for millennia.

And would continue to be.

Less than two weeks and Persephone would claim her place at my side, fixing everything that had fallen apart in her absence. Thanatos was right in that I could take her sooner. It wouldn't fix everything the way her awakening would, but us being married would start the process. If nothing more, it would allow me better control over my death magic.

Control that I desperately needed.

I couldn't afford to appear weak. Even with Thanatos at my side, I didn't want to think about what our odds would be against a swarm of The Night Children if Hypnos managed to wield another spell against me.

But Persephone needed to bond to me willingly. All woven threads needed consent. I could convince her, use the souls hanging in the balance to get her to agree. That had been my plan from the beginning—the only plan that made sense. But the thought of her flinching from my touch had my stomach twisting.

I needed her moaning my name, her legs wrapped around my waist as I buried myself between her thighs. I wanted her to writhe beneath my touch, eager to spend eternity at my side. Even now, I hated the distance between us. It felt unnatural, like a coil of unease had taken root in my stomach.

I let traces of my magic stretch, sending tendrils out to find her, like how I'd tracked her in Cocytus. Her presence was subtle, a mere brush of heat in my quickly cooling realm, but it was there. My little witch was safe in Elysian.

Persephone was captivating. The way she made me feel alive was intoxicating. I wanted her more than I'd ever wanted another. More than I had wanted anything. But most of all, I was desperate for her to *see* me.

Persephone was the only partner to want me without knowing my title. And fates damn me, but I would sacrifice both our realms to have her look at me with something other than fear and hatred again.

Thanatos sighed, as if he knew exactly what I was thinking. "We should go before we're discovered."

He started down the citrine lined path toward the cave's opening with the light of the midday sun reflecting off the clear waters beside us. Persephone would be exploring the Elysian designated for women and children only. It was the safest place in The Underworld, and she had Hecate and Kassandra with her. So, why did I feel so uneasy?

Darkness descended before us, halting us in our paths. The shadows solidified, revealing a broad chest and sharp cheekbones. Dark hair reached to his shoulders, the black top and thick boots more akin to The Night Children than to his father's preferred silver attire: Morpheus.

"Did Hypnos send you?" Thanatos asked as I stepped beside him. His hands were loose at his side, but tension was visible in the slight twitch of his fingers, and the increased cadence of his heart. He was ready for a fight, just as I was.

Morpheus's golden eyes ringed in red bounced from him to me, his lips quirking in an arrogant smile that revealed just the hint of fangs, proof of his father's affair with the princess of The Night Children. "My father would be interested to learn you're this near, Lord Hades. He's been eager for a meeting with you for some time."

"I've been busy," I snapped. His smile grew.

"I've heard." Morpheus toed the edge of the Lithe, his black boots crunching along the yellow stones. "You finally found your witch. Even dragged her through The Underworld if rumors are true. Tell me, Lord Hades, why such an extensive tour of Tartarus and Cocytus?"

My jaw ticked, but Thanatos spared me from answering. "We've come to invite you to the happy couple's engagement celebration."

"Is that so?" Morpheus said, golden eyes blazing as he placed his hands in his pockets. "And here I thought this little visit was for the wraiths. You've let them wander too freely, Lord Hades. They've grown strong. There are whispers that one attacked your future queen."

My eyes narrowed. *How did he know so much?*

"Of course, I silenced such gossip. Can't have those in my father's court believing such lies. If word got out that the great Lord Hades couldn't protect his intended..." Morpheus shook his head. "Some would see that as an invitation to challenge the throne."

I flitted forward, my fist closing around his neck before he could fade into the shadows. "Is that a threat?"

"Not at all." Morpheus's grin stayed fixed in place without a flicker of fear scenting the air. "More of a warning between friends."

My eyes narrowed as my fingers lengthened into claws.

"I don't advise starting a war with my father, Lord Hades," he said, lifting his chin as beads of blood welled up. "Especially when your little witch is battling death magic as we speak."

"She's safe in Elysian with Hecate," Thanatos replied coolly, but I let my tendrils of darkness stretch, searching for her flame of life. She was, indeed, still in Elysian, but there was a sharp spike of frost clashing with her fire.

Morpheus's lips stretched, his grin showing off the sharp, pointed tips of fangs as he watched my dawning horror.

"She's unawakened, is she not?" he whispered, his voice dipping with something akin to seduction. "Not even Demeter would be able to contain an active flare of death magic."

"Stop," Thanatos growled, his open palm connecting with Morpheus's chest and sending him sprawling out of my grasp.

Shaking my head to clear it from his influence, I bared my teeth at Morpheus's bloody neck, peering over Thanatos's white wings to see that the thin slices left behind from my nails had already healed. "You dare to use your night magic on me?"

Morpheus ran a hand through his disheveled hair, tilting his head to the side and exposing the mess I'd made along his collarbones. He didn't bother standing, choosing to remain on his knees with his gaze fixed on Thanatos.

Of course. Using his power of persuasion had only been another ploy to get Thanatos's attention. Morpheus stayed rooted to the spot beneath Thanatos's feet, peering up at the God of Death as if he could go back in time and fix what he had broken.

Tearing his gaze away from the angel of death, he met my glare with regret still swirling in his eyes.

"Time is running out, Lord Hades."

PERSEPHONE

POWER FLOWED THROUGH MY FINGERTIPS, POURING INTO THE
earth around me. I felt it trickle down, like the cleanest water
purifying the stained soil. It wasn't only the plants that sought
life, but the earth itself. All the nutrients had been consumed,
burned through like a freshly lit match rendered to ash. It was
useless. Dead... but the kindling remained. All it needed was a
spark.

"You're reaching your limit," Hecate said. "That's enough."

But it *wasn't* enough. Coils of darkness rose, reaching,
ravenous for more. A cry tore from my lips as its icy grip locked
around the thread of my magic, like claws digging into flesh. It
pulled, dragging me across the line of healthy grass into the
maimed field. I stumbled, my knees crashing into ice and ash
and sharp shards of ice slicing into the flesh of my palms as I
fought to regain control.

More, it called, my arms nearly buckling from the force of its
draw.

I could vaguely hear Hecate screaming in the background,
could make out bright flashes of light flaring through the dark

clouds surrounding me, but I was alone. No one could reach me through this storm of darkness.

Red curls tumbled around my face, pieces matted to the sweat coating my forehead, as I forced my gaze to rise. My breaths came in short, ragged bursts as I stared down the swarm of blackness before me. There was only a small circle of soil beneath my hands and knees, the only patch untainted.

Inky strings stretched from the swarming black mass before me, wrapping around my wrists, consuming more of my life force. Instead of pulling away, I dug my hands into the earth, fingers curling in the soils and forced more of my magic out.

"Persephone," Hecate shrieked, her voice frantic and fracturing with fear, but I couldn't stop. The life magic *wanted* to go just as much as I wanted to give it, both of us intent on cheating death.

I was so close. Only a few more drops...

The next push of power tore at my insides, screams ripping through my lungs. I could feel the fibers of my life thread being ripped apart, but then my power reached the roots. And the magic caught.

Life surged before me, exploding from the ground in great bursts of green. Light burned through the darkness, the clouds of death dissipating as withered stumps stretched into full trees. Plump apples filled their branches as pops of yellow flowers covered the forest floor. They were everywhere, as far as the eye could see.

Dandelions.

I caught a glimpse of Hecate rushing forward, the halo of light around her eyes hovering over me, blocking out the two pairs of wings growing closer in the skies above, before darkness spotted my vision and I fell into the surrounding blossoms.

≈

"WE CAN'T DELAY THE CELEBRATION ANY FURTHER." THANATOS'S voice cut through my sleep, the bite to his words worsening my already terrible headache.

I blinked my eyes open, closing them against the glare of light. In the few seconds I managed to see, I noted the same minimalistic decor from the first room I'd been taken to.

"And don't even think to suggest canceling it. There's already talk circulating."

"Then silence it," Hades snapped.

"I can't quiet every soul in The Underworld."

"And *I* can't force Persephone to wake," Hades seethed.

"Can you two keep it down," I grumbled, draping an arm across my eyes as I attempted to turn away from them. "I'm trying to sleep."

There was a beat of silence before the world turned upside down. My stomach clenched as my body dipped, but then the scent of sweet frost and darkness was there as Hades's arms came around my waist, crushing me against the hard planes of his chest.

I winced, the small gasp causing him to withdraw.

"Where does it hurt?" Not waiting for me to respond, he turned to Thanatos, barking orders. "Get Hecate."

"She's attempting to contact the elders in The Crystal City—"

"Now."

Thanatos's crystal blue eyes narrowed as he clamped his mouth shut. With that look, I realized that despite his narrow frame he was just as lethal as Hades. His white wings stretched, looking like he might call Hades on his bullshit, but then his gaze shifted to me.

"You very nearly killed yourself by expelling that much magic. Luckily, Hecate was able to stabilize the frayed ends of your life thread, but if she'd been a minute later—"

"Thanatos," Hades cut in.

"No," he bit back as my pulse raced. My head was throbbing, but I couldn't look away. "You would have died, Persephone. And the both The Realm of the Living and The Underworld would have been fucked."

"It was my fault." All turned to find Hecate striding through the doors. "Persephone wanted a chance to defeat the death magic. Regardless of her being unawakened, I decided against warding it and allowed her to try."

Hades looked like he might eviscerate her right there, but she strolled confidently forward until she reached my side.

"As everyone can see, I was correct."

I lifted a brow at her but otherwise kept my mouth closed as her hand came to rest on either side of my head. Heat blossomed beneath her touch, soothing the icy migraine until all that was left was a dull throb. Flexing my muscles, I noted that the rest of my body felt healthy.

"Now that that's taken care of," I said as I got out of bed. "I'd really love a shower before we discuss how and why Hecate was contacting the elders of The Crystal City."

Hecate's eyes widened, her gaze snapping to Thanatos as he lifted his shoulder in a shrug.

"I thought she was asleep."

"She needs to know, anyway," Hades cut in. "We're running out of time to ease her into this."

"I agree," I said as my gaze bounced between them. My eyes narrowed as their guilty expressions became more apparent. "We're getting married in twelve days. It's only fair that I know what I'm getting into."

Thanatos and Hecate shifted uncomfortably, but Hades held my gaze, offering me his outstretched hand as I pushed the cotton covers back and stood.

"You've accepted your place at my side?"

"I thought we'd been over this," I said, batting his hand away, not liking his accusatory tone. I wasn't sure why he was acting as if he cared about my well-being, but I wasn't about to let him off the hook that easily. "Despite you being a vile, lying demon, if I don't bond with you, both realms suffer. You've made it quite clear I don't have a choice."

"You stabbed me," he seethed.

"Well, you kidnapped me," I growled, fists clenching. "I'd say we're even."

"Not even close, little witch." Hades's jaw ticked, the veins along his forearms standing out as the temperature cooled. "After knowing everything, you ran. And that stunt in The Elysian Fields? You insisted on putting your life in danger—"

"I stopped the death magic. Magic, I might add, that is supposed to be under your control, *oh dark one*."

"You shouldn't have interfered. Hecate had it under control."

"By doing what?" I seethed, leaning into his threatening glare. God or not, I wasn't afraid of him and wouldn't be intimidated into cowering. "By walling off the section of land that was dying? By letting it rot when I could save it?"

"Yes," he snarled, the blacks of his eyes expanding as the ghost of wings at his back threatened to appear.

"This wasn't some corner of hell, Hades. This was in Elysian. In paradise—"

"And I would watch it burn a thousand times over to know you were safe."

Hades stilled; his eyes went wide as if the confession had been pried from his lips. The room seemed to tilt as my thoughts swirled, too quickly to make sense of them. He was acting as if my life mattered to him... no. I was only seeing what I wanted to. Hades had been using me from the start. I was only ever the missing piece to a puzzle left unfinished for far too long.

He lied to me the moment he met me. Stolen me from The Realm of the Living and meant to use me just as everyone else in my life had. For some gods' forsaken reason, I'd thought that despite everything, I'd stumbled upon someone who might actually see me as something worthwhile. That a part of Hades looked as me and saw a person who mattered.

But the truth was, he would've said anything to get me here. I couldn't believe anything had been real, because if I hoped, if I opened that aching part of my soul and was once again proven wrong, it might just kill me.

"Well," Thanatos said after the silence had stretched far too long. "I think it's safe to say Persephone is feeling well enough to attend the ball tonight."

"Agreed," Hecate added, following as the two of them headed for the door. "I'll have preparations made."

And with that, they fled the room.

I blinked, somehow managing to look past the anguish in Hades's gaze long enough to remember how to speak.

"What ball? To celebrate our engagement?"

"Yes. Followed by our wedding... in three days' time."

38

PERSEPHONE

THREE DAYS. THE THOUGHT RACED THROUGH MY MIND AS I SAT ON the edge of the cushioned seat placed before the gilded vanity. Toying with the sleeves of the silk robe Hecate had found for me, I let my mind drift to Hades. I only had three days until I was bound to the God of The Underworld. Gods above, no wonder he had been so worried. So angry. I'd nearly slept through my awakening.

"You're lucky you woke at all," Hecate cut in, her ability to read my mind uncanny. My eyes narrowed on her as she looked through the table of cosmetics in small jars and rows set before the mirror.

"Can you read my mind?"

"No. Your emotions are far too easy to read in your expressions." The soft smile faded as she reached for a deep red lipstick. I lifted my chin under her command as she painted the vibrant color across my lips. "But to continue on what you were thinking, I was afraid you wouldn't wake."

She pulled back, allowing me to study the shade in my reflection. It was beautiful, highlighting the greens of my eyes while somehow not clashing with my hair. After another moment, I worked up the courage to meet her eyes.

"I needed to do it."

She inhaled deeply, but gave a small, sad nod as if she understood. "In the last century, death magic has been growing stronger, but I've never once seen it manifest a physical form like that."

My breathing hitched as I recalled the feel of its icy tendrils wrapping around my wrists, the sharp barbs digging beneath my skin. I glanced down, finding the place along my wrists slightly raised and pink.

"I healed you as quick as I could, but the cuts were deep." Hecate's words were soft, as if she were soothing a bird about to take flight. "You'll have the scars forever."

"I hadn't realized how close I was to..." The pads of my fingers traced the jagged lines, a lasting reminder of just how dire the situation had become. "Death magic can't go unchecked. I know Hades said our union was important, but Demeter always told us he wanted destruction. That the devastation was orchestrated by him to further The Dark Faction's power."

"Those you call The Dark Faction—demons—are witches who have mixed bloodlines with The Night Children," Hecate said. "There are variations among any group, but most are not as deplorable as you imagine. They do not derive power from destruction, nor does Hades. Though death magic is a part of his being."

"I've seen villages destroyed and innocents killed. The Crystal City, my childhood home... I was told every bad thing in my world was because of Hades and his horde of demons."

"And now?" Hecate asked, not allowing me to look away. "After everything you've learned about Hades, what do you believe his character to be?"

Memories of the worry flashing through his eyes when I'd

awoken last night rose to the surface, along with half-a dozen others: Hades had saved me from the Lethe and carried me up the mountainside of Tartarus so my feet wouldn't burn. He'd encouraged me when facing off with Kampe, despite my magic paralyzing him. Hades dove in front of the hydra to shield me, carried me across The Mountains of Mourning, and had followed me into the pit of Cocytus even after I'd stabbed him.

Maybe I was going crazy, because a piece of my heart squeezed at the worry flashing in his eyes last night.

Hades had lied to me the moment he'd opened the earth beneath my feet and dragged me to The Underworld, but he'd always kept me safe. He could've let me drink from the Lethe that first day. He could have forced or threatened me a number of ways, but he hadn't.

He had even been kind when telling me the truth about Demeter, sparing me the harsher aspects of what no doubt was a monstrous ordeal. Hades was my demon, bloodthirsty and dark, but mine nonetheless.

"I think marrying him might not be so bad after all," I muttered, hardly believing what I was saying.

But admitting to myself that I wanted him, didn't mean he wanted me. The moments between us that had seemed real were all part of his plan. He'd orchestrated the entire thing. I was meant to fall for him... and I had.

"Why did you run?" Hecate asked, breaking the silence that had stretched between us. I glanced up, prepared for judgment in her gaze, but there was only burning curiosity. "Cocytus is a horrible place to be sure, but you had already made it through the edge of Tartarus and The Mountains of Mourning. I even understand wanting to prove a point by jumping, but why not wait for him?"

My stomach twisted as my fingers found the cool crystal around my neck. I thought back to that moment, when it felt like everything was closing in around me. When I'd realized I'd abandoned Lark to the ruthlessness of Demeter and Cyrus.

"I needed to return to The Realm of the Living."

Hecate opened her mouth, but I continued before she could lecture me.

"Not forever. Just long enough to free a friend from my mother—Demeter's grasp." Because I was done calling that narcissistic bitch my mother.

"My *only* friend," I corrected. "Larkspur was punished by Demeter and forced to be a servant a few years ago. I'd been so lonely before her, but Lark and I hit it off right away. We both knew what it felt like to be different and unwanted.

"The plan was always to escape together, but Lark sacrificed herself so that I could get away. Lark has the power of persuasion."

"She's a witch with the blood of The Night Children?" Hecate asked, her brows lifting.

"I'm not sure," I admitted. "I've asked, but she's never been open about her family. In fact, until the night of my escape, I hadn't known she had a sister. That's why she had to stay behind, to ensure Demeter didn't punish her sister."

My stomach twisted as I gripped the edge of my crystal. Hecate noted the reflex, lifting the gold chain out of my silk robe to gaze at the fire opal cradled within.

"Did you select this?"

"Yes," I said. "It's one of the only things I've selected for myself. It was right before we left The Crystal City. I was only seven at the time, but it called to me. I know it's not a normal conducting stone, but Lark was able to place a location spell on it whenever we'd sneak out."

"Did she?" Hecate asked, but it didn't sound like a question. Her lips pressed thin as her brows furrowed. "Fire opal is a very rare stone to select. You were trying to return to The Realm of the Living for her, for Larkspur?"

"Yes."

She dropped the necklace, taking a step back as she studied my face. "And you thought jumping through hundreds of feet of snow at the lowest, most hopeless part of The Underworld was the time to go looking for a way out?"

"When you put it like that, it sounds crazy."

"It sounds illogical and impulsive," Hecate corrected. "And though you have some dark inclinations, I wouldn't use those words to describe you."

"I do make rash decisions sometimes," I admitted.

"Only when there's a realistic outcome, or if someone else's life is on the line, like in Elysium."

"Lark was in trouble," I insisted. "She's been in trouble this entire time."

"Exactly," Hecate countered. "She has been in jeopardy the moment you two ran. What changed in Cocytus?"

My hearing went a little fuzzy as I fought to think back. "I don't know. Hades had just told me I needed to wed... Hades. It was the first time I believed him, realizing that my life would never be my own."

"And that made you want to run?"

"No. I knew I couldn't leave our realms to suffer, but then I thought of Lark and I couldn't leave her." I shook my head. "The only other friend I had was killed, Ruby. She was my sister in every way that mattered. Ruby had dreams of rising to High Matriarch, of leading our coven into a new era, but when her awakening came... She was the first to be claimed. I know now that was all a lie. Demeter must have killed her like she did all the others, but Lark was different. She always wanted out of the coven. Wanted freedom."

I stared up at Hecate, feeling like I was reaching for a thread only to find a tangled lump of yarn. "I was going to come right back, I'm sure of it..."

"I believe you," she soothed, squeezing my hand. "Just, wait until after the bonding to return. Or at least after you and Hades finally give in to each other. It will be safer for all of us."

"Safer if we sleep together or wed?"

"Both. Getting married and being with each other physically will start the binding process. But your threads won't be solidified until you complete the awakening. Think of it like weaving a blanket together only to leave the end untied. One pull and the whole thing would unravel."

"So, sex and marriage will give us access to most of our magic, but it will be unpredictable?"

Hecate nodded. "And unstable."

"But completing the awakening and pledging my life to his will seal it and restore balance to our realms?"

"Sort of," Hecate explained patiently. "You will need to pledge your *magic* to the realms upon your awakening to restore balance, but yes. Vowing yourself—your life and soul—to Hades after the wedding and sleeping together will keep *your life* safe."

"As in, I'll become, what? Immortal?"

"Precisely." Hecate smiled like a proud teacher as she browsed the cosmetics once more. "Your life thread will be fully woven with a god's and forever bound."

"So, my awakening is the key to stabilizing everything, but until then…"

"Physical intimacy and marriage are the best way to bolster your power," she finished.

My cheeks heated as I thought about what we'd done in the pools, wondering if that counted.

"Yes," Hecate answered, again with the mind-reading abilities. "Had you not taken to each other, I doubt your powers would have been as accessible. Same goes for Hades."

"Do we have to love each other?" I asked around the butterflies in my stomach.

Hecate swirled a narrow brush in a jar filled with shimmering dust. "Both of you need to share your magic and your bodies. I was worried at first, but I don't think it will be a problem. Personally, I hope you two decide to make tonight's engagement party a real celebration."

"As in get married tonight?"

She shrugged. "It would simplify things. Your union has already been blessed by the gods and woven by the fates. All that's left to do is recite the vows and fuck."

My face flushed but Hecate didn't seem to notice.

"Hades won't bring it up, and an extra day with more magic probably won't make a difference, but you never know." She tilted her head, her eyes returning to the opal around my neck. "The paths between our realms are sealed at the moment, but I'll look into a way to help with Lark."

"Thank you," I breathed as hope flooded my veins. If there was any witch powerful enough to save Lark, it would be Hecate. A weight settled in the pit of my stomach as she offered me a kind smile. "I'm sorry I ever believed you would murder witches."

Her smile faltered as she turned away.

"I hate that Demeter has been so convincing. She's taken my teachings and twisted them for her own gain. With the balance between life and death magic being off, I've been confined to The Underworld. Only recently have I been able to reach The Crystal City coven, and even that communication is strained."

I pulled in a sharp gasp, hardly daring to breathe. "There're still witches in The Crystal City?"

"Only those clever enough to hide from Demeter's initial split from the coven. She killed everyone else. Demeter is nothing if not thorough, as you know. She went far enough to change your name and destroy all grimoires that opposed her views. I plan to restore the covens to their former harmony once things are as they should be, and my magic returned to full power. I only hope it's not too late."

39

HADES

What the fuck was happening to me? Persephone saved Elysium, defeated a wild burst of death magic that would have destroyed the section of The Underworld meant to be a sanctuary for women and children… and I felt only rage.

No, not rage. Fear.

Gods below, it felt like a dagger had sliced through my chest and embedded itself in my heart only for it to be twisted, ripped out, and plunged in again.

Nothing could get the image of her being dragged through ash out of my head. Persephone had been surrounded by clouds of impenetrable death magic. I'd flown as fast as I could, sent my own death magic and shadows to clash with the ones consuming her. I'd tried to pull the magic inside of my soul— Still, it hadn't been enough.

But then the blackness had faded. And Persephone had crumpled to the forest floor. She lay there on a bed of dandelions, the light slowly fading from her skin, and the only thought racing through my mind was that I'd give anything to save her. The Realm of the Living, The Underworld, my immortal life—all of it. Just to see her live.

"She's ready for you," Hecate called.

I glanced up from the obsidian floors toward the grand staircase where Hecate waited. The ornate banister was adorned with blacks and golds, the precious minerals shimmering in the light of the candles around the room. This was my private sitting room, one where Persephone was to join me before we greeted our guests.

Hecate eyed my outfit, her shrewd gaze tracking the subtle accents of deep greens and golden filigree I had added to my otherwise black tunic. I looked up through dark lashes, the twisting in my stomach settling as she gave a small nod of approval.

"I'll see to our guests as you two... catch up." With that Hecate swept from the room

My pulse picked up as the soft patter of heels echoed along the obsidian floor, the faint traces of Persephone's heartbeat reaching me right before she stepped into the light.

Gods below, she was stunning.

The tips of her pointed heels peeked out from beneath golden silk, the slit extending high along her thigh. Forest green thread woven into vines trailed along a neck line that dipped to her navel, the vines swirling and looping across the bodice, hugging every perfect edge of her body.

Her chest rose with a deep breath, drawing my eyes back up to the flush along her skin. To the darkening blush along her cheeks. Hecate had used golden pins set with diamonds to arrange half her hair up, creating the illusion of a crown. Tomorrow, a real crown would grace her head. And she would be mine forever.

I'd resisted taking her that night in the springs, but gods did I want to drop to my knees and worship her. To lick every delicious inch of her body until she was making those sweet noises, trembling with pleasure as she moaned my name.

It wasn't until I met her eyes that I remembered she hated me.

"Good evening, little witch." Her breathing hitched as sweet vanilla scented the air. Despite everything, Persephone still wanted me, at least in some way. "Or should I start calling you my queen?"

"We're not wed yet, Hades." Her heels echoed as she descended the steps, and I swore she added an extra sway to her hips just to taunt me.

Persephone had been brave enough to place her life on the line to protect my kingdom. She was powerful, and good, and saw the world in a way that I couldn't quite understand: with hope.

I had only ever thought to secure our threads. I'd planned on tricking her into it if needed, but Persephone made me think finding a true Queen of The Underworld was possible.

"Soon, my queen," I promised, catching her hand as she stepped from the last of the stairs. Magic flared at our contact, pulsing through our bodies as if it too were seeking to weave our threads. It felt like the purest energy. Like the magic of every living thing coursed through her veins and into mine.

A small gasp fell from her lips as the heat shifted into something warmer. Something far more captivating. Her pupils dilated as she dragged her bottom lip between her teeth. My gaze dipped to the movement. How I wanted to taste those lips, to nip and lick until they were swollen. To see them bruised and battered from being wrapped around me.

Persephone snatched her hand away, baring her teeth as tears welled in her eyes. "I don't need your help. We'll marry and bond, I'll even let you fuck me, and then all of this can be over."

I stiffened as something painful in my chest squeezed. "What if I don't want it to be over?"

"Stop *lying*!" she screamed, her voice breaking on the last word. She turned to run, but I was there before she could, backing her up until the stairs were at her back.

"I'm not lying, Persephone." My heart raced, my body humming with the unfamiliar state of being vulnerable—of feeling anything at all—but it was nothing compared to what my little witch was going through. Her cheeks were damp, eyes ringed in pink, and that beautiful bottom lip of hers trembled as she fought for control. I wasn't going to let her catch it.

"I haven't felt anything in so long."

Persephone shook her head as her gaze dropped from mine, but I eased her chin back up.

"Not until you. At first, I thought this was a product of your magic, of your power resurrecting my withering body, but then I saw death magic surround you in Elysium. I had to *watch* as the shadows consumed your life force while I was helpless to reach you. And then the darkness cleared. The forest and fields were alive once more… but you fell."

Her breathing hitched, sobs shaking through her body, as I stepped closer. She lifted a hand to my chest, keeping me at a distance, but she didn't stop my hand wrapping around her waist, tugging her closer.

"You saved Elysium. The world was thriving, and my people were safe, but you… You were so still. At that moment, I didn't think about the balance, or the repercussions. I couldn't see past the way your eyes had closed. Couldn't fathom an existence where I might never see the exact shade of green in your eyes again."

Tears fell as the pad of my thumb traced the curve of her cheek.

"Give me your anger, little witch. Glare at me with hatred and fury, with infinite loathing. I'll take it all, every scowl. Every curse. So long as you *live*."

40

PERSEPHONE

How did he do that? One minute, I was content in my anger. Justified even. And then the next...

Against my better judgment, I leaned into his touch, still not daring to open my eyes, but his palm was warm on my cheek, wiping away the last of my tears.

"I don't regret lying to you, little witch. I can't, not when it brought us here."

My fingers curled into his tunic, the effort I'd been putting into keeping him at a distance dissipating as my eyelids fluttered open. The blacks of his eyes had expanded, hinting at the dark god within, but where I'd once seen only cool detachment, there was now burning desire.

Desire for me. Not for the earth witch to restore balance, or the future queen of The Underworld, but *me*.

My gaze dropped to his lips as my tongue darted out to wet my own. Hating him was easier than trusting this—whatever *this* was—between us. I should focus on all the reasons I had to keep my distance, but then he bent. His lips brushed the edge of my cheek, trailing kisses down my neck. His tongue teased the sensitive spot along my collarbone, and I felt the last of my resolve crumble.

"Say you'll be mine," Hades whispered.

His teeth scraped over the top of my breast, and I arched into him. My life magic flared as he followed the sharp neckline of my gown, tasting between my breasts. His lips dipped lower with each frantic beat of my heart, before he dropped to his knees before me.

"Let me worship you forever."

Dark eyes blazed up at me, the shadow of monstrous wings stretching out behind him. My hands dropped to his shoulders as he worked under my dress, his fingers teasing up the back of my calves. The sight of him—the God of The Underworld, power incarnate—staring up at me with desperate longing, with insatiable hunger, had my thighs trembling. And when his fingers continued their exploration up beneath the gold silk, brushing against my bare pussy, I didn't stop them.

Hades groaned as he felt the slickness between my thighs, my own whimpers joining him as he pressed two fingers in. He pumped once, twice, before withdrawing, the evidence of my arousal clear as he held his finger before my lips.

"Open your mouth," Hades rumbled. "Taste what your god does to you."

Heat flared in my cheeks, warmth pooling lower, as I parted my lips and sucked, tasting myself on his fingers.

"Such a good girl," he praised. "Lie back, little witch. It's time I had a taste."

Not trusting my legs to hold me up much longer anyway, I sank onto the steps, watching as Hades's ram horns shimmered into being.

"What about the party?" I breathed, my pulse racing as he pressed the golden silk up, until the smooth material pooled across my waist.

"Let them wait."

Hades parted my thighs, exposing all of me to his hooded gaze. My chest heaved as I watched him lick his lips, his eyes eclipsed in black, before he buried himself between my legs. His tongue licked up my center, languid and savoring each stroke, letting me know he enjoyed this just as much as I did.

I propped myself up on my elbows, watching him work my body tighter. The coil of pleasure built as his tongue flicked and swirled over my clit, the scrape of his teeth adding to the mix of sensations. Moans fell from my lips, my head dropping back as I wrapped one of my hands around his horns, holding him where I needed him most.

A hungry growl rumbled through him, the vibrations tightening that delicious tension building between my thighs further.

"So fucking sweet," Hades breathed, positioning my heels over his shoulders before cupping my ass. This time when he tasted me, it was punishing. He fucked my pussy with his tongue, using his thumbs to part me further as he tasted all of me. As he savored every sweep of his tongue. And then his fingers were there, stretching me as his tongue flicked across my clit.

"Oh gods," I panted, grinding against his face.

"I'm the only god you'll ever need, Persephone." A third finger joined, the pain of the stretch only adding to my mounting ecstasy. "Who does this body belong to?"

"You," I moaned.

"Me," he growled, the heat of his breath fanning across my pussy as his fingers pumped. I was so close. Hades moved from my pussy to my breasts, pushing the edges of my gown aside until his mouth closed around my nipples, one and then the other.

"Hades, please," I begged, staring down at the god ravaging my body. His wings had manifested, tucking in close behind him, and there was no hiding the spiraling ram horns or his black eyes. He was a beast, everything I had been taught to hate. And I craved him all the more for it.

"You're so fucking beautiful when you beg." I whimpered as the pace of his fingers increased, as he lowered himself between my legs once more. "Now, be a good girl and come for me."

His mouth closed over my clit, sucking just as his fingers curled. My hips undulated against him as I gripped his horns, the orgasm tearing through me. Electricity sparked from my fingertips, and I could feel it weaving into both of us, connecting us further. A rush of desire, heat, and an aching devotion flooded through my veins, prolonging the waves of pleasure rocking through my center.

"This is what you do to me, little witch."

His fingers eased through the last of the aftershocks as my mind slowly drifted back to my spent body. He gathered me to him, pressing tender kisses to my chest, my neck, to every inch of my body, as if he were reassuring himself that I was here.

"I love you, Persephone. You've taken all that I once was and changed it forever." He cupped my cheek, the pad of his thumb tracing the splash of freckles there. "The world above may burn. The realms could splinter and fall, and still my soul would find yours. In each life. In every rebirth. Until the end of time, I will love you."

Tears pricked the corners of my eyes as I felt something in my chest lock into place. The beating of my heart matched his, the pulse humming in his chest beneath my fingertips now in perfect harmony with my own.

"I love you," I breathed, needing to say the words out loud. Our heartbeats skipped, causing his lips to tug into a sheepish grin still coated in my come. I watched fascinated as the black of his eyes gave way to cerulean blue. His ram horns and wings faded from view and still he held me as I stared, marveling at what fate had orchestrated for us. "Until the end of time."

41

HADES

"ARE YOU READY?" I ASKED, LOOKING DOWN AT PERSEPHONE poised on my arm. The makeshift crown had remained in place through everything we'd just done, a promise of what was to come. Her skin was flushed, the scent of me clinging to her even now. I felt our threads link, sensed the moment when she realized we were more than pawns in fate's game. Our souls were two halves of a whole, the frayed, battered shards finally starting to mend.

Fuck everything else. I wanted to take her to my bed and sink into her needy pussy. To bend and fuck, to take her in every way imaginable and then do it all again. But my little witch was vulnerable until she was fully awakened, and her safety was the one thing I wouldn't risk.

Morpheus had warned Thanatos and me about his father. I had no doubt Hypnos was here, sniffing out any weaknesses he could exploit. It was best not to give him one.

"Yes," she answered, her gaze moving from the set of double doors before us to me. "Are you? You look ready to murder someone."

"If only," I muttered. "There are some who would like nothing more than to see me fail."

"Us," Persephone corrected, her fingers weaving with mine. My eyes widened as a surprised smile stretched across my face.

"Us?"

She nodded. "Do we have anything to be concerned with?"

My spine stiffened reflexively. Morpheus had all but confirmed Hypnos was the one responsible for the spell that had left me weak upon returning to The Underworld. Hecate suspected that the only reason I'd survived was because of Persephone. Her magic had weakened whatever spell he had cast. He was definitely one to be concerned with, but Persephone and I would be wed and bonded tomorrow, and my little witch awakened when the hour struck midnight. Judging by how late it was, we had a little over twenty-four hours before all threats were nullified.

"Nothing to worry about," I reassured her, leading us through the doors before she could think to ask why I didn't meet her eyes.

Persephone

I CLEANED UP AS BEST I COULD BUT THERE WAS NO DISGUISING the scent of me still clinging to Hades or the way subtle traces of frost and darkness hovered around me. It was more than what we'd done physically, too. It felt like our threads had started the joining process, the first few pieces locking into place when we'd spoken of our feelings. Of our love.

Hades loved me. And I loved him. Tomorrow, I'd be his wife and the full might of my magic would manifest. There was nothing to worry about, but I couldn't help but sense that something was off.

Hades led me through the double doors, bringing us to the

edge of the throne room filled with dancing couples. There were a number of creatures, from winged harpies to beautiful gorgons, and I swore I spotted a group of centaurs in the fields beyond the windows. Beaded gowns and precious stones glittered in the candlelight, separated from the group of dark wings and shadows at the far end. Everything stilled upon our entry. The music halted and conversation quieted as each being dropped into a low bow.

My grip on Hades's arm tightened as his wings unfurled, tendrils of darkness billowing out around us. The cerulean blue of his gaze vanished as the great ram horns upon his head spiraled into being. His lips twisted into an arrogant smirk, one that promised pain to anyone who dared to cross him. Hades was the embodiment of every horror story, of every whispered fear uttered into a silent night. He *was* power.

All stayed bowed as Hades led us through the throne room, his shadows flanking us in a torrent of night. Sharp inhales and curious eyes glanced up as we passed, the throng of spectators scenting what we'd done.

Everyone in this room knew I'd had the God of The Underworld between my thighs moments ago. Where I would've felt exposed before, now I felt liberated. It was a subtle shift in perspectives, but a pivotal one. If I were to be Queen of The Underworld, to rule at Hades's side over the monsters of this realm, I needed to own it. Fear was a weakness that would be exploited, one that would jeopardize Hades's power. And I refused to be a weakness for him.

With more confidence than I felt, I crafted my own sinister smile, lifting my chin as we stepped up the dais. Every being in the room turned, watching through inclined positions as Hades guided me to his throne.

My heart skipped a beat as he placed me among the obsidian shards, before stepping back himself. Shadows swirled around us, the dark making the golden silk of my gown and the makeshift crown upon my head stand out further as The God of The Underworld dropped to his knees.

Murmurs erupted through the throne room.

"Silence," Hades commanded, his voice threateningly low as the darkness thickened. "Your queen has not given you leave to speak."

I swallowed as the waiting creatures of The Underworld focused their attention on me. Hades's shadows brushed the curve of my cheek, caressed the edge of my collarbone, letting me know he was with me. That he would be with me forever.

Taking strength in our bond, I sat up a little straighter. "The party may resume."

A genuine smile broke across my god's face as he stood. Hades tilted my chin up, parting my lips with his tongue as the music started. He tasted like frost and darkness with the faintest hint of me still lingering on his lips.

"You did well, little witch," he rumbled low enough for only me to hear. "There will be dancing and dinner, and then we'll be free to indulge in each other."

His shadows drifted between my legs, brushing against my pussy. My breathing deepened as my nipples hardened, the scent of my arousal turning a few heads in our direction.

"Unless you didn't want to wait."

"Hades," I breathed, not sure if I wanted him to stop or continue. He grinned as if he knew exactly what I was feeling.

"I once teased you with the idea of exhibitionism on the shores of the Lethe. Of fucking you in the forest for all to see. But what if we were in a throne room?"

Tendrils of darkness wrapped around my ankles, anchoring them to the throne. The large slit in my gown stretched as my knees were pushed apart. Hades stood before me, his body and shadows concealing my naked center from the eyes of his court.

"Say 'yes', Persephone. And I'll have you riding my face in front of everyone."

I glanced around him, noting the heated looks turned our way. More than one of them were women staring in disbelief as Hades's shadows made me bite my lip against another moan. Jealousy pricked as their hungry gazes took in the vastness of his power. Of how his attention was fixated on me.

I'd already given my heart to Hades, had decided to give my body, but he was just as much mine as I was his. And I wanted everyone in this room to know who he belonged to.

Looking up into his eyes, I sat up and scooted to the edge of the throne, my legs still held wide for his shadows to tease. He lifted a brow as my hands came to his thighs.

"I have a better idea," I breathed, undoing the laces of his pants until his straining cock was free. His hand fisted in my hair, tilting my head to meet his gaze.

"I won't be gentle," he warned, the blackness of his eyes growing deeper some how.

"Let them watch," I breathed, licking my lips as his cock twitched. "Let them see how much their queen can take."

42

HADES

I'D MEANT TO BE THE ONE WORSHIPING PERSEPHONE BEFORE OUR people. To have her thighs wrapped around my face as she rode my tongue, using my horns for balance.

But my little witch had other plans.

Her green eyes stared up at me from the edge of my throne as she wrapped a hand around my cock, guiding my tip to her lips. My hands fisted in her hair as she licked up my length.

"Use me, Hades," she breathed, hitching her dress further up as she spread her legs for my shadows.

I tugged on her hair, pulling a gasp from her lips as I leaned down. I dragged my nose up the length of her neck, dropping my voice low for only her to hear. "Careful what you ask for, little witch."

My shadows lashed out, tying her wrists behind her back as others wrapped around her neck, forcing her mouth open. My cock was filling her in the next second. She gagged, her body pulling back, but I didn't let her go anywhere. I watched as saliva fell from the corners of her pouty red lips, dripping down her chin as she fought for breath. My shadows parted her thighs, sinking into her pussy as I fucked her face.

Fuck, I love the way she whimpers.

"So fucking beautiful," I growled, watching as tears streamed freely over her cheeks. "Look at the way your body begs to be used."

My fingers tightened in the curls at the nape of her neck as I thrust my hips forward, losing all control. My cock hit the back of her throat, my shadows pinching her nose closed, cutting off her air completely. Her green eyes widened as she thrashed against me, but I didn't let up.

"You're doing so well, Persephone. Taking what I give you."

Her pussy clenched around my shadows, her body tensing, spurring my own on.

"Swallow all of me, little witch. Every drop."

She moaned as I thrust deep into her throat, releasing the shadows around her nose and neck. Her body was trembling with her own orgasm, but she fought to drink every bit of me down, fighting for breath through her nose, until I eased my cock from her mouth.

Her eyes were puffy, face flushed, and lips swollen. A halo of red curls framed her face, the crown titled but still in place upon her head. She looked like a fucking goddess. I leaned forward, my thumb dragging across the edge of her mouth.

"Every. Last. Drop."

She closed her lips over the tip, tongue swirling until it was clean.

"Good girl."

Persephone

A large figure with golden hair and blue eyes sat at the head of a long table, merrily sipping red wine from a silver goblet. His grin was pulled tight, his silver sleeves rolled up to reveal toned forearms. Power emanated from him, captivating all those nearby. All, except for a vaguely familiar, shadowy figure to his left.

"The revolting god at the head of the table would be Hypnos, the God of Sleep," Hades whispered through his smile. After our display, I'd thought about freshening up, but Hades encouraged us to stay, relishing the way his scent clung to me. "Without him, mortals in the above would go mad."

"And those in The Underworld?" I asked, shifting on the hard seat of the throne, watching as couples spun across the dance floor.

"We enjoy sleep, but don't require it," Hades answered, his hands resting on my shoulders from behind.

I surveyed Hypnos, not liking how large the crowd was around him. He smiled easily and talked smoothly, a dangerous combination for an enemy to have. Because there was no doubt in my mind that Hypnos was an enemy. He'd yet to approach the dais and congratulate us, as most if not all the others in the room had.

My gaze shifted to the shadows beside Hypnos, finding a pair of golden eyes ringed in red locked on mine. The red around his irises confirmed he was one of The Night Children, one that had fed recently. Any who wielded their particular brand of power was forced to drink blood. I tried not to think about how much blood he must've consumed for the scarlet rings to be as bright as they were.

He lifted a brow at my gawking. I blushed, unable to look away as his head tilted to the side, eyes dropping to where I clutched the fire opal around my neck. It warmed under the pads of my fingers, the heat growing in intensity until I was forced to drop it. Chest heaving, I rounded my shoulders, letting the necklace dangle in the air before me.

"What's wrong?" Hades asked, coming to my side as he searched my body for an injury. Tentatively, I reached up, only to find the stone cool to the touch.

"Who is that?" I asked, my gaze darting back to the dark-haired man with the golden eyes ringed in red, who now appeared to be in deep conversation with a woman seated across Hypnos's lap.

Hades followed my gaze, lips turning down. "That's Morpheus, son of Hypnos. Why?"

The woman threw her head back, long black hair swaying as she laughed, batting Morpheus away playfully. He smiled with a hint of fangs showing, the gesture more predatory than anything as he lifted her diamond-covered wrist to his mouth, pressing a kiss to the inside.

"My crystal felt hot, but I must've been imagining it."

"Trust your instincts, Persephone," Hades said, eyes narrowed as he studied the crystal around my neck. "They're normally forgotten memories from a past life trying to warn you. Regardless, I've delayed our introductions long enough."

Ignoring the twist in my stomach, I accepted Hades's hand, the two of us stepping into darkness only to appear across the room a moment later.

"Hades," Hypnos beamed. The woman on his lap fell silent, slinking off as the God of Sleep stood. She was careful to keep her face hidden from view, but there was a lingering scent of something earthy that had the fine hairs on the back of my neck standing on end. "How kind of you to join us. For a moment, I was worried something terrible had befallen you."

"Come now, father," Morpheus smirked, his red-ringed gaze drinking Hades in before turning toward me. "It's clear the happy couple were merely getting a head start on the bonding process. Their scent is practically a cloud around them: Vanilla with a hint of frost."

My cheeks burned, but the sour expression on Hypnos's face was strangely reassuring.

"Yes," Hypnos muttered, turning his eyes on me. "I heard I missed quite the show." His gaze roved over the makeshift crown somehow still pinned in my hair before dipping to the gold chain I hadn't realized I was gripping. "What an interesting piece of jewelry, Lady Persephone. Might I have a closer look?"

"You can see just fine from there," Hades said, his hand protectively dropping to my waist. I leaned into his touch, taking comfort in the thickening shadows around him.

Hypnos lifted a brow at the display of power. "Of course. The crystal must be very valuable. I'd take care not to misplace it."

I could have sworn Morpheus pulled in a sharp breath, but his face was a sheet of practiced control, giving nothing away.

"It's good to see your power so clearly manifesting, Lord Hades," Hypnos said, but there was nothing kind about his smile as he retrieved his goblet from the table, swirling its contents before taking a long sip. "I'd heard rumors they were waning. That you'd been trapped on the banks of the Lethe, no less."

My pulse raced as sparks of anger—not of my own making —simmered in my veins. Hypnos was pushing Hades. Testing him. And it looked like he'd just hit the mark. Judging by the cruel twist of his lips, he knew it, too.

"Such a joy the rumors are false, isn't it Morpheus?"

"A joy to be sure," Morpheus answered dryly, those dark eyes boring a hole into my soul.

"With the earth witch now returned to us, our realm will be healed in no time."

"Lady Persephone," Hades corrected. "And after tomorrow, you may choose between Queen Persephone or Your Grace."

Hypnos's smile grew tight at the edges, the tips of his fingers seeming to shimmer with a soft light as a thin layer of very fine powder collected beneath. A few of the others seated at the table beside him pushed to stand, a dozen leathery wings shimmering into being. More than one of them offered threatening smiles showing off their red-ringed eyes and sharp fangs: The Night Children.

Where in gods' names were Hecate and Thanatos. It looked like a fight was about to break out any moment. But then Morpheus stepped forward and dropped into the most exaggerated bow imaginable.

"Lady Persephone, Queen of The Underworld, we are overjoyed to have you among us. You bless us with your life, with your magic, but most importantly, your beauty." Morpheus winked, the cocky tilt of his lips far more endearing than it should have been. He was just the type of guy Lark would've gone for. The thought of her flashed through my mind as he lifted my hand to his lips, pressing a soft, lingering kiss to the back of my hand.

"Enough," rumbled Hades, but The Night Children were mimicking Morpheus's antics, bowing to one another in exaggerated supplication as he had me.

"How foolish of me, Lord Hades." Morpheus's voice dripped with false innocence as he pivoted, dropping to his knees. "Would you like me to kiss something of yours?"

My eyes widened, more from curiosity than jealousy, but Hypnos yanked his son back before Hades could respond.

"You are prince to The Night Children, heir to The Sleeping Realm, and *this* is how you behave?"

Morpheus was prepared with a witty reply, but a flash of white wings along the periphery caught my attention. Thanatos strode forward with Hecate at his side.

Her shrewd gaze took inventory of the situation for all of a second before she snapped her fingers. Waitstaff carrying great platters of food poured from the kitchen, forcing everyone to claim a chair.

"Perfect timing," Morpheus drawled, leaning into a particularly attractive server, much to Hypnos's dismay. His father's cheeks darkened from red to purple, but Morpheus didn't seem to care as he took a seat, fork and knife already in hand. "I'm starved."

43

PERSEPHONE

I HADN'T REALIZED HOW HUNGRY I WAS UNTIL THE FIRST COURSE was served. It was a simple salad dressed with walnuts, crumbled feta cheese, and a drizzle of honey-glazed pomegranate seeds, but my mouth was watering the moment it was set before me.

Reaching for my fork, I dug the metal tongs through the center, the rumble of my stomach spurring me on, but Hades's hand covered mine before I could raise the bite to my mouth.

"Wait," Hades said, his voice low enough for only the four of us to hear. Hecate and Thanatos had joined us at a small table set in front of the throne immediately upon their entering with Thanatos seated to his right and Hecate to my left. A quick glance their way showed that both were staring at me.

"Why?" I breathed, matching his tone. "You think someone would try to poison me here?"

"No," Hecate answered, though Hades had yet to look away. "You haven't eaten anything since you've passed into our realm. Your life magic and my healing magic has sustained you thus far, but if you *do*…"

"You'll be tied to The Underworld forever," Thanatos finished.

"Isn't that the whole point with our marriage and bonding tomorrow?" I asked, trying to lift my fork as my stomach growled.

"Yes, little witch," Hades said. "But even with our threads woven, you'd be able to come and go as you pleased. You would be Queen of The Underworld, and therefore no longer hindered by the same restrictions others are. Consuming food would tie you further to this realm, making it impossible for you to step foot from The Underworld for half of the year."

I blinked.

"Being that you're still alive and born a powerful earth witch from The Realm of the Living, you'll never be fully trapped here," Hecate added.

"That and when your life threads are woven, you'll become immortal," Thanatos said, starting in on his own salad. "Although, taking a piece of The Underworld into your being would allow your essence to merge with this realm."

"Merge?"

"Yes," Hades confirmed, finally removing his hand from mine. "Goddess of The Underworld."

My heart skipped as I dropped my gaze, focusing on the juicy pomegranate seed set atop deep green leaves. I was already giving my body, my magic, my entire life-force to Hades, but there had still been a way out. This would take that away. I needed to save Lark... but hadn't I already decided my future was here?

Looking up, I took in my surroundings. The four of us had an uninterrupted view of the room now that the dance floor had been cleared, making the divide in loyalties obvious. Despite Hades's reassurances, Hypnos's influence was concerning—or was it Morpheus who commanded most of the attention?

Either way, The Night Children clustered around the two of them, flanked by a rather large cluster of gorgons. On the other side of the room, sat spirits adored in battle leathers and military regalia, along with most of the harpies. Members of The Dark Faction were split, but I could practically see the tension in the room as the two groups sized each other up.

This was to be my kingdom. My home. I could save its existence by pledging my magic to this realm and to Hades, but I wanted more than survival. I wanted peace.

With a deep breath, I focused my gaze on the god next to me, staring at the cerulean blue irises surrounding the darkest black. And lifted the fork to my mouth.

Honey and pomegranate filled my senses, the delectable tastes rolling over my tongue. It was better than anything I'd ever eaten, like the freshest drop of dew had been gathered and mixed with joy. Closing my eyes, I moaned, licking the remainder of the dressing from my lips.

"Gods below," muttered Thanatos as Hecate laughed, but it was Hades's low murmured promise that had my eyes snapping open.

"If you keep making sounds like that, I'll have to start on my own meal."

My cheeks pinked as I swallowed, staring at the open desire swirling in his gaze. "It's delicious."

His lips twitched.

"Wait till you try the champagne."

AFTER MY THIRD GLASS, THE PARTY WAS WELL UNDERWAY. EACH course of the night had gotten progressively better, from the lemon-and-thyme tarts sprinkled with goat cheese, to roasted lamb seasoned with garlic and rosemary, and finally to the buttery baklava stacked with honey and nuts. All the while, bottles of champagne and sweet flavored wine flowed freely.

Hypnos had left as soon as dessert was served, taking the gorgons and most of The Night Children with them, all except Morpheus. He was busy flirting with a curvy, dark-haired harpy.

"Don't let him worry you," Hecate said, tugging my arm as she led me toward the dance floor. We joined the line in the center of the room where couples paired off, facing one another. "Hypnos has been trying to find a way to usurp Hades for decades. He might have succeeded if you hadn't been found."

My eyes widened as I glanced toward Morpheus who was slipping deeper into the shadows with the harpy on his arm.

"But," Hecate said, gathering her hands in mine as the first notes of the song began to play. "You are here. And you love him."

A timid smile stretched across my lips as I glanced toward Hades. He was with Thanatos. The God of Death looked like he was relaying something important, but Hades's burning gaze was fixed on me.

"I do love him," I whispered. The champagne had my inhibitions down, letting the words flow freely. His pupils dilated as if he'd heard me.

"See? Nothing to worry about." Hecate spun me around, breaking my eye contact with Hades as we turned with the other laughing couples. "Less than twenty-four hours, you two will be married. A few hours more, and I can bestow my blessing upon you at your awakening, completing the bonding process, and saving both our realms."

My stomach fluttered as she dipped me to the music.

"With balance reestablished, I'll lead you to The Realm of the Living where we can free Lark and hold Demeter accountable for all that she's done."

The fuzziness from the champagne cleared a little as we

continued with the dance, stepping back and then together again with the others. "Everything was going to be okay."

Hecate nodded, but there was a frown lingering on her lips. "It should be, but I can't shake the feeling that this is the calm before the storm."

"What is that supposed to mean?" I asked, dropping to a curtsy as the song ended.

"I'm not sure," she breathed, shaking her head as we moved off the dance floor. "But I've learned to rely on my instincts. And right now, they're telling me to keep my guard up."

A large shadow fell over the two of us. Pricks of electricity danced across my skin as the scent of frost and shadows swirled in the air around me.

"May I cut in?"

I turned to find Hades with his hand outstretched, palm waiting for my answer. With a smile, I placed my hand in his, turning to find Hecate had already left.

"I've missed you, little witch." Hades pulled me close, my body flushed with his as he inhaled the scent of me.

"It's been one dance," I laughed, but I leaned into him, loving the way our hearts synced.

"Then it has been one dance too long." he said, guiding me to the center of the floor as we waited for the music to start. "Stay with me tonight. Not in the queen's rooms, but in mine. In *ours*."

My breathing quickened as his hand dropped to the low of my back, the other cupping my cheek.

"Yes," I answered with too much enthusiasm. Pink tinted my cheeks, the pad of his thumb dragging across the color as his lips tilted into a wicked smirk.

"So eager," he said, his voice dipping low. "We'll have fun tonight, my Persephone. I promise you that, but first, we dance."

44

HADES

Fucking perfect. That's what Persephone was. Dazzling, radiant—a fucking goddess among mortals. She was the candle amid endless darkness. A diamond gleaming among lumps of coal. No one was worthy of her, not even to gaze upon her beauty. Not even me.

I was nothing but a shadow, having grown hollow and depleted like the wretched wraiths wandering the cursed kingdom of Cocytus. I'd thought it was death magic leeching life from me... but I'd been fading for far longer than I cared to admit.

As the ruler of The Underworld, there was always something I needed to do. A personification I needed to embody for my siblings or my people. Punishing, harsh, benevolent. It had been centuries since there had been anything other than duty and obligation.

Until Persephone.

She bathed my reality in light. In life. But it was so much more than her magic. It was *her*. Her goodness. Her hope. I had been existing in a bland sheet of gray, but Persephone saw the world in vivid shades of color.

I glanced down at her, marveling at how bright her smile was as I spun her through another turn, her freckled cheeks rosy from the champagne and the dancing of the night. She'd left her red curls down after she'd tasted me on the throne, but the golden pins remained in place.

They were real diamonds, a gift for my future bride, not that Persephone knew that. She wasn't one to be swayed by the jewels of The Underworld, but I planned on giving her the finest of everything, proving to the realm that she was so much more than the savior of our realm. She was *everything*. The source of each and every facet of brilliance in The Underworld.

"That was so much fun. You didn't tell me you were such a good dancer," Persephone panted, her green eyes flashing to Hecate as they darted around the boisterous ballroom. "I hadn't realized how lively The Underworld was."

Thanatos had followed Hypnos the moment he left, but most of The Underworld had yet to tire. It had been a while since the spirits of my realm had much to celebrate. The promise of balance restored, death magic controlled, and a royal wedding were each things that warranted a proper party. Together... I'd be surprised if the spirits quieted in the next month.

My lips twitched as Hecate appeared next to Persephone. "It's easy to lose yourself when you're surrounded by wonderful energy. Alas, I must call it a night. I need rest before the big day tomorrow. After all, each witch's awakening is a blessing from my lifeline."

Persephone's brows furrowed as the three of us moved to the edge of the room. "Meaning an ember of your magic is gifted to each of us?"

"When midnight strikes," Hecate smiled, catching the frown tugging on Persephone's lips. "He magic gifted is nothing that weakens me, though I am more aware of the recently awakened witch for a few days."

"Aware how?" Persephone asked, her eyes darting to me as her cheeks pinked.

"Nothing that intimate," Hecate laughed. "It's more of a presence. Sometimes I can even sense where witches are, depending on the person."

"And when a witch doesn't survive?" Persephone asked, her voice growing soft. "When Demeter decides a witch isn't strong enough to live, what happens?"

Hecate's smile dropped, a vast hollowness opening within her gaze. "I feel each and every death that comes to my line, newly awakened witches, even more so."

"We will avenge them," Persephone vowed, the fire burning in her gaze eager for a fight. "Soon, I'll have the power to defeat Demeter and set things right."

"Soon," Hecate agreed. "Enjoy tonight, Lady Persephone. In less than twenty-four hours, you will be fully awakened. The next day, we go to war."

45

PERSEPHONE

"Finally, I have you alone." Hades dragged his nose up the length of my neck as he pressed me against his door. I leaned into his touch as the last of the champagne swam through my veins.

Gods above, did he feel incredible. His lips pressed against my thrumming pulse, the skilled caress of his fingers drifting up the inside of my thigh as his other hand wrapped around my waist. Each point of contact sent electricity tingling through my body.

My hands wrapped around his neck as he worked the gold silk of my dress up.

Yes. I couldn't believe I'd stayed away from him for this long. I needed to taste him again, to feel him lose control.

Savoring the way his hooded eyes widened, I turned us, pressing him against the wall. "What are you up to, little witch?"

"I miss your taste."

His pupils expanded as I knelt before him, working his laces free. He pressed his palms flat, the muscles along his forearms straining as his pants pooled at his feet. Wrapping my lips around his tip, I guided him inside my mouth, staring up at him as I took him deeper. Hades groaned as I pulled back, running my tongue along the length of him, before swallowing him again, until he was pressed against the back of my throat.

"Fuck Persephone," he growled, his hands lifting from the wall to tangle in my hair. Then his hips were moving, fucking my face as I fought for air, finding stolen breaths in between thrusts. I did my best to hollow my cheeks, letting him use me, spurred on by the primal sounds spilling from his lips.

Only I could make him feel this way. Only I could make the great God of The Underworld tremble with need. Desperate for *me*. His queen.

Hades yanked hard on my hair, pulling a gasp from me as he withdrew, forcing me to look up at him from my knees. His eyes were fully black, simmering with something dark and hungry. Something primal.

His fingers pinched my chin, tilting my face from side to side, inspecting what he'd done to me. I could feel the dampness along my cheeks where tears had fallen. My jaw was aching from his rough treatment, my lips swollen, and my knees were starting to hurt from where I'd knelt on the obsidian floor, the golden material of my dress bunched around my thighs. But all I could think about was how I wanted more.

"You're so fucking beautiful on your knees for me," Hades rumbled as my thighs clenched. "I bet you're wet for me already, aren't you, little witch?"

My chest heaved as I stared up at him, unable to nod with the grip he still had on my chin.

"Feel yourself," he said, releasing me as he took a step back to watch. "Slip your fingers into your needy pussy and tell me how much you wish it was me."

My cheeks blazed, but I did as he said. Spreading my knees, I lifted my dress slowly, knowing he would track every movement. I let my fingers drift up, closing my eyes as I imagined Hades's hands in their place.

I was wet, my thighs slick with want. Letting my dress fall to the side, I circled my clit, my breasts heaving as that delicious coil low in my belly started to grow. My nipples were hard, my body flushed as my fingers worked.

It was only when I heard Hades's growl of frustration that I let a finger sink inside me. Then his hand was around my wrist, holding me inside before I'd even had time to blink my eyes open.

"Such a naughty little witch."

My pussy squeezed around my finger as I stared up at him, knowing I'd purposely found the longest way to carry out his command. A way that would torture him just as much as it did me.

"You never said I couldn't have fun first," I breathed, tilting my pelvis to grind my clit against my palm.

A low growl rumbled in his chest as his nostrils flared. He yanked my hand free, holding my slick finger up between us before his lips closed over it. His tongue swirled as he licked me clean, savoring the taste.

My breathing quickened as our pulses raced. The scent of my arousal was heavy in the air as he slipped my finger free from his mouth, licking his lips for any lingering traces. His gaze dropped to the fabric between my legs for only a moment before he gripped the golden silk and ripped.

It split down the middle, the gown held up only by the thin straps across my shoulders. My mouth fell open as Hades made quick work of those too, until the scraps of my beautiful gown were laying in tatters around my knees.

"Stand up."

Embarrassment burned across my cheeks even as my nipples hardened, but I pressed to a stand, lifting my chin as he circled me. My pulsed raced, my breasts aching as I fought to control my breathing. I was exposed, naked and bared before him as he inspected every inch of my body, standing in nothing but my fire opal necklace and the make-shift crown pinned in my hair. By the time he finished circling, I was practically panting with need.

"Next time I give you a command, I expect you to carry it out right away. If I tell you to pleasure yourself, I expect you naked and spread before me in the next breath." His hand cupped my pussy, pulling a gasp from me. "This is mine, little witch."

His palm pressed against my clit, applying just enough pressure to have me grinding against him in response.

"Every inch of your body is mine to do with as I will." His fingers slid through my slickness, teasing my pussy but never entering. "I will take this from you tonight."

Hades pressed a finger into me hard, adding a second one as he pumped, before pulling back to a teasing touch.

My moan turned into a whimper as my pussy clenched, desperate for release. My breathing hitched as his chest pressed against my back, using the wetness between my thighs to reach further.

"This too, little witch." I stilled as the pad of his finger circled my ass. "We have work to do before you're ready to be fucked here."

My body clenched as he pressed against me, but then his shadows were there. They were everywhere, pinching my nipples, circling my clit, filling my mouth as I moaned into the darkness. All the while his finger stayed at my ass, working in slowly as my body loosened.

"There," he breathed against my neck, his finger gently gliding into me. "You would let me do anything to this body, wouldn't you Persephone?"

I nodded, tilting my pelvis as I tried to take more of him.

Every nerve ending was on fire, electricity dancing across each place his magic touched my own.

"You'd let me fuck this tight hole right now if I wanted."

"Yes," I breathed, pressing back against him.

Hades kissed my neck as his other hand replaced the shadows between my legs. He slipped two fingers into my pussy, dragging a moan from my lips as my legs shook with the effort it took to stand. I was stretched like I'd never been before, used and worshiped at the same time. Hades could have bent me over and fucked me every which way and I would have thanked him, so long as he let me come.

My body clenched as he worked, the pressure building. "Please, Hades."

An animalistic growl vibrated through him. "So fucking beautiful when you beg."

I was close. So close.

"Do you want to come, Persephone? Knowing that my fingers are stretching you. Filling you. That the God of The Underworld, King of Demons, is the only one able to make your body tremble like this."

I whimpered my agreement arching my neck as I stared into his eyes, shamelessly grinding against him as the wave of pleasure crested.

"Come for me."

He kissed my lips, stealing the last of my breath as his fingers curled. The orgasm tore through me, each moan swallowed by a sweep of his tongue, a press of his lips. My legs gave out as he worked every last wave of pleasure from my body. It felt like I was floating, like I was nothing but ecstasy. I had detached from my body and was hovering in clouds of euphoria.

I felt his arms around me as he carried me to the bed, felt the smoothness of the sheets against my skin as he laid me down. And then the heat of his breath was on the inside of my thighs as he licked up toward my center.

My consciousness returned to my body enough for me to look down, finding dark curls poised over my soaking pussy.

"What are you doing?"

"Cleaning up my mess," Hades breathed, his hands pressing my legs apart. "We're just getting started."

46

HADES

Persephone's eyes widened, that sexy fucking blush blooming across her cheeks as I pressed her legs apart. Seconds ago, she was bouncing on my fingers, begging me to take her however I liked, but now that the effects of the orgasm were fading she was back to being nervous. Self-conscious even.

As if I didn't crave every inch of her. As if I wasn't going to taste and fuck and brand myself on every piece of her soul. I looked down at her pussy, fucking soaked and waiting for me. I allowed the whisper of my wings to show. Her breathing hitched as I lowered my mouth, her breasts heaving, her nipples hard and pink from my earlier attention. Red curls fanned out around her, with the crown of diamonds still pinned in place.

Like the fucking queen she was.

"I'll get on my knees every day for you, little witch, worshiping your body like the goddess you are."

A needy whimper fell from her lips at the first swipe of my tongue. She tasted like sunlight and honey—like the only heaven I'd ever need.

She was my grace.

My life.

Everything I never knew I needed and so much more than I deserved.

Positioning her thighs over my shoulders, I gripped her ass, tilting her toward my face. Like a starved man served his favorite meal, I devoured her. Ravaged her. Until she was panting and writhing beneath me, her hands locked around my ram horns as she rode my face.

"Gods, Hades," she moaned, tugging me closer.

"Yes," I said, sinking my fingers into her tight pussy as I teased her clit. "I'm your god, Persephone."

She arched her back, her breaths coming in short, ragged bursts as the climax built.

"Say it," I commanded, adding a third finger. She gasped at the fullness but didn't pull away. Such a good girl. I intended on fucking her properly tonight. It was important she was ready for me, because I wouldn't be gentle. "Tell me I'm your god. That I'm the only one to ever make you feel this good."

"Hades," she begged as I pumped, allowing my fingers to graze that sensitive spot within.

She looked down at me with one of her hands still wrapped around my horns as my mouth remained poised over her clit. I wondered if she knew she held all the power here. That if she told me I was nothing, that I was a placeholder until she found something better, that I would still bow to her. I would pledge my life—my eternal soul—to her again and again even if she could never promise me the same.

"I'm yours," she breathed, and I thought I would die from how my heart squeezed. "All of me. Everything. My entire world. It's you, Hades. It's only ever been you."

My wings burst into being as something clicked in my chest. I stared up at her green eyes marveling at the beauty before me and sent a thanks to the fates for bringing her into my life.

"Then come for me, my goddess. Show me how loud your god makes you scream."

I closed my lips over her clit and sucked as my fingers curled. She screamed my name as her pussy clenched around me, pressing her center into my face as I continued to work her through her orgasm. Lapping at her slit until those soft little pants grew louder once more.

I climbed up her body, kissing the curves of her stomach, the swell of her breasts. My teeth grazed the edge of her nipple before tasting the soft skin in the curve of her neck, licking just over her pulse that beat in time with mine.

"Forever, Persephone," I vowed.

"Hecate mentioned we could've gotten married tonight. That doing so would've helped with our magic, even before my awakening." She glanced up, tracking the pads of her fingers drifting down my chest to the upside down torch branded over my heart.

I stilled, waiting for her to meet my gaze. "Yes. If we spoke the sacred vows, our threads would start to weave, but won't seal until you're fully awakened."

She looked up through thick lashes. "But they *would be* woven. Braided but not fastened."

Shifting to my side, I caressed the edge of her cheek, noting the faintest hint of a blush. "Yes."

Persephone breathed deeply, turning into my touch to press a kiss against my palm. "Marry me, Hades. Right now. I want to feel our souls joined as our bodies are."

My eyes blazed as she met my gaze. Her head was fanned out around the pillow, a halo of red. Her skin was still flushed from her latest orgasm, and the scent of her sweet arousal hung heavy in the air.

"I give myself to you, Persephone." Gently, I removed the crown of pins from her head, setting them aside for what was to come. The air became charged, buzzing with power. I pressed a kiss to her forehead, feeling our magic reach for one another.

"All that I once was, I yield to you."

My lips brushed her cheeks, my nose grazing her own as I hovered over her lips.

"All that I will be is yours. From now, until the end of time, we will be as one."

The heat of her breath washed over me as she uttered her promises back, each word adding to the mounting charge in the air.

"I give myself to you, Hades. All that I once was, I yield to you. All that I will be is yours." She swallowed, her gaze locking with mine as the electricity pricked across our skin. "From now until the end of time, we will be as one."

A gasp stole from her lips as our magic snapped together, linking our threads. The blazing fire of her life magic sizzled against the cold frost of mine, the dark and light threads braiding together seamlessly. Electricity cracked in the air, light sparking in small prisms as my shadows rose in turn.

I could feel her. The desperate need of her body. Her love. Gods below, the power of her love was infinite.

I stared down at her as her fingers traced the brands across my chest. She was exquisite, her green eyes amazed as sparks danced beneath her touch.

"There's no escaping me now, little witch," I vowed, nudging her knees apart to position myself at her center.

"You already own all of me, Hades," she breathed, dropping her knees to open herself further. "Now, show me what it means to be fucked by a god."

"Yes, my queen."

I thrust my hips forward, savoring the way her body tensed at the intrusion. Her eyes widened, her pouty lips parting around a gasp as I claimed her. She moaned as my lips closed over her nipple, her head falling back as I switched to the other. Fuck, if I didn't love the way her nails dug into my ass, willing me to take more, even as my cock split her in two.

"Open your eyes, Persephone. Look at how your body was made to take me."

She whimpered as she watched my cock enter her swollen pussy. I groaned at the way she clenched around me, feeling her mounting pleasure as if it were my own.

I pulled out flipping her over onto her stomach, her hands stretched over her head. Lifting her perfect ass into the air, I ran my fingers from the slickness of her pussy to the tight hole of her ass. She pressed back against me, eager for any type of friction I would give her.

"Such a good fucking girl," I murmured, holding a finger over her ass as I lined my cock up. I pressed my finger in at the same time I thrust my hips forward, watching as her body opened for me. "You're a part of me now, Persephone. Woven into every fiber of my being."

She moaned as I increased my pace, keeping my hand at her ass while my shadows worked her clit. Our pleasure synced as our breathing grew ragged, the wet sounds of our slapping bodies intensifying as our rhythm grew frenzied.

I wanted to take her deeper. Rougher. To own and punish. To praise and adore. I needed to bend and abuse her body until she was trapped in a haze of pleasure so thick she'd never come down.

"Oh gods," she moaned, her hands gripping the sheets for purchase as I fucked her savagely. "Hades."

"Not yet," I growled, shifting us until she was straddling me, our lips inches from one another. "I want to watch as you come undone around me."

I gripped her ass, lifting her up and down as she bounced on my cock. This angle was deeper, each thrust causing her clit to grind against my pelvis. My shadows swirled around her, not leaving an inch of her body unattended to. She gripped my arms, her nails digging into my skin as her thighs clenched.

Our magic grew, the sparks along our skin shifting to a

raging fire, one that threatened to burn me in an ecstasy so potent I might just die from it. I saw the same realization in her gaze, watching as her decision mimicked my own.

"Come for me, my queen."

Her body trembled as mine pulsed, our bodies finding euphoria together as we welcomed in the inferno of magic that wove our threads. Light danced across her head, shimmering pieces linking, until a golden crown shimmered into being. I felt the chill of shadows gather between my ram horns, growing heavier as our magic blended, until I was sure my own crown of darkness had emerged.

All the while, our bodies moved, writhing together as the waves of pleasure continued. It felt like the greatest high—a release so strong it was nearly painful. But every part of me was alive and humming with energy. All past notions of love and joy were decimated. *This* was what it meant to live. To love.

There would only ever be my Persephone from now until the end of time.

My goddess.

My queen.

My wife.

47

PERSEPHONE

HADES TOOK ME OVER AND OVER AGAIN UNTIL IT FELT LIKE I WAS suspended in a permanent state of euphoria. Until every cell in my body was alive and drunk on pleasure. We'd crashed only an hour or two ago, both of us spent and sore—but something tugged me from sleep.

The heavy weight of Hades's arm was draped across my stomach, holding my back flushed against his chest. I felt safe here, wrapped in his touch... but there was a flicker of heat along my chest that had me blinking my eyes open.

I disentangled myself, being sure not to wake him, before padding across the obsidian floor toward the door. My skin pebbled with the loss of Hades's touch, my nipples hardening as a shiver worked down my spine. I reached for the robe draped over the back of his chair, the white silk fabric cut to my size. A soft smile tilted my lips as I vaguely registered there was a matching black one next to it, as if Hades had planned on us wearing them after exiting the shower. We'd both chosen to sleep naked last night, but the thought he must have put into this had me slowing just as my fingers reached the gilded door handle.

Where was I going? The sun hadn't yet risen, and the formal marriage ceremony wasn't until this evening. I should be resting...

My breathing hitched as a flash of heat seared between my breasts. My necklace was hot, the fire opal painfully so, but before I could tug it from my neck, a wash of calm came over me. The pads of my fingers traced the smooth edges of the crystal, my brows furrowing as I tried to understand why my pulse was racing.

The opal had never been painful before... and it was fine, now. I must have imagined it—a gasp stole from my lips as a pulse of magic shot through my fingers.

Lark. I needed to find Lark. Something was wrong.

I fled the room, rushing down passages and dipping through corridors until a narrow, wooden door was set before me. A small, frantic piece of my mind worried that I didn't know how I'd gotten here, or what was beyond the door, but then that familiar tugging was back.

It was only a door. And somehow I knew it would lead me to Lark. Set me on a path back to The Realm of the Living where I was needed.

The handle burned bright as I turned the knob, opening into an overgrown path. Cold night air whipped at the thin material of my robe as my bare feet crunched dead leaves and twigs. Thorns bit into the soles of my feet but I barely felt the pain, too consumed by the impulse to run through the emaciated trees surrounding me.

My breath puffed in the air as I reached for the first of the mangled trunks. A rush of magic poured from my fingertips as the bark beneath my touch brightened, the dull gray transitioning into a rich brown. Brittle branches gave way to lush green leaves and red-orange blossoms. Plump, red fruit swelled as my power swept into the grove, the scent of fresh pomegranates filling the air.

My lungs heaved with the energy it took to revive them. My brow was damp and coated with sweat despite the frost. I wanted to return to bed, to curl up in Hades's arms, but I was compelled forward, spurred on by a whispered command urging me to hurry.

Newly strengthened branches clawed at my shoulders and legs as I moved, as if they too wanted me to turn back. Gusts of wind shook the leaves, hollowing in icy bursts as I pushed into the small clearing at the center of the grove, stumbling before a monstrous tree.

The trunk was easily as wide as I was tall with the center hollowed out and humming with power. The gnarled branches stretched high into the sky, its leaves a rich shade of green with a shimmering golden hue along the edges.

Whatever my magic had done for the rest of the grove, it was helpless here. This was an ancient site, a place that stood outside the scope of time and space. One that was here long before the power humming in my veins was even created.

Plump pomegranates rocked along the tree's lower branches as the wind raged. Shadows and ice knocking a few of the largest ones down. The fruit split open to coat thick, gnarled roots with scarlet juice and seeds.

My hair whirled around me as I clung to the edges of my robe and the fire opal around my neck, closing my eyes against the torrent of wind. When I blinked them open, my toes were positioned just before the hollowed trunk.

I fought for breath as my stomach twisted, my body teetering forward despite the cold dread sliding down my spine. My heart thundered in my ears, my legs trembling as I fought against the urge to step forward. Whatever waited on the other side felt desperate. A frenzied type of hunger that suggested it wanted to slice me open just to see what was on the inside.

An echo of my name carried on the wind, the deep cadence of the voice cutting through some of the fog clouding my mind.

Breathing deeply, I concentrated all my will on my legs and took a step back.

"I told Cyrus the compulsion wouldn't be enough. Even with Demeter's power amplifying the spell on your little charm."

The crystal around my neck burned, clouding my consciousness in a thick haze. It felt like time had slowed, like I was running through sand. I fought against the need to step through the tree's hollow, but then my world tilted.

Hands shoved against my side, sending me careening toward the vast darkness at the center of the hollowed tree buzzing with primal power.

A scream built in my chest as I caught a glimpse of the dark-haired woman who'd pushed me, and the tear-dropped diamond dangling from her wrist. She was the same woman who'd been seated across Hypnos's lap yesterday... and that bracelet. It was identical to the one adoring the wrist of the witch who'd been plotting my death with Cyrus.

I should have recognized the voice sooner. But it wasn't possible. Even if she were still alive, she'd never hurt me. We were friends—more like sisters.

Dark strands of her hair whirled around her as her blood-red lips tilted into a grin. "Time's up, Korae."

Her name was whispered in disbelief as I fell into the awaiting abyss. "Ruby?"

48

HADES

I woke to darkness, my heart hammering in my ears. The sheets were damp with sweat, every muscle in my body tensed and poised for a fight. All notions of sleep vanished as I rolled to the side, instinctively looking for Persephone only to find the bed cold. And Persephone gone.

A heavy weight settled in my stomach as my pulse spiked from a fear that was not my own.

Something was wrong. There may have been a time when she would have fled, but I knew to my very core that Persephone would never leave on her own. Not after all that we'd just shared. Persephone was my queen—my wife—and I intended to get her back.

In a wash of shadows and frost, I snatched my discarded pants and tunic from the floor, inhaling the traces of Persephone still clinging to the fabric. I followed her scent of vanilla and wildflowers now mixed with frost, like a forest on the verge of spring, and paused only as I reached a small corridor where Hecate was waiting.

"Persephone, she's—"

"Gone," Hecate answered, her face set in a grim frown. "I

wasn't sure, but I think a witch is compelling her, possibly through her necklace. I was on my way to your rooms when I caught a whiff of magic."

"Life magic?" I asked, leading the way down the narrow passage as I followed traces of my wife's scent.

"No," Hecate answered from behind me, her voice wavering with uncertainty. "It feels similar to The Night Children's compulsion but mixed with magic from The Realm of the Living."

"How is that possible," I seethed, the temperature around me cooling as Persephone's fear rattled through our loosely woven threads. If she were fully awakened, I'd be able to find her in a moment. Instead, I was forced to follow her trail, the next piece of the path only shimmering into view once I was near. "No one is allowed to cross into The Underworld if their threads have yet to be cut. I should have felt it."

"There is much that shouldn't be happening at the moment," Hecate said, keeping pace with me as I turned down a worn stone path that angled downward. We must be beneath The Dark Palace, having somehow found a connection to the lost tunnels. "If I were to guess, I'd say Demeter was behind this."

With a curse, I flitted through the darkness, stopping only when I came to an old wooden door. It squeaked on its hinges, the metal rusted and worn as it swayed in the wind. Soft light from the approaching dawn filtered in through the small opening. Persephone must have gone this way.

I burst through the door, the chipped wood splintering in my haste to catch her. I glanced around, searching for my queen. The Dark Palace was in the distance, its golden walls shimmering as the last of the stars faded overhead. Fresh grass sprang beneath my feet, the swath of green so at odds with the withered life surrounding it, evidence of Persephone's life magic, but my attention was snagged by the dark figure standing just to my left.

"Fine morning for a stroll through the grove, is it not?" Morpheus was wearing the same tunic from last night, but the edges were rumpled, and his dark hair disheveled as if he hadn't spent the night sleeping. He was relaxed, his hands loosely in his pockets and gaze fixed on the horizon—as if I wasn't moments away from killing him. "Especially with a heated fire opal to keep you warm."

"Where is she," I snarled, grabbing his throat.

He managed a smirk, his golden eyes ringed in red and sparking with mischief. "I always knew you'd be into airplay, My Lord, but we haven't agreed on a safe word."

My grip tightened, only to be stayed by Hecate's spark of magic around my wrist.

"He's fucking with you, Hades. We can't afford a war with Hypnos."

Morpheus's smile grew, revealing a hint of fangs despite his toes barely grazing the ground. "Don't tell me there's someone else you'd rather have your hands on, Dark God."

My eyes narrowed as my jaw clenched. "I will not ask again."

"Hades," Hecate breathed, her eyes wide with horror. "The grove. Persephone is in the grove."

Morpheus crumpled to the ground as I turned, following Hecate's gaze. The once decaying trees were flourishing, their vibrant branches heavy with plump pomegranates.

"No," I breathed, realizing what awaited at the heart of the grove. Dense clouds heavy with shadows and frost darkened the skies overhead as true terror gripped me for the first time. I was humble enough to be wary of The Hollow, to realize that even a being such as myself couldn't control whatever force governed it. "This is Demeter's doing. It must be."

"But you two are already married," Hecate said, her eyes snagging on the dark crown glinting between my ram horns, no doubt realizing Persephone must have her own display of power atop her head. "Demeter might try to force her to choose the Earth Coven, but she's already married to you. She can't bind Persephone to Cyrus, meaning—"

"The High Matriarch can't lay claim to all of the little goddess's powers," Morpheus said, his hands in his pockets as he stepped to my side.

"If Persephone reaches The Hollow, if that bitch gets her hands on her..." Hecate swallowed as the color drained from her face.

"She'll kill her."

49

HADES

I WAS ALREADY MOVING BEFORE THE THOUGHT OF PERSEPHONE'S death could take hold. A storm born of death magic and vengeance swirled overhead as I dashed through the trees. My wings were helpless here. The grove was far too dense to see through from above, but the branches seemed to whisk me forward as I ran, guiding me toward the center. Toward Persephone.

She was close. So close. I could feel her panic—her *fear*.

"Persephone!" I bellowed, catching a glimpse of The Hollow up ahead. I threw my magic out in a torrent of icy wind in an attempt to slow Persephone down, willing the trees to pull her back to me. But the compulsion gripping her was strong, far too strong to have been placed by a stranger. She was being led to The Realm of the Living—to her death—by someone she knew. Someone she trusted.

"Time's up, Korae."

The voice slashed through the air as I stepped into the clearing. The Hollow was as powerful as ever. It was ancient, one of the first creations of this world. Some had used it as a portal between our worlds, but each passing was a risk. The great tree was connected to more than the space between The Realm of the Living and The Underworld.

And Persephone was falling right into it.

I felt the moment her life passed from my realm. The second she was taken from me. The frantic, beating muscle in my chest squeezed, my pulse freezing as I raced forward, waiting for her essence to reemerge in The Realm of the Living.

There was a blur of dark hair following Persephone into The Hollow—the witch who'd lured Persephone here. I reached out, intent on seizing her, to make her death as slow and agonizingly painful as possible, but The Hollow flared with magic just as my fingers wrapped around the ends of her hair.

I was thrown back as light seared from the open crevice in the trunk. My body slammed into the ground, gnarled roots and freshly sprouted grass breaking my fall. A dull throb ached across my ribs. It felt like half of my body had been scorched by the sun, but all I could focus on was the dark strands of singed hair clutched in my fingers—And the strong beating of my heart.

Persephone was alive.

Branches snapped in the distance, the sound of racing footsteps growing louder. I fought for breath pushing to my knees as I felt the effects of soothing magic working to heal me.

Persephone's life magic was racing through my veins, our marriage allowing our powers to be shared. If she lived to see her awakening, our magic would be forever entwined and her life tethered to that of an immortal god. She would have both my power and my immortal soul protecting her.

I only hoped Demeter was arrogant enough to think she could somehow still claim her daughter's magic for herself.

"Gods below," Hecate panted. "She's gone."

I glanced up, finding her wide-eyed gaze fixed to the tree behind me as I dragged my body into a standing position. Half of my tunic was charred, the skin beneath it blistered and raw, but the pain had dulled. "She made it to The Realm of the Living."

Hecate's chest heaved as she swallowed. The air still pricked with electricity as the veins in the massive tree shimmered with power. The hollow crevice at its base was sealed with tortuous vines, making it impossible to follow even if I dared.

I turned away from the grove, needing to return to The Dark Palace and find a way of reaching my wife before anything happened to her.

"Who did this?" Hecate asked.

I shook my head as I offered her the strands of hair clasped between my fingers. "A witch. I couldn't see her face, but I have no doubt a tracking spell would lead us to Demeter."

Hecate nodded, taking the strands from my hand, before falling in step beside me. "I can't travel to The Realm of the Living until midnight when Persephone is awakened and the balance is restored, but I think I understand how she was controlled."

"How?"

"Did she ever tell you why she jumped from the cliffs of Cocytus? Or why she fled even after you'd told her about her role in restoring balance?"

I shook my head, jaw ticking as I waited for Hecate to continue.

"She felt an overwhelming urge to save her friend, Larkspur. At first, I thought it was misplaced guilt for not saving her childhood friend, a witch who Demeter killed at her awakening, but now I'm not so sure.

"She's never gone without her necklace—the fire opal. Even when she sleeps. You said yourself, those from The Realm of the Living can't cross into The Underworld without risking the fates' wrath. Demeter wouldn't take that risk, but I think she had a curse placed on Persephone's necklace. Persephone would be returned to the coven—"

"And Demeter would be safe from the fates," I finished, running a hand through my hair as I passed among the pomegranates. Scarlet stains littered the ground, seeds and juice spilling from the slaughtered fruit. "She'll try to claim Persephone's power, at least what remains to be claimed."

"I can track her."

My gaze narrowed on her. "Persephone had no personal effects here. Even her clothes—"

"I took a link from her necklace when I was inspecting it," Hecate said. "I had my suspicions, and when Persephone refused to leave it with me, I took matters into my own hands."

Hecate lifted the dark strands of hair, her lips pressing into a thin line. I watched as worry melted away, leaving only burning anger in its wake. Hecate was the mother of all witches, a teacher, a friend… but when those she cared for were in danger she transformed into the most ruthless of monsters. She was a woman who knew no fear—no limits—when it came to protecting those she loved.

"Between the gold link and the connection you've already started, the charm will lead you to her."

But I heard the uncertainty dripping from her voice. The poorly veiled fear that Demeter wouldn't bother keeping Persephone alive once she laid eyes upon the golden crown shimmering on her head.

"Hurry."

50

PERSEPHONE

THE FIRST THING I WAS AWARE OF WAS THE THROBBING PAIN IN MY head and the cold floor against my cheek. My body was stiff, the rough stone doing little to ease the soreness in my muscles. There was a trickle of wetness clinging to my brow, the fluid still warm. It wasn't until I blinked my eyes open that I realized it was blood.

I pressed onto my forearms, the small movement causing the world to tilt as I squinted against the late morning light streaking in through the bars.

Bars?

Gods Above, I was in a dungeon. And not just any dungeon... this place felt familiar. I could sense the forest beyond the stone walls. I could hear their pine branches swaying in a gentle morning breeze and could practically smell the wildflowers a few paces further. I was in The Realm of the Living, trapped and caged like an animal by the very coven I'd grown up with. The Earth Coven had found me.

Dozens of witches had been sacrificed for Demeter's greed. I had no intention of joining them. Gingerly, I sat up, allowing the pads of my fingers to trace the gash along my temple still trickling blood. It throbbed and a large knot had formed, but Lark always said swelling on the outside was better than on the inside.

Lark.

She was probably trapped down here, too. Maybe I'd be able to find her. Together, we might get out of this alive.

Fighting off the wave of nausea that threatened to upturn my stomach, I forced myself into a standing position. The world tilted and I stumbled, clutching the thin scraps of my silk robe together in an attempt to find warmth. A sheen of sweat coated my brow with the effort it took, but I steadied myself against the rough wall. I let my magic search, slowly combing over each stone of my prison. There was always a weak point. I only needed to find it.

There. It was nothing but a small crack in the mortar, but I could feel the flicker of life humming within. Deep tree roots hovered on the other side. I coaxed my magic onward, wishing I could speed up time and be a fully awakened witch.

Voices came from the hall, forcing me to abandon my efforts. I dropped into a sitting position, pressing my back against the crack that I'd formed a moment before they entered.

"Look what we have here." The arrogant tone of Cyrus's voice grated on my nerves, but I forced my chin up as he came into view. His long blond hair was tied back, highlighting his sharp cheekbones and pale skin. He wore a dark green tunic and matching pants with his sword hanging from his hip—the closest thing to battle leathers that I'd seen him in.

He wanted my fear. Like Demeter, he was used to controlling others by it. He was nothing but a green witch—a grounder. I should have been able to stand a chance even if my powers weren't fully awakened.

The amused smile splashed across his face shifted to rage as his light blue eyes landed on the shimmering crown upon my head. I didn't want to fear Cyrus. Or Demeter. I wanted to prove that they hadn't broken me, that I was a witch—a queen to The Underworld—and capable of handling so much more than them. But the unfiltered hatred blaring down at me through Cyrus's eyes had my pulse quickening, despite myself.

"Ruby was right. Our little Korae is nothing but a filthy whore."

"My name is Persephone."

"I see you've been listening to Hades's lies," Cyrus scoffed. "Your mother was right to keep you away from him—"

"That bitch is not my mother," I seethed, jumping to my feet. My heartbeat thundered in my ears as my vision spotted, but I planted my feet and glared at Cyrus with every ounce of hatred I could muster. "She's the reason magic between The Realm of the Living and The Underworld is out of balance. *Demeter* is the reason death magic has attacked countless towns, killed hundreds of innocents."

Cyrus barked a laugh, the harsh sound echoing off the stone walls. "You're crazier than I thought. The Dark Faction drains life from The Realm of the Living, Korae. You're just too stupid to realize Hades used you."

"No," I breathed, feeling the sting of my magic gather at my fingertips, only the power felt different. It felt colder, like the type of burn that only comes from the darkest, bitterest frost. "Hades has been trying to save our realms."

"He told you what you wanted to hear to convince you to fuck him," Cyrus snapped.

"I didn't need convincing."

"You fucking whore," snarled Cyrus, baring his teeth as he gripped the hilt of his sword. It looked like he meant to silence me once and for all.

"Don't," a feminine voice said. Her fingers appeared from the shadows behind Cyrus, wrapping around his wrist to stop him from drawing his blade.

A chill ran down my spine as my stomach twisted. I'd

expected to see the tear-drop diamond along Ruby's wrist, the dark tendrils of her hair, but her wrist was bare. A swath of forest-green fabric covered her body, the hood drawn low to conceal her identity. The same cloak I'd seen dozens of times. Instinctively, I took a step back on trembling legs, my body seeming to process what my mind refused to believe.

"She's been bewitched by Lord Hades, but she may yet be useful."

"No," I whispered as her voice washed over me. A voice that had promised to run away with me. One that had sacrificed herself to *protect* me.

"I can feel her power already. Despite marriage being off the table, she might yet pledge her gifts to the Earth Coven, strengthening us against The Dark Faction."

She waited for Cyrus to nod, for his blue eyes tinged with the same glazed look I'd seen on a dozen others when she used her forbidden gifts.

And then the hood fell back, and Lark turned to face me.

51

PERSEPHONE

"Hello, Persephone."

"Lark?" Her name left my lips as she turned. Umber curls tumbled free as her pleading hazel eyes met mine. Here I was racked with guilt for not saving her, and all the while Lark had been working with Cyrus. Gods above, did that mean she'd been working with Demeter this entire time, too? "Have you been spying on me?"

"Finally catching up, are you?" Cyrus sneered over Lark's shoulder, his hand still gripped on the hilt of his sword.

The unbridled hatred in his eyes should worry me. Nothing was as dangerous as a self-righteous narcissus who knew he would avoid any and all consequences for his actions. Though I'd wed Hades, our thread was not yet sealed. I was still mortal.

A flick of Cyrus's wrist, a well-placed strike, and I'd be done. But death—returning to The Underworld as a spirit—might be preferable to knowing that my entire relationship with Lark had been a lie. A set up from Demeter to keep me in line.

All those times we'd snuck out, the late nights we'd spent talking, divulging our deepest, most earnest wishes for what our lives might one day be if we could escape the coven and carve out a bit of happiness in this lifetime. All of it—had been a lie. A ploy devised by Demeter to better control me. Lark's gentleness and kind words had been nothing more than kindling for my birthday pyre set to light in a few hours.

I'd been entirely alone my whole life without a soul who'd loved me.

Except for Hades.

Everything else might be a lie, but not him. Not my God of The Underworld. My demon.

I needed to stay alive for him, for each and every soul in The Underworld and The Realm of the Living who were counting on balance being restored.

"Hades may be a lot of things—vengeful, merciless, the embodiment of death magic—but he is not a liar." Disgust curled my upper lip as my gaze bounced between Lark and Cyrus.

"Keep telling yourself that, Korae." Cyrus's gaze roved over the thin fabric of my robe, each swipe of his eyes making me feel dirty. "It was the necklace."

"Cyrus," Lark warned but she might as well have been talking to the wind.

"That's how dear, little Larkspur controlled you."

"I had this long before Lark." I clasped the fire opal in my palm, shaking my head. "I claimed this stone in the caves of The Crystal City when I was just a child."

"Yes, but Lark was able to link her stone to yours," Cyrus grinned, enjoying my agony. "She waited patiently, biding her time over the years as she earned your trust. Trust is needed to ensure the bond between the two necklaces was strong, giving our dark witch the ability to channel her magic through it."

My eyes widened, tears already gathering at their edges as I turned toward Lark. Her face was a mask of control, but she didn't deny anything he said. *Gods above.*

"You compelled me to return here? After everything you saw them do to me, all the promises we made of escaping... *Why?* Why help me escape only to force me right back to where it all started?"

The necklace had felt special, the one thing in this world that was just mine. That was meant for me... but even that had been twisted, tainted and warped for Demeter's benefit. Chest heaving, I yanked the opal, snapping the gold chain and throwing it at Lark's feet.

"You've taken everything from me. You might as well have this, too."

Lark flinched as the chain rattled, looking as if she might bend to pick up the fire opal, but her spine stiffened as Cyrus turned. He came up behind her, wrapping his arms around Lark's waist as if he'd done it countless times before. Bile burned the back of my throat as nausea threatened. Was she sleeping with him?

"All you had to do was stay put for a few more weeks," Cyrus said, his lips brushing the back of Lark's neck. Her nostrils flared, but she didn't push him away. Didn't compel him to stop. "All of this could have been avoided. No matter. Once Demeter is done with you, you're mine. I'll have you beneath me, Korae, one way or another."

He dragged his tongue up the side of Lark's neck. "I wonder if she'll scream my name as prettily as you did, Larkspur."

"Everyone dies," I said, my voice low and steady. "And when you do, my husband will be waiting."

The air pricked with energy, and I could have sworn Lark's eyes flashed black, but then she turned, running her hands along Cyrus's chest to link behind his neck. He gripped her ass, pulling her body flush with his as she leaned forward to whisper in his ear.

"Such vision," Lark cooed, the sweetness of her voice turning my stomach. "Demeter is lucky to have you at her side, Cyrus.

Not many men of your caliber would be content waiting for her when we have everything we need to move forward, but you're different."

"Gross," I muttered. Lark flashed me an irritated glare as Cyrus's attention snapped to me, but she was speaking again before I could respond.

"She's promised you High Patriarch of the coven, hasn't she? A position just as powerful as her own."

Cyrus's eyes started to glaze over as he nodded.

"Demeter will need guidance on what it means to share power. Reminders that your time is just as valuable as hers. She's lucky she found a partner as humble as you. Someone willing to bow to her timeframe."

Lark's fingers roved through his hair, caressing the sides of his face, his temples, until Cyrus pushed her away. The bars of my cell rattled as Lark connected with them, but Cyrus didn't seem to notice. Her chest heaved, but she was moving before Cyrus realized what she was doing.

"Demeter and Ruby should be here," he growled.

"They should," Lark whispered, matching the urgency in his voice as she captured his hands.

"We have twelve hours until Korae's magic awakens. We should've already started bleeding her."

Bleeding me? Fuck, that didn't sound good.

"You're right," Lark said in the same soft tone. Her compulsion was working, but I couldn't figure out why. "You're always right, Lord Cyrus."

"I'm going to find them and demand they return. We can't afford to lose this much magic."

Lark nodded. "Show them that a High Patriarch waits for no one."

With that, Cyrus dashed from the room. Lark slumped against the bars of my cell, evidence of how powerful that spell must have been.

Before she could think of running, I wrapped my arm around her neck and squeezed.

52

PERSEPHONE

"Tell me what the fuck is going on, Lark," I said, easing up on the pressure around her throat so that she could answer.

"Gods above, Persephone." Lark tapped on my forearm that was currently pressed against her larynx. "When did you get so aggressive."

"When my only friend compelled me away from my husband in the middle of the night and then delivered me to a coven intent on murdering me." I seethed, tightening my grip and forcing her shoulders back. "Especially after learning Ruby, in fact, wasn't killed by Demeter. Like you, she's been apparently plotting my death for years."

The silence stretched between us for a long moment before she spoke. "The key to your cell is in my left pocket. Cyrus won't be gone for long, and I can see we have a lot to talk about."

My pulse was rapid and weak, and my vision had started to spot, but I kept my forearm around her neck as I slipped my other hand into her pocket. A key was there, just as she said. "Open it."

She turned; her cheek pressed to the bars as her fingers

worked the metal into the lock. There was a click and the door swung open.

Lark looked at me for the first time, her eyes snagging on the stain of blood that matted my hair and dripped down the side of my face, before shifting to the golden crown shimmering across my head. It was faint, a ghost of what it would be, but it was all the proof she needed.

"Did he force you?"

I made to move out of the cell, but she stepped in front of me, blocking my path. My aching muscles tensed for a fight, despite being on the verge of passing out. Cyrus could return any moment with Ruby and Demeter in tow. If I was still here when they arrived, I wouldn't survive.

"Hades didn't force me to do anything. *You* did."

She flinched, the reflexive movement causing my brows to furrow.

"I did use the necklace to channel my compulsion," Lark started. I lifted my chin, pressing my lips shut as I waited for her to continue. I was wasting time listening to her, but I needed to understand why she'd betrayed me. "And I did compel you to return to The Realm of the Living."

"Were you ever a friend to me? Do you even really have a sister or was that a lie, too?"

"Yes," Lark breathed, and I wanted to believe her. "The things we talked about, our hopes for the future, that was all real. But... Demeter did have me spy on you."

My nostrils flared as that icy fire tingled along the pads of my fingers. Lark lifted a brow at the display of magic, hastily rushing through her explanation.

"I only ever told her what I needed to in order to keep my sister alive. I *hate* Demeter. And Cyrus. I hate all of them more than you can imagine. If you believe nothing else, believe that." Her chest heaved as she held my gaze.

"Then why drag me back here knowing I'll be killed?" My

voice broke as the extent of her betrayal sunk in. "You may like getting fucked by Cyrus, but I sure as shit—"

"Don't you dare judge me," Lark snapped, anger and humiliation flashing across her face. "You have no idea what I've had to do to survive here, to win back their trust while you were playing princess in The Underworld."

Her cheeks flared a deep red, her eyes blazing. My heart cracked as I felt the truth of her words ring in the air between us. I wanted to comfort her, the way I might have done if we were still friends, but she'd brought me here to be slaughtered. Whatever we had once had, I could no longer trust her.

"They showed me where the ground had split. Where Hades had taken you. All the stories said he was pure evil. Even my mother's family warned against his ruthlessness." Lark frowned, her gaze flicking up to my crown. "I thought I was saving you from a worse fate. I can see now that I was wrong."

"You're saying you did this for my own good?" I laughed, the humorless sound hanging between us.

"Partly. But I would have brought you back even if I'd known you were happy."

"Unbelievable," I huffed, attempting again to leave. Lark blocked me. Despite the amount of magic she'd used, she looked like she could go a few more rounds.

"For my sister to live. To be free of Demeter, I'd sell my body and soul ten times over."

The silence stretched between us as the air buzzed with magic. Irritation shifted to unease as I realized she wasn't going to let me out of here.

"Lark, listen to me." My pulse was racing, the ache in my head pounding with each beat, but I couldn't afford to appear weak. Not when it looked like Lark was seconds away from following through on her promise to Demeter. "As soon as my magic is awakened, we can take on Demeter together. I'll help you find your sister. Hades will help, too."

Lark only shook her head, lifting her hand as she took a slow step toward me. "Demeter has my sister, Persephone. She'll be released from her imprisonment if I deliver you before your awakening. Demeter wants you to pledge your magic to The Earth Coven."

"That's never going to happen." I fought to keep my voice steady as I stepped further into the cell, trying to maintain space between us. One brush of her fingers on my skin and she would send her compulsion through me. "My magic is the one thing that can save our realms. If I pledge it to anything other than restoring balance, death magic will continue to spiral out of control and destroy both The Realm of the Living and The Underworld."

"My little sister has been trapped for nearly four years. She was young and naive, too gentle and far too good for this world. I can't pass up my last chance to save her."

"Lark, please," I pleaded as my back hit the cold stone. There was nowhere to run. I was cornered, but I wouldn't go down without a fight. "Don't make me do this."

"I promise I'll stop Demeter before she can harm you." Lark's voice dripped with regret, but it wasn't enough to sway her decision. "I love you, Persephone. Your friendship was one of the few good things in my life, but I must protect my sister. I've already failed her once."

Having no other option, I reached for the pricks of magic along my fingertips, sending it out in a torrent of shadows aimed at Lark's chest. I darted to the side as her screams filled the dungeon. My heart leapt as I rushed toward the hallway, desperately trying to ignore the bile burning the back of my throat.

Lark's fingers dug into my shoulder before I reached it, jerking my body back into hers. Her other hand was around my throat before I could utter a word.

"You don't want to fight me, Persephone. I'm your friend.

We're like sisters."

No. No. No. I knew she was using compulsion; I could feel the fog closing in around me, but this was so much stronger than anything we'd played at before.

"Please," I tried to beg, but only a whisper fell from my lips.

"Shh, it's going to be alright."

A whimper escaped me as she turned my head to look into her eyes. I couldn't stifle the scream that tore from my throat as I gazed upon the bloodied, raw tissue along her cheek and chest.

The shadows I'd sent after her had eaten away the skin, gnawing and burning tissue with their touch—the power of death magic. But the raw, blistered muscle and tendons were already healing—much too fast for that of a normal witch. My eyes widened as I met her gaze, finding her irises ringed in scarlet... just like the eyes of The Night Children before they fed.

"Do you see why this is my only chance?" Lark said softly. "I'm punished for my magic. For something I had no control over. Demeter will never free me as long as my mother's magic runs in my veins, but my little sister isn't like me. She has a chance at a real life. The chance we never got to take."

My knees weakened, causing my body to sag against her. Lark caught me, easing my listless body to the ground.

"Don't worry, Persephone. Sleep."

It felt like I was caught in the strongest current. I was fighting with all my might to stay in the shallows, to remain on shore, but the tide was too strong. My eyelids closed as my mind drifted, forgetting why I'd been so worried in the first place.

"You'll see. I can save us all."

53

HADES

"WHERE IS THANATOS?" I GROWLED, PACING THE LENGTH OF Hecate's room as she finished with the amplification spell. Everything was taking way too fucking long.

"I sent Medea to search for him," Hecate said as her brows pinched with concern. "No one has seen him since he left to trail Hypnos."

"He's been gone all night?" I asked. She nodded. "We could bring Morpheus in. I'd be happy to put him through a round of questioning."

Slamming my fist into his smug face sounded incredible. I needed to do something. Anything. I couldn't stand another moment of waiting around while Hecate worked. I had tried to return to The Realm of the Living without her help, to the forest I'd first taken her from, but the path was blocked. I was trapped here, just like the rest of the miserable souls. Everything now relied on Hecate's ability to override the death magic gripping our realm and allow me passage.

"Torturing Morpheus won't help, Hades." Hecate set down the amulet containing the golden link from Persephone's necklace in favor of the moonstone.

"It would help *me*," I grumbled as she placed the opalescent stone in a small basin filled with clear water and obsidian shards.

"We can't afford a war with Hypnos," Hecate repeated around a weary sigh. "And there's no evidence he's connected to Persephone's abduction."

I lifted a skeptical brow in her direction as she chanted over the water, sprinkling its surface with a mixture of mint, nettle, and comfrey. "Someone powerful enough blocked all movement between the realms. Beside my siblings in The Above, there aren't many who can wield such power. And we both know only Hypnos would risk a slight of that magnitude."

Her brows furrowed as the spell completed, the moonstone flushing to a shimmering bluish glow as Hecate retrieved it. The light within flickered and then died, just like the others. Hecate deflated, her face falling as she stared at yet another failed spell.

"If Hypnos is working with Demeter, if the two of them are powerful enough to ward off the realms and steal our queen... nothing I do will work."

My spine stiffened. "You're the mother of all witches—of all magic in The Realm of the Living. You'll be able to break whatever enchantment they've placed."

"Not if Hypnos blended his power with Demeter's. Especially this close to the awakening. Until Persephone's power manifests and she swears herself to you, magic will continue to spiral out of control, making it harder to wield." Hecate shook her head. "The only person who will be able to cross is..."

"Thanatos!" A feminine voice called from the hall. My head snapped to her echoing footsteps, her silhouette darkening the door of Hecate's laboratory a moment later. "Lady Hecate, Thanatos has just returned. And he needs your help."

~

"THANATOS," HECATE CALLED AS HER KNUCKLES RAPPED AGAINST the wooden door. She'd done all she could for me. A location spell confirmed Persephone was with the Earth Coven, but each of Hecate attempts at breaking the barrier between our realms had failed. We needed Thanatos.

Silence answered her.

There were lingering hints of cinnamon in the air, a telltale sign of Thanatos's magic, but it was tainted with something sharp and foul. My body tensed as I recognized the smell of metallic tang doused in smoke—The Night Children.

Pushing past Hecate as she made to knock again, I burst through the door and swept into the room. My magic gathered at my fingertips, ready for a fight, as I flung my shadows out. But there was only Thanatos alone and bare before his floor-length mirror.

His pale body was streaked in red, the scarlet stains coming from what appeared to be dozens of bite marks and fingernails. His once pristine feathers were matted with patches of coagulated blood, the russet brown blending with bright red patches. Purple bruises had started to form, peppering his back and thighs with evidence of what he'd endured.

Thanatos's great wings closed around him as he turned to face us. A few feathers broke free, drifting to the floor as I gaped. The worst of the cuts and claw marks had a clear ointment applied over them, but even with his healing, they looked painful. My breathing hitched as I registered the haunted look in his eyes—one borne of anger, grief, and a flicker of shame.

Swallowing against the wave of bile burning my throat and the urge to slaughter every member of Hypnos's cursed kingdom, I focused on Thanatos and took a cautious step forward.

"Was this Hypnos's doing?"

"In part," Thanatos answered, this throat bobbing. His tongue swept out, licking his split lip. "The woman that was with him at the ball, she's a witch capable of astral-projection.

Hypnos asked her to wait for him in The Night Forest while he bathed. I should have known it was a trap."

"The Night Children?" Hecate asked, her voice shaking with fury as she peered around my shoulder. I fought to contain the darkness billowing out, but frost cracked across the windows as the temperature in the room dropped.

Thanatos's wings hitched higher, tucking close around himself as he met Hecate's worried gaze. "The Night Children's Southern Faction."

"An entire faction?" Hecate gasped, her eyes going wide.

My fists clenched as Thanatos nodded once more. He'd been taken, *used*, by over a hundred Night Children. Judging by the placement of his wounds, I'd bet my soul he was used for more than just blood.

Ice crystalized against the floors and walls as my wings snapped wide. I was already at the window, shadows gathering around me before Thanatos's voice stilled me.

"They're dead."

My spine stiffened as I turned to face him, but this time there was a fire kindling in his gaze. It grew as he spoke, smoldering with hatred and righteous retribution.

"All of them. They took everything from me..." His voice broke as tears pricked at the corners of his eyes. "Teeth and claws. Knives. They drank and fucked until I was nothing but an empty vessel. Until I was rendered limp, too drained to even keep my eyes open."

My nostrils flared as my body shook with the need to slaughter them. To hunt down each of their miserable souls and resurrect them just so I could peel each layer of skin from their body. I needed to hear their screams and pleas of mercy, only to find newer, crueler ways to punish them.

And I would.

"They didn't realize the God of Death couldn't die." Thanatos lifted his chin, seeing the rage play across my features.

"I waited until enough of my strength had returned, until the horde of them were satiated, drunk off my body and blood... And then I tore them apart."

"Good," Hecate said, her body trembling nearly as much as mine. "I'll fetch you a tonic to regenerate your health. As much as I'd enjoy condemning each and every forsaken soul responsible for harming you right now, we need your help. We think Demeter and Hypnos have been working together. They've managed to seal the passages between realms."

Thanatos's gaze snapped to mine. "Persephone?"

I stared into his eyes, hating that I had to place this upon his shoulders after everything he'd been through. Because I knew he would tuck every piece of his agony away to save her. To help me. With a deep breath, I forced the words from my lips.

"She's been taken."

54

PERSEPHONE

DEMETER'S SHRILL VOICE CUT THROUGH THE FOG OF MY MIND, rousing my consciousness despite my sluggish body. I forced my breathing to remain even, controlling each rise and fall of my chest as I willed my pulse to stay calm. Maybe I'd be able to overhear something that would get me out of this mess.

"You will never summon me, Cyrus. You may hold a title once we are through, but the power will remain with me as the High Matriarch. I can't take any chances after what happened to Ruby."

"I thought she would have returned when Perseph—Korae—did. I didn't realize..."

"Of course you didn't," Demeter snapped.

The sounds of her heavy footfalls vibrated across the stone floor, louder than the shifting slippers behind her. I dared to open my eyes, looking between thick lashes to glimpse the two witches at her back. Both were clad in olive-colored tunics with light features—green witches. Regardless of Cyrus being head of their coven, they looked ready to carry out whatever command Demeter issued.

"Hypnos will be furious that Ruby's soul is lost."

"Forgive me High Matriarch," Lark said, her voice alone causing my stomach to twist. "But perhaps it's a good thing Ruby didn't return. She believed she was next in line for your position as head of our coven, and though she was loyal to you, even the most patient person has their limit."

"True," Demeter mused, and I could practically hear an evil grin tilting her lips. "Astral-projection always has its risks, doesn't it?"

"Always," Lark said, matching her tone.

Lark had betrayed me. *Compelled* me. Just like Ruby. Just like the woman I'd called a mother for twenty years. I'd wanted to believe I wasn't alone in this life. That Ruby had really been my friend once-upon-a-time, or that Lark and I would've managed to escape the coven all together. I needed to believe someone cared... And maybe I was hoping for someone to rescue me, to see my struggles and take it upon themselves to fix my world. For someone *else* to fight my battles.

But I realized that I didn't need anyone.

Hades would always love me. I believed that to my core. He was probably on his way right now to slaughter all of them, and while that soothed the edges of my battered heart, I knew that *I* had all the power I would ever need to rescue myself.

I was my own savior. Wife to Lord Hades. Goddess of The Underworld. *I* was the key to restoring balance between our realms. The strongest earth witch in centuries. It was time to show them who Queen Persephone really was.

I let Hades's magic gather at the tips of my fingers, felt the swell of power accumulate as I feigned sleep, listening to the three of them talk.

"You've proven useful, Larkspur," Demeter said. "You need only compel my daughter to pledge her magic to The Earth Coven when the clock strikes midnight, and your sister will be free."

"Then, Korae will be mine," Cyrus added as the temperature

dropped around me. Frost grew on the stones beneath my cheek, webbing out from my hands.

"Yes, yes," Demeter said. "Korae will be yours to use however you like in a matter of minutes. As soon as Larkspur secures her magic."

I'll never be used by anyone again, I thought as I rolled to my knees and aimed all my gathered magic through the bars toward the woman who dared to call me 'daughter'.

The shadows struck right above her chest, gnawing away at a barrier surrounding her. The rest of the shadows ricocheted, splintering off to hit the two witches behind her.

"No," I breathed, my head spinning as I watched death magic claim them. I didn't feel bad for ending their lives, only for the power that it had cost me.

Their skin thinned, burning away in great, gaping swaths. Deafening screams erupted from the witches as muscle and fat were exposed, giving way to tendons and bone beneath. Death magic continued eating away at them, obliterating every fiber of their being, until their cries of agony subsided. And only dust remained.

Demeter had used them as a shield, their energy deflecting the brunt of my magic. I'd failed and lost the element of surprise. A cold sweat coated my brow as my vision spotted. That strike had taken everything from me.

I panted for breath on my hands and knees, searching for any remaining tendrils of magic that I could use. Reaching for *anything* that might save me from Demeter's wrath. But only smoke remained.

A few hours more and I would've been awakened with a vast well of power at my fingertips. My life thread would have been sealed to Hades; my soul tethered to his in every possible way. I would've been immortal.

But midnight had not yet come. I was weak and powerless before Demeter. Just as I'd always been.

"You dare wield filthy death magic against *me*? After everything I've done for you. Everything I've sacrificed." Fury sparked in Demeter's eyes, the flames of hatred growing wildered as they flicked across the crown shimmering atop my head. Her vicious gaze locked with mine as the buzz of her power grew. The fine hairs on my arms rose as electricity pricked.

"Get her," Cyrus growled. Each word dripped with promised revenge, causing my stomach to twist. He would punish me for killing the green witches, but I couldn't think about that, now. Not when Demeter looked like she might finish me off before he got the chance.

Lark's gaze bounced between us, and I could have sworn there was genuine worry in her eyes. "High Matriarch, please let me—"

Demeter threw her hands out, the force of her spell colliding with the metal bars of my cell. The wall cracked and fissured along the edge, until the bars fell forward with a loud clang.

"I always knew you were a whore, Persephone," Demeter seethed as she took another step forward.

"Please," Lark said, stepping before her with a low bow. "Don't trouble yourself with retrieving her. Allow me."

Demeter's spine stiffened as her lips pressed thin but whatever protection she'd once carried had dissolved when the witches had died. Her shrewd gaze swept over me—over my crown—and she gave a small, tight nod.

Lark wasted no time. She swept into my cell, stepping over the rubble and displaced bars until she was kneeling at my side.

"No," I breathed, scrambling back from her touch.

I could feel a shift in the atmosphere, practically taste the magic waiting to enter my body. Midnight was near. I was so close to freedom, to having the power to change *everything*.

My fingers sparked as shadows gathered, but Lark's hands gripped my wrist before I could wield them.

"Don't fight." The power of her compulsion rippled through

me, sapping the last of my managed strength. She leaned down, brushing bloodstained curls back from my brow to whisper in my ear. "As soon as I have my sister, we *will* destroy them, just like we always said we would. Trust me."

But I didn't trust her.

Lark slipped her arm around my middle, dragging my limp, useless body out of the darkness of the cell. And as my legs scraped across crumbled stone and displaced bars, I couldn't help but feel like Demeter had already won.

55

PERSEPHONE

THE MOMENT MY BODY CRASHED TO THE COLD STONE AT Demeter's feet, a golden circle shimmered into being. A sharp inhale sounded behind me as the gilded light surrounded Lark and Demeter in a brilliant halo, linking the two of them before fading.

"Our bargain is complete," Lark breathed, her voice dipping in disbelief.

Demeter rolled her neck as she surveyed me, her lip curled in disgust. My pulse was frantic, but I couldn't fight. Not with Lark's compulsion gripping me.

"Lift her," Demeter said.

Cyrus stepped forward, pulling me into a standing position. Demeter's hand lashed out, striking my cheek hard enough to send me sprawling across the stone floor. A high-pitched ringing sounded in my ears as the world spun. My lungs heaved as I ignored the throbbing in my head and concentrated on taking my next breath.

Hecate's magic was near, waiting until I was able to accept it. Just a little longer and I would be free—

Demeter's foot connected with my stomach, my body rolling

as the metallic taste of blood coated my tongue. Each breath caused a sharp spike of pain on my left side, probably a fractured rib.

"Don't break her," Cyrus grumbled. "I don't want to wait before I have my fun."

Bile burned the back of my throat as my stomach twisted. I'd kill myself before I let him touch me.

"Such power wasted on someone so weak." Demeter prowled forward, light collecting at her fingertips as magic swelled in the air. I felt my own body reaching for power, like a dam on the verge of breaking. "It's time, Larkspur. Compel her to pledge her magic to The Earth Coven."

"Where is my sister?" Lark asked.

My pulse thundered in my ears as currents of electricity coursed through my veins. I rolled to my side, feeling my body heal under the hum of power. I had seconds—seconds—until I was able to claim my power. Lark stepped in front of me, shielding me from Demeter's view.

The High Matriarch's gaze snapped to her, her upper lip curling. "Our bargain was for that little brat to go free."

"She is not here." Lark's fists clenched as swirls of darkness gathered.

"I never said anything about delivering her to you," Demeter sneered. "Good luck finding your way to The Underworld."

"No." The word fell from Lark's lips as she drew back.

"Yes," Demeter said, her eyes narrowing. "And I'll do worse to you if you don't compel Persephone this instant."

Lark swallowed, her throat bobbing. For one moment, I thought she would refuse, but then she unclenched her fists and knelt beside me. One of her hands brushed hair away from my damp brow, like a mother soothing a frightened child. I wanted to scream, to fight, but she'd taken away my ability to do anything but comply.

Her hazel eyes were lined with tears, as I felt the familiar weight of my fire opal settle against my chest. "This is your true conduction stone. Wield it as you please."

Her compulsion broke immediately.

"You ungrateful bitch," Demeter snarled. "Cyrus!"

He rushed to her side, grabbing her hand as he grounded her. The charge of magic grew as the earth rumbled. Heeding Cyrus's call, the stone floor split and fresh musty soil appeared. Gnarled roots and torturous horned vines whipped toward Lark in vicious lashes. Her skin split beneath their assault, fresh drops of blood spraying the ground as she fought to get away.

Her shoulders bowed as she screamed, her own magic rising to meet Demeter's challenge. Streaks of shadow covered her body, whisking her away to the edge of the room in a wash of night.

I used the distraction to get to my feet. My head was throbbing, and my ribs were sore, but my vision had cleared. The veil between worlds, the one that concealed the depths of my powers was slowly falling away as midnight neared.

The vast depth of my magic felt like blurry edges slowly coming into focus. Like instead of being stranded in a desert, thirsty and alone, the fire opal was creating a small fresh-water oasis. Holding the necklace over my heart, I welcomed the heat radiating from it, calling to Hades's power until mine was ready.

Magic gathered at my fingertips as I thought about all of the pain I'd suffered at the hands of my would-be mother. Of all the bruises and blood, of the endless tears I'd shed for her. She'd told me I was worthless my entire life. Powerless and weak. That I was the worst type of disappointment.

All I had wanted in my short miserable life was to matter. To be seen—*really seen*—and considered someone who was allowed to exist.

Hades had stolen me away, but I'd found my salvation there in the darkness. I'd learned strength wasn't just a matter of physical power, but of resilience. And Demeter had been sharpening *that* skill my entire life.

With a thundering scream, I unleashed the blast of frost and darkness from my hands, aiming it at Demeter's chest. She turned just as a flash of green deflected the brunt of my magic toward the ground, the pulse of death magic eroding stone and earth. Cyrus had flung his magic in front of her.

My eyes widened as the scorched dirt turned black. I recoiled as roots withered under my magic, feeling the earth shudder from my touch. Chest heaving, I reached for the heat within me, for the warmth of life magic humming beneath the frigid cold of my husband's power and willed it to the surface.

The decaying plague stopped. And then reversed. Roots wound through the earth, growing thicker by the second, as thin stalks sprouted. Warmth flooded my body, electricity buzzing across every inch of my skin as I fed the plants.

"Ground her!" Demeter yelled. "We need to kill her before she fully awakens."

Cyrus stayed routed to the spot, eyes wide as the earth answered my call.

All my senses sharpened as my magic poured into the ground. My pupils dilated, my gaze darting between the beads of sweat across Cyrus's brow to the hammering pulse in the curve of his neck. His chest was still heaving with the effort it took to intercept my earlier curse, and there was a sharp, bitter scent coating the air around him—fear.

Cyrus was a green witch who'd grown powerful by murdering other witches with Demeter's help, but no amount of magic would grow him a spine. He was a coward, through and through. It was time he paid for his crimes.

Vines unfurled across the rough stone floor, lashing out under my command. The smell of blood around me grew as barbs dug into his ankles, winding further up his legs. His screams were music to my ears, a lovely lullaby that I'd remember forever.

I stumbled back as a wave of fatigue crested over me. Blinking against a mounting loss piercing my chest, I watched as the vines withered. The deep greens transitioned to brown, the thick, flourishing plants shriveling as their energy was claimed. As it was siphoned into Demeter.

"Cyrus is grounding—acting as a conduit," Lark shouted, her face appearing through the shadows against the wall. "Demeter is feeding off your magic. Call on Hades's power."

My eyes widened as I took in the subtle glow to Demeter's skin. Her head was thrown back, her eyes closed, but her hands were open and extended, absorbing all the magic I was using.

Lark pressed off the wall, sending tendrils of shadows toward Cyrus. Each one bounced off an invisible shield, particles of light blazing to life before crumbling under each strike.

I focused on pulling Hades's darkness to the surface, but the torrent of life magic felt like a flood. Like only the edge of the dam remained upright while the vast majority of water raced through the gaping hole. And every drop was making Demeter stronger.

"I can't stop it," I breathed as Lark darted forward, each step matched with a blast of shadows. The life magic was building in me, but Demeter pulled from the source just as quickly. Like a wound poisoned by the venom of a snake's fangs, the bleeding didn't stop. I was hemorrhaging magic.

Dropping to my knees, I gritted my teeth as I wrestled with Demeter's power. But it was no use. I was losing.

"Hang on!" Lark yelled.

She flew at Cyrus in a wash of smoke and shadows, closing the remaining distance between them. A loud crack sounded as her fist connected with his face, his neck snapping sharply to the side before crumpling to the floor. She was over him in the next breath with a sharp dagger raised above his head and then plunging through his chest.

Blood gushed from the wound as Lark withdrew her blade. She was on her feet without a moment's hesitation, lifting her chin to face Demeter.

My world tilted as Cyrus's chest stilled, the puddle of blood around him growing. I searched Lark's face for regret, for guilt or shame or even a slight flicker of uncertainty over having just taken a life. Red coated her face and chest, eerily reflective of the ring around her irises, but she was calm. Composed even.

"No," Demeter seethed as the raging river of magic left my body slowed to a trickle. "You stupid girl. I should have killed you years ago."

"Yes," Lark said, squaring her shoulders with the dagger clasped in hand. "You should have."

Shadows sprang forward, but a flick of Demeter's wrist had cleared them. Lark's chest heaved as she sent another at her. And another, each one buying me time as I tried to coax the last embers of my magic to ignite. Tears pricked at the edge of Lark's eyes as she hurled another blast, one born of hatred and the dawning hopelessness of our situation. I forced my legs under me, willing my body to move just as Demeter cut inside Lark's attack.

"Time to correct past mistakes." Demeter's cruel laugh filled the dungeon as her fingers closed around Lark's neck.

56

PERSEPHONE

PUSHING PAST THE NUMBNESS IN MY LIMBS, I THREW MYSELF forward, knocking them to the ground. My shoulder crashed to the floor and the taste of blood coated my tongue, but Lark was already standing, racing toward Demeter with the slim dagger clasped in her hand.

I pressed my palms flat against the stone, willing new vines to grow from the cracked floor. They answered. Thin roots rose, lashing out at Demeter. She rendered each to ash with little effort, but I sent more—dozens—wrapping around her wrists, her legs, squeezing her chest. Willing each of them to hold on.

Gods Above, we just might make it.

Lark dove, thrusting forward with the tip of the blade aimed at Demeter's heart.

"Enough!" Demeter yelled. A network of light flared around her, sealing into a shield like the one Cyrus had wielded. Lark's blade splintered upon contact, the force of the blow blasting her backward.

Lark flew through the air, her head cracked against the stone floor hard enough to have the ground vibrating beneath my feet. A strangled cry left my lips as her eyes stayed closed, the mangled sound pitching higher as a red pool grew around her limp form.

I reached for her on instinct. Even after everything she'd done, I couldn't let her die. There was a familiar tugging of life magic leaving my body, draining what little energy I had left. Wisps of shimmering gold light wrapped around Lark as I willed her broken body to heal. I focused on the fissures along her skull, the swelling of the fleshy brain tissue below. I forced more of my magic out, shredding my own life thread to mend hers.

I didn't see Demeter until her hands were around my throat.

"It's time." She smiled down at me with anything but kindness.

My heart thundered as heat radiated from my fire opal. It acted like a conduit, allowing vast pulses of magic to seep into my body, pumping through my veins in fiery bursts. It felt like I was being burned from the inside out.

"Your awakening is finally upon us. Swear yourself to The Earth Coven—to me—and I might let you live. Or die. The choice is yours."

"Never," I snarled, but the word cut short as Demeter's nails pierced the soft flesh of my neck.

Pain shot through me, but worse than that was the overwhelming fatigue rolling over me. I blinked away the fog, fighting to stay present as I realized what was happening. Somehow, Demeter was acting as her own conduit.

"Yes," she nodded. She must have seen the surprise flash in my eyes because her grin widened. "The Green Coven and I have shared much. I can pull from you, dear Persephone. It won't be nearly the amount of magic as it would've been if you'd given it freely, but I'll make do."

I could feel my fragmented body growing weaker with each second. My gaze darted toward Lark's still form, her blood pooling out to link with the puddle surrounding Cyrus's mangled body. Dead roots littered the dungeon floor, their withered corpses unresponsive to my will.

Demeter would drain me. I was going to die, and I was all alone.

"I pledge my magic..."

Demeter withdrew her nails, allowing me just enough room to breathe. Tears tumbled down my cheeks as I forced the words out. "To the Earth Coven."

A spiteful smile stretched across her lips as she basked in my defeat.

"And to The Green Coven. I pledge my magic to the Cosmic Coven, the hedge witches, The Dark Faction, the lone witches, and all those in The Crystal City," I continued as I let the last of my feeble attempts at slowing the flow of magic go.

It raced out of me in a torrent of power, but with that freedom, I was able to grasp the cold shadows of Hades's magic. She could drain every ounce of life magic from me, but Demeter couldn't touch the darkness. Shadows billowed out around me in a vast cloud. I used them like a shield, cutting off Demeter's access to my magic as I scrambled back.

"I pledge my magic to The Realm of the Living. To The Underworld. And every soul caught in between. I pledge my magic to restoring balance between the realms."

Light punched a hole through the wall of darkness I'd crafted, revealing a wild, infuriated Demeter. Her golden hair was raised with the charge of magic she wielded. Blood dripped from her nose, burst vessels staining the whites of her eyes. All traces of reason had gone. Only ceaseless rage remained.

Shadows closed over the opening she'd made, but for each area I patched, another gap opened. Each blast of her magic forced me to take a step back. Every blow, another retreat, until my heel bumped into the cool stone of the wall. My pulse hummed in my ears as I fought for breath, trying to find a way out.

I stepped right, only for vines to rip up the floor and embed themselves in the wall, narrowly missing my face. I turned, but curling roots were there, too, braiding an impenetrable wall. My stomach clenched. Demeter had me trapped.

"I pledge my life to Hades, God of The Underworld." Somehow I found the strength to meet Demeter's gaze as she bore down on me, making a promise to myself that I wouldn't die with fear in my heart. "I vow to be Hades's wife. His Queen. To weave every strand of my life thread with his, binding our souls forever."

Electricity sparked in the air around me as the vows left my lips. Power—such power—was hovering above my body, just out of reach...

Demeter shook her head, her face warping into a manic grin as she took the last step forward. My shadows swirled around her, trying to hold her back, but she cut through them with a flick of her wrist. Blood dripped from her palm where she gripped a piece of sharp metal—a shard of Lark's shattered blade.

"If only Hades were here to complete the vows."

A scream tore from my throat as the tip of the blade sliced between my ribs.

HADES

"I ACCEPT PERSEPHONE AS MY WIFE."

The words were little more than a growl as I tore through earth and stone to reach her, following the tugging within that would lead me to her side. Power hummed in the air the moment midnight struck, the cloud of magic only growing stronger as I hoisted myself through the last of the rubble.

"I pledge my life to her. I vow to be her King. Her god. To weave my magic and immortal soul with hers until the end of time."

The magic between our realms shifted as I climbed onto the cold floor of a dungeon. The metallic scent of blood was heavy in the air, mixed with damp earth and the unmistakable feel of magic. But Persephone's awakening was complete. She would be safe—

Every last drop of warmth in the room froze as her screams echoed through my bones, the agony of her cries shattering something in my chest. I locked eyes with her through the torrent of shadows, my gaze dropping to the splash of red across her lips. A matching stain coated her chest, growing wider in the heartbeat it took for me to comprehend what had happened.

I started toward her, but Demeter's arm jerked forward before I could reach them, shoving the blade deeper between Persephone's ribs. Her body shook, blood dribbling from the corners of her mouth, but the pain that had been swirling in her gaze moments before was dissipating.

A subtle shifting of the wind indicated Thanatos had manifested behind me, shaking out debris from his wings, but my gaze was fixed on Persephone. And the small twitch of her lips as her eyes met mine.

She grasped the hilt of the dagger, stumbling forward as Demeter took a step back. Her red curls fell like a curtain around her face, her shoulders bowed, but she remained standing. Slowly, she lifted her head, those fierce green eyes locked on Demeter as she withdrew the dagger from her chest. Blood oozed from the wound for only a moment as I flitted to Persephone's side, before shadows and light blended over the gash and sealed it shut.

"No," Demeter muttered, more breath than voice as she took another step back. "It can't be."

"Is that how you killed all the others?" Persephone's head tilted her head to the side as if amused at the horror permitting the air. "By sliding a dagger between their ribs?"

Demeter swallowed, taking another step back. Her breath fanned out in front of her with each panicked gasp as she shook her head in disbelief.

"Sometimes," Thanatos answered.

Demeter's head snapped toward us, her blue eyes wide and ringed with light. She had been siphoning off my little witch, consuming Persephone's life magic—as if she had the right to it. As if she were destined for anything other than eternal suffering.

The white feathers of Thanatos's wings brushed my

shoulder as he stepped to the other side of Persephone, the three of us forming a line with my little witch at the center. Thanatos's fists clenched with the need to claim Demeter's soul. Her death was near, hovering in the atmosphere.

"Mostly, it was a blade across their throats," I finished.

"Everything I did was for the coven," Demeter stammered as she scrambled away from the three of us, tripping over Cyrus's cold body. His blood smeared across her gown, her palms streaked and muddied with it as she crawled back. "Korae, please. I'm your mother. Everything I've ever done was for your own good."

Shadows stretched under my command, binding Demeter's arms to her sides and holding her in place. She thrashed under my dark magic, but she was helpless against the cold anger fueling them. Weak and useless to do anything but watch as my little witch raised the dagger to her throat.

"My name is Persephone."

The sharp edge of the blade dragged across Demeter's neck, a sheet of red coating her chest as blood flowed. Persephone watched, her golden crown shimmering atop her fiery curls. Grime coated her body, the thin scraps of her robe hardly concealing the torment that had befallen her... but she stood proud, watching, until the High Matriarch slumped forward and was still.

Persephone

IT FELT LIKE HADES'S DARKNESS WAS BLENDING WITH MY LIGHT, like our souls had melded into one. Hot and cold. Life and death. I felt his emotions—the twisting guilt churning with his simmering rage as his shadows let Demeter's body fall. He'd wanted to save me, to protect me from everything that had happened, but as I looked down into Demeter's vacant gaze, I realized I needed to be the one to end this.

After years of mental torment, of bruises and broken bones, of believing her every time she told me I wasn't good enough... it had finally ended. And not because I'd waited for another to slay the monster for me. I'd had the strength within myself the entire time. Even before my awakening, I had the power to change my life. To break free from the lies and misery that had been forced upon me and forge my own future.

"Hypnos helped her ward the realms." Hades's voice was soft, gentle even, as if he were afraid I'd turn the blade on him.

Not taking my eyes off Demeter, I asked, "Where is he?"

"Gone," Thanatos answered. "We have reason to believe The Night Children were working with him and Demeter. A witch named Ruby was with him, the same witch who was sitting on his lap at the ball. I followed her through his kingdom, thinking she would lead me back to him and reveal their plans. Instead, I was led into an ambush."

Something in the tenor of his voice pulled my attention away from the body on the floor. My brows furrowed as I met Thanatos's gaze. He was strong, just as stoic as ever, but there was a slight shifting on his feet, a subtle rustle to his wings. Something had happened in the northern parts of The Underworld. Something horrid enough to shake the God of Death.

My gaze bounced to Hades, catching the nearly imperceptible shake of his head. Questions would have to wait.

"Ruby is lost," Hades said. It was an obvious change in topic, but Thanatos seemed grateful for it. "The portal in the pomegranate grove is dangerous. Hecate thinks she's been displaced in time, or perhaps sent to an alternative realm. Either way, she's no longer a concern of ours."

"We need to return to The Underworld and present a united front to the realm," Thanatos added, all traces of vulnerability displayed moments ago vanishing. "Magic is already finding balance as your life force revitalizes the withered, decaying parts of The Underworld and The Realm of the Living. We need to capitalize on it and show them this is because of their new queen."

A groan sounded behind them as Lark rolled to her side. Her hair was matted with dried blood, streams of it tracking down her neck. Her lip was split and there was dirt and splashes of Cyrus's blood clinging to her gown, but when she blinked her eyes open, her gaze was clear.

The coil of dread in the pit of my stomach loosened as she glanced at the bodies at our feet before meeting my gaze.

"It's done?"

"Yes."

Hesitantly, she forced her shaking legs to stand. "My sister?"

I shook my head. "She never appeared. I think Demeter was telling the truth when she said you'd have to retrieve her from The Underworld."

Anguish twisted Lark's face as her shoulder bowed. "What I did to you was fucked, but—"

"You'll be taken to The Dark Palace to face questioning from Hecate," Hades cut in. I lifted a brow in his direction. "She's requested to speak to the witch who charmed your necklace."

Lark's face paled as her eyes widened.

"This soul is ready," Thanatos called, kneeling beside Cyrus's body. "The other should be along shortly."

"I want them taken directly to Tartarus," Hades rumbled, pausing only long enough for me to nod my agreement.

"Keep them parted," I added. "I don't want either to have any form of comfort, not even in sharing their torment."

"Yes, my queen."

Thanatos dipped his head as he reached for the flickering shade lifting from Cyrus's body. The ghost blinked, dazed until he spotted me. A moment of realization flashed across Cyrus's spirit, his soul seeming to fade and reappear.

"No you don't," Thanatos rumbled, his magic seizing Cyrus's soul before he could flee, and then the two of them were gone in a flash.

"Let's go," I said, turning toward Hades.

"Wait," Lark said, gaze bouncing between me and Demeter's crumpled form. "Don't you want to see the look in her eyes when she realizes she's dead? She's brought nothing but pain and suffering to everyone. She's killed dozens of innocents."

I followed Lark's gaze to the vacant stare of the woman I'd called mother, recalling every horrible memory I had. I hated her. Loathed everything she stood for and all that she'd once been... But she was the only mother I'd ever known.

Shaking my head, I reached for Hades, allowing the fatigue of the day to catch up with me as his arms wrapped around my waist, holding me up.

"It's over," I said. Warmth hummed along Hades's and my woven life threads as I met Lark's fierce gaze. "I want nothing more than to never look upon her face again."

58

HADES

We passed through the realms easily with Persephone tucked close to my side and Lark clinging to her hand. I'd wanted to kill Lark immediately, but Hecate insisted Persephone would want to keep her safe despite her betrayal. It seemed she was right.

Shadows cleared as the three of us appeared in Hecate's sitting room. She was standing, her black floor-length gown crafted from obsidian scales that highlighted the serpents snaking up her arms. The tattoos were a reminder of who she was—the mother of all witches. A goddess in her own right.

Hecate promised me she would see to Lark, uncover the depths of her betrayal without placing Persephone in an unfavorable position. It didn't seem brutal enough for what she'd done. Lark deserved to be punished, sent to Cocytus with the rest of the traitors, but as Hecate's eyes narrowed on the young witch, her vast powers crackling through the air, I knew I could trust Hecate to uncover the truth.

"Meet us in the throne room in two hours," I said, not moving my hand from around Persephone's waist. Her lips tugged down into a small frown as she looked between Lark and Hecate before settling on me. "Hecate had agreed to keep Larkspur company while we freshen up. The four of us will meet with Thanatos and Morpheus soon, but first…" My gaze softened as I swept my thumb over Persephone's blood-smeared cheek. "Let me take care of you."

She must have seen the earnest need swirling in my gaze because the worry knitting her brows together over Larkspur's fate softened.

"Okay," she breathed.

Not wasting another moment, I allowed my shadows to transport us to my room. I left her side only long enough to turn the shower on, before holding her to me once again.

Persephone was alive. She was safe—*had* saved every soul in The Realm of the Living and The Underworld… but it had been too close. Far too close.

"I missed you," she whispered, unbuttoning my tunic.

My heart raced under her touch, her thrumming pulse beating in time with mine. Gods below, had I missed the brush of her fingers, the spark of life that zapped between us. I gathered her hand in mine, pressing her palm flat against my chest as I leaned into her touch and just… breathed, allowing the sweet scent of vanilla and wildflowers to fill my lungs, easing the worry that had terrorized me these past hours.

"It's okay," she said, her lips moving against my ear. "We did it."

"*We* didn't do anything," I amended, tilting her chin up and pressing a kiss to the healed cut along her cheek, before allowing my lips to brush against the trickle of blood along her temple. "You, little witch. *You* defied the odds and upheld the Fates' will."

I dragged my nose down the slope of her neck, my tongue lashing out over the tender place where her pulse hummed. "My queen. My goddess."

Her breathing hitched as I tasted her skin. The unimaginable had almost happened. I'd almost lost her. But my little witch had been strong enough to save us all.

"I know I don't deserve you," I breathed. "But I will spend every moment of my immortal life striving to be worthy."

I TOOK MY TIME WORSHIPING HER, MARVELING AT THE WAY HER skin pebbled under the stream of the hot water, at how her cheeks took on a rosy glow after her first orgasm, her eyes growing hooded with satiated desire.

Down on my knees, I buried my face between her thighs, ravaging her once more. This incredible creature was mine—*mine*—forever. I would be able to hold her in my arms whenever I pleased. To lick and taste, to ring those sweet little moans from her lips every day.

Her fingers dug into my hair, one hand gripping a ram horn while the other braced herself against the shower wall. I looked up at her as my tongue swirled, loving the way her breasts heaved, the nipples hard and peeking out beneath her wet, red curls.

I had washed every inch of her body, erasing all traces of the pain she'd suffered. There were other wounds, ones that I couldn't scrub away, but I'd be there to help repair those too, when she was ready.

"Hades," she moaned, her back arching as her thighs trembled. I felt the coiling desire through our bond, scraping the edge of my teeth over her clit just when she needed me to. Her legs tightened around my face, her hips undulating as I lapped at her core as she detonated, delighting in the taste. I would never have enough of this.

Before the orgasm ended, I was standing, capturing her lips with mine while I slid my fingers into her.

"Two down," I breathed, nowhere near finished with her. "Let's see how many more you can stand."

59

PERSEPHONE

I'd lost count how many times Hades had made me come. All I knew was that my body was sore in places I'd never thought possible. He'd taken me in the shower, in the sitting couch, against the window overlooking our kingdom. We'd eventually made it to the bed, but I'd been floating by that point, so lost to the ecstasy he'd coaxed from me that I'd even enjoyed when he used his shadows to fuck me.

"We could still turn back," Hades murmured in my ear, the heat of his breath sparking that delicious coil low in my belly.

My cheeks flared with his whispered promise, but as much as I'd like to remain tucked away and tangled in his embrace, I needed answers.

"We're already late," I chided, but my voice was breathy, my body recalling how good it felt under his touch. I'd somehow managed to shower and get dressed without giving into Hades's temptations, which was a miracle in itself. I knew he would make good on his promises, that he would keep the others waiting forever if I asked him to.

Tearing my gaze from his, I fixed the edge of my dress before looping my arm through his. "We need to know if Thanatos has discovered anything further on Hypnos's whereabouts."

"And see how Lark is fairing under Hecate's watch?" Hades asked, lifting a knowing brow in my direction.

I shrugged but knew he felt my pulse quicken as we entered the throne room. Lark had lured me to the Earth Coven, throwing me at Demeter's feet even after knowing it might cost me my life, but she'd freed me in the end. Had fought *with* me against Demeter and Cyrus. And that was worth something, wasn't it?

"Oh good," Morpheus said as Thanatos, Hecate, and Lark turned toward us. "You two are finally done fucking. I thought for a moment you'd forgotten about us."

My cheeks blazed, but Hades strolled forward, guiding us toward the massive throne the others had gathered around.

"Priorities," Hades said with a smug smile. He led me up the dais and into a second throne next to his, one crafted from oak and embedded with precious stones. One just for me. "My queen."

Hades gave a slight dip of his chin as I sat. His eyes were fully black, his bat-like wings and ram horns proudly in place, and I found I liked the look of them. I liked the feel of them beneath my hands as I rode his face even more. His lips twitched as he felt the flush of desire rush through me, but he held his tongue and took a seat in the obsidian throne next to mine.

"Why is he here?" Lark asked, eyes narrowed on Morpheus.

"*He* is here to help you deal with Hypnos." Morpheus's lips twitched into a lopsided grin, showing off the hint of fangs.

"Why would you do that?" Lark pushed. Her spine was ridged with her arms crossed over her chest.

"Who better than his son to usurp him?"

"So eager for the crown?" Her gaze narrowed in suspicion.

A flicker of excitement shone in Morpheus's eyes as he

strolled toward her, looking as if he were a cat having found a fluffy mouse to play with.

"Maybe," he shrugged, his eyes trailing the length of her body, forcing me to take a good look at her for the first time.

While I'd been wrapped in Hades's touch and soaking in the shower, it was clear Lark had been kept waiting like a prisoner. The back of her hair was coated with dried blood from the wound that had nearly killed her earlier. Her skin was pale and riddled with bruises and cuts, but it was the sprays of scarlet across her dress that seemed to snag Morpheus's attention.

"Well, aren't you a vision in red." He licked his lips. "Tell me, little monster, do you like the taste of blood as much as you like wearing it?"

Lark recoiled as if he'd slapped her, the color draining from her face.

"Enough," Hecate said, stepping forward to shield Lark. "Larkspur has already been through a great deal tonight and has proven herself loyal to Queen Persephone."

I inhaled a sharp breath, my hands gripping the carved handles of my throne.

"Truth serum?" Hades asked, but Hecate shook her head, her lips pressing thin.

"She opened her mind to me."

Thanatos cocked his head to the side, appearing to have waited for this bit of information. "Compelled?"

"Willingly," Lark answered before Hecate could.

She lifted her chin under Thanatos's assessment, not intimidated one bit by the God of Death. She held his gaze a moment longer before turning toward me. That harsh exterior cracked as she took a step forward, and then another, until she was positioned just before the dais.

Hades tensed beside me, his large wings twitching, but I covered his hand with mine, willing him to let this play out. It wasn't like she could kill me. I was immortal, now.

"She would never hurt you," Hecate said. Pain flashed across Lark's face as guilt showed on mine.

"She already has," Hades growled, the temperature in the room dropping as shadows swirled around him.

"Enough with the frost, Daddy Darkness." Morpheus stood by Lark's side, placing his hands in his pockets as he glanced down at her. "Hecate says the little monster has already opened her mind *willingly* to her. If she had any ill intentions, we would know."

Lark's chest heaved as her eyes glazed with the sheen of tears, but she wouldn't let them fall. Before I could go to her, she dropped to her knees before the throne, bowing her head as she spoke to the obsidian floor.

"The plan was always to escape. That's why I ran with you as far as I could go... to see you safe." She shook her head, sitting back on her heels, staring at her palms in her lap. "Psyche was taken six years ago as punishment for my father rejecting Demeter's advances. She was only fourteen. I've been Demeter's prisoner for nearly as long, having been subjected to her torments just as you have. Worse sometimes. But I refused to give up. I kept fighting, knowing that the horrors I was facing could be only a fraction of what my little sister endured."

"I'm sor—"

"Don't say you're sorry." Lark's gaze snapped to mine. Her cheeks were damp, but a familiar fire was burning in her eyes. "It makes it seem like my sister's fate is sealed and I refuse to believe that."

Swallowing, I nodded, but Hades wasn't moved.

"You compelled my wife to return to The Realm of the Living against her will, forcing her to return to Demeter who tried to drain her of magic."

"Not to mention ushering Persephone toward the portal through the pomegranate grove," Morpheus added, seeming impressed rather than horrified. "Such risks taken with her best friend's life."

"It was my only chance," Lark cut in, fists clenching as she glared up at him. "Haven't you ever had a person you'd do anything for? Crossing the void between realms, working with a sworn enemy, and yes. Even risking my best friend's life. I jeopardized the fate of both our realms for the chance to save my sister. And I would do it all over again if it meant Psyche's life would be spared."

Her chest heaved as the two of them stared at one another. Lark's cheeks were tinged with pink as all the frustration and anger in the last few years rose to the surface, but Morpheus only looked on with cool curiosity.

"And where is this sister of yours?"

Darkness gathered along Lark's palms as she pressed to a stand. "If Demeter was telling the truth, Psyche is free of her punishment, but remains trapped in The Underworld."

Morpheus cocked his head to the side. "Do you know which kingdom in particular, or do you plan on securing yourself a permanent spot here."

"I have no intention of dying if that's what you're implying."

"I wasn't implying anything, little monster. A stubborn, bloodthirsty little witch like yourself will die the moment you step foot out of The Asphodel Plains. Based on Hypnos's entanglement with the Earth Coven, I'd wager your sister is trapped somewhere in the north."

Lark's nostrils flared, but she didn't argue.

"Hypnos has her?" I asked, my gaze bouncing between them.

"It seems our goals align," Hades said after the silence had stretched. "For now. I've never known Hecate to be tricked. So, I am forced to trust that you have pure intentions, Larkspur. But even the best intentions can lead one astray."

Hades looked to me, but I didn't have an answer for him. I understood why Lark did it. If I were honest with myself, I'd probably have done the same thing if Hades had been in danger. But that didn't make trusting her any easier. Perhaps the two of us could mend what had been broken one day, but it would take time.

The thread linking me to Hades pulsed with a soothing warmth as he picked up on my warring emotions. I let his presence calm me, allowing my husband to share the weight of this decision.

"With your recent betrayal to the queen, you will not be allowed free passage through The Underworld."

Lark's eyes widened, beseeching me to reconsider. "Persephone, please—"

"Morpheus will search the north for traces of his father, as promised, and will report any findings of your sister."

"I can't sit around when I'm this close—"

"I'll take the little monster with me," Morpheus cut in, the ever-present smirk on his face markedly absent. He looked at Lark with a seriousness I hadn't thought he was capable of. "If we are to trek through the north in search of my father, you'll have to listen to my guidance."

Hades opened his mouth to protest, but Hecate stepped forward. "I second the plan. Morpheus will accompany Lark in The Underworld. As collateral, I offer myself up for any wrongdoings she commits."

Lark's mouth fell open as her gaze snapped to Hecate in stark disbelief.

"Are you sure you want to do that?" Morpheus asked. "She looks like she could get into quite a bit of trouble."

Lark snapped her mouth shut as she glared at him, but Hecate continued to hold Hades's gaze. "I trust her."

Hades shifted in his throne as his wings bristled, looking like he'd just sucked on a lemon. His gaze bounced to Thanatos on the edge of the room, but the God of Death only shrugged. After a long moment, Hades sighed. "Fine, but the second you disobey or defect for any reason, I'll cast your soul into The Realm of the Living and bar any passage to The Underworld until your lungs heave their last pitiful breath."

Morpheus rolled his eyes as Lark nodded.

"So dramatic," Hecate muttered with a faint smile on her lips.

I exhaled, letting go of the tension in my shoulders as things settled into place. Demeter was defeated, the Earth Coven free once more, and Lark... It hadn't happened how I'd imagined it, but both of us had escaped our lives of imprisonment.

Gazing around the throne room, I saw only hope staring back at me—except for Thanatos. His light blue eyes were still glued to Lark, slightly narrowed as if he were waiting for her to attack. But he shook his head and turned toward Hades.

"It's time to present our new queen to the souls," Thanatos said. "By now, they've no doubt felt magic stabilizing, but it's important to show them you are unharmed. News of Hypnos's betrayal is circulating. We must show The Underworld there's nothing to fear. There's already a large crowd gathered in front of the palace."

"They've been waiting this whole time?" My eyes widened as I glanced toward Hades.

Morpheus smirked. "Not to worry, Queen Persephone. A marriage needs to be honored."

"So does an awakening," Hecate added with a grin as she led the others from the room. "The Underworld is in a state of celebration. Half of the souls out front are engaged in scandalous acts at this very moment."

My cheeks heated as Hades stood, offering me his hand with an amused glimmer in his eyes. "I'll be at your side the whole time, little witch."

"I'm a queen, now," I said, feeling his shadows stir as I accepted his hand.

Darkness closed around us, opening moments later to a

golden balcony. We were far enough back from the edge that the boisterous souls beneath couldn't spot us, but the entirety of The Asphodel Plains stretched out before us.

The once barren landscape had transformed. Lush, green grass swayed over rolling hills spotted with wildflowers. The pomegranate grove in the distance sported thick branches full of plump red fruit. I could even make out the edge of Elysium where death magic had once nearly claimed my life—it was healed, all traces of the scorched earth gone.

"Yes. You are Queen of The Underworld," Hades said as one of his arms wrapped around my waist. "But you'll always be my little witch, the only person capable of thawing my frozen heart. I love you Persephone. Ruling a kingdom has its challenges, tending to the entire Underworld even more so, but no matter what difficulties come our way, we'll face them together."

I leaned into his touch, letting the warmth of his chest and the beating of our synchronized hearts ease my nerves. We had a long road ahead of us, but I wasn't afraid. Hades would be with me, supporting me, despite how perilous the journey might become. He saw all of me, the good and the bad. Despite it all, Hades loved me. And that made all the difference.

With a deep breath, I thought of all we'd overcome and all we had yet to do. Gripping his hand, I breathed out, letting go of the past and stepped forward toward the future.

ACKNOWLEDGMENTS

Thank you first and foremost to the readers who love dark greek mythology retellings as much as I do. I loved helping Persephone find her strength and Hades his humanity.

Thank you to my group of fellow authors and my incredible, wonderful, best person in the world Editor Sam who made this book possible. I'm forever grateful for your support.

Thank you to my besties for letting me talk for hours about made up worlds and fictional characters. Thank you for helping me find my own strength, and never letting the shadows win.

ABOUT THE AUTHOR

C.L. Briar believes books are always better than reality, and that one of the greatest offenses a person can commit is interrupting reading time. When she is not busy dreaming up dark fantasy worlds and plotting destruction, she can be found drinking coffee in her backyard with her three young daughters, and hound dog.

ALSO BY C.L. BRIAR

The Storm of Chaos and Shadows Series

Storm of Chaos and Shadows

Storm of Blood and Vengeance

Storm of Death and Darkness

Storm of Mist and Monsters

The Sinful Seasons Series

Morpheus and Thanatos: A Prequel

Spring's Descent

Summer's Seduction

The Seven Deadly Sins Series

Envy

Wrath

Lust, Greed, & Gluttony

www.ingramcontent.com/pod-product-compliance
Lightning Source LLC
Chambersburg PA
CBHW020933260626
47169CB00006B/1695